*A Little Class
on Murder*

By Carolyn G. Hart

A Little Class on Murder
Honeymoon with Murder
Something Wicked
Design for Murder
Death on Demand
A Settling of Accounts

A Little Class on Murder

CAROLYN G. HART

A CRIME CLUB BOOK

DOUBLEDAY

New York · London · Toronto · Sydney · Auckland

A Crime Club Book
Published by Doubleday, a division of
Bantam Doubleday Dell Publishing Group, Inc.,
666 Fifth Avenue, New York, New York 10103

DOUBLEDAY and the portrayal of a man with a gun are trademarks of Doubleday,
a division of Bantam Doubleday Dell Publishing Group, Inc.

Library of Congress Cataloging-in-Publication Data
Hart, Carolyn G.
    A little class on murder / Carolyn G. Hart.
        p.   cm.
    "A Crime Club book."
    I. Title.
PS3558.A676L58   1989
813'.54—dc19   89-1141
CIP

ISBN 0-385-26452-6
Copyright © 1989 by Carolyn G. Hart
All Rights Reserved
Printed in the United States of America
September 1989
OG

To Professor Mack R. Palmer, my old friend and former colleague, who teaches the kind of journalism I believe in

*A Little Class
on Murder*

1

OPEN STACKS. A boon to scholars and to those surreptitiously in search of esoteric knowledge.

The reader in the shadowy, out-of-the-way carrel stifled a whoop of delight. Here it was in exquisite detail: how to put together a bomb, a nice little bomb timed to explode at precisely the right moment. In a manual on guerrilla warfare, courtesy United States Army. The coffee-spattered cover was a dull green. Such an innocuous-appearing pamphlet, but full of means to maim and destroy. Right here on the shelves of the Chastain College library.

2

EMILY EVERETT WAS HEAVY. That's how she put it to herself. Heavy. But she couldn't help it. She didn't eat that much more than other people. Why did everyone else have to be thin? Why should it make so much difference?

She tugged on her bra and her enormous breasts quivered. Damn thing choked her. Something always hurt. Her back. Her feet. She sighed and reluctantly hoisted a thick stack of yellow folders. She stared at them with loathing, then slowly shuffled across the office. She hated filing, almost as much as she hated typing. She hated working while going to school.

The main office door burst open and a slim redhead bounced up to the counter. "Hi, Emily. Is God back yet?"

"Mr. Burke is out of the office this morning," Emily replied stiffly. Who did Georgia Finney think she was? But Emily knew the answer. Georgia Finney was Sports Queen, chief photographer for *The Chastain College Crier*, president of her sorority. And gorgeous, with a brilliant shine like maples in the fall.

Emily fastened malicious, resentful eyes on Georgia's cheerful face, and said in an innocent tone, "Oh, Georgia, I saw the notice that Professor

Crandall and his wife are having the Student Press Association over next week. Won't that be fun?"

And Emily felt a thrill of triumph, because the look in Georgia's eyes— fleeting but so revealing—was a compound of fear, misery, and despair.

3

THE HARDEST PART was coming home to the down-at-heels apartment house with its faded green stucco exterior and hummocky grass. Charlotte Porter walked stiffly, her thin shoulders rigid. Shards of glass from a broken beer bottle glistened in the late fall sunlight on the cracked sidewalk.

In her mind, she carried an image of a gracious house, an old and dignified house high on a bluff overlooking the river. Never a grand house, but so human and so filled with memories.

But here, it was easier not to think of Jimmy.

Spilled cola made the front steps sticky underfoot. Those loud Stemmons children. But what could be expected, no father, and a mother working two jobs. Not like Jimmy, who had been the center of her universe with every care she could give. The vestibule door was ajar. The Stemmons children again. Too young, too much in a hurry, too unruly to remember to close the door. Charlotte nudged it open wider with her elbow, her hands full with her purse and her briefcase.

Shifting the briefcase to one hip, she fumbled in her purse for her keys and poked the tiny one into the front of her mail slot. A massive wrought iron mailbox had weathered sixty years on the shady porch of Riverway.

The usual mail. Sudden tears blurred her eyes as she glimpsed the ornate writing on one square white envelope. The annual University Women's Thanksgiving tea. She'd not missed attending for more than a quarter of a century. A mistake that the invitation had come, obviously, because she'd dropped out of her clubs, all of them. She no longer went to the luncheons, every second Wednesday of the month, every third Thursday, with their high fluttering chatter of women, so like the evening chorus of birds settling in the treetops, and their familiar programs on quilts or silver, lace or church history.

She'd told everyone, when she'd moved to the apartment house, that it was financial reverses, that dreadful stock market drop.

No one knew how the money had gone, how desperate she'd been.

She jammed the invitation, circulars, and bills into her purse, opened the second door, and started up the narrow wooden stairs, the treads covered with cracked linoleum.

What a tacky, hateful place.

But she could just barely manage the rent and continue to make restitution.

At least, no one knew about that.

She couldn't bear it if anyone knew about that.

4

COULD LIFE BE SWEETER?

"Agatha," Annie announced to her cat as she stepped down from the ladder, "marriage is marvelous. I recommend it."

The sleek black feline atop the coffee bar paused in the fastidious cleansing of a pink-padded paw to regard Annie with unimpressed amber eyes.

Annie wasn't surprised at the lack of response. Salmon soufflé would garner Agatha's respect, but not the irrelevant (to food) musings of her owner. And Agatha would assuredly take exception to that designation of possession. She had no sense of humor and a clear sense of her own preeminent position at Death on Demand.

"The finest mystery bookstore this side of Atlanta," Annie announced, picking up her adored feline and stroking her silky black fur.

With the ease born of long practice, Agatha draped herself comfortably over Annie's shoulder, yawned daintily, and focused her inscrutable gaze on the back wall.

Following Agatha's glance, the bookstore owner observed with pleasure the new watercolors she had just finished hanging over the mantel on the west wall. She could always count on drawing the island's most omnivorous mystery readers (and upping sales for the day by at least thirty percent) on the first of every month. They hurried in for a glimpse of the mystery paintings. Competition was keen. The first person to correctly identify all five paintings by title and author received free coffee for a month and a free book. (New, of course. Some of her first edition collector's items were pricey indeed, such as Michael Innes's *Christmas at Candleshoe*, $75; J. D. Carr's *The Murder of Sir Edmund Godfrey*, $150, and Harvey J. O'Higgins's *The Adventures of Detective Barney*, with a Goldstone bookplate, $160.)

As Annie contemplated the paintings, she grinned. Was there anything more fun than the mystery combined with humor? Sometimes wry, sometimes dark, sometimes wacky, but always trenchant, the humor in the mystery limned society's pomposities and posturings with wicked delight.

And these watercolors illustrated some of the best in murderous humor, American-style.

In the first, a young man in a white coat, cap, and apron loped down a brick sidewalk in the light of a street lamp. Running beside him was an elderly man, the image of Shakespeare. He carried a lion's head and a black homburg and was impressively fleet of foot for a man of his age.

In the second, three children hunkered close together in an obviously conspiratorial consultation as they peered out from behind a bush at a pink villa, guarded by a young policeman in uniform. The oldest member of the trio was a tall teenage girl with fluffy brown hair and enormous brown eyes. Listening attentively to her were a delicate blonde with smoky gray eyes and a small boy with a dirty face, unruly brown hair, and a hole in the sleeve of his jersey.

In the third painting, the youngish man walking up the dark street had an air of diffidence and indecision. Everything about him was round—shoulders, stomach, forehead, and spectacles. Deep in thought, very deep in thought, he was totally oblivious to the black car cruising up the street, the gun poking from its window, and the splintered hole in the trash can he'd just passed.

In the fourth painting, the skinny, angular, fairly athletic male with the deep tan, scruffy shorts, and bare feet struck a discordant note in the formality of the elegant panelled library. A darkly handsome man in a business suit sat behind the desk. He held up, for his visitor to see, a .38 caliber Smith & Wesson.

Without warning, Agatha turned and, smoothly as a ballerina, sprang back to the coffee bar. Art, her attitude clearly indicated, was not a matter which deserved a feline's undivided attention. Muscles bunching beneath her sleek black coat, she flew from the coffee bar to a nearby table and disappeared behind a stack of Sue Grafton's latest, all autographed by the author.

In the fifth painting, the woman police officer was young, tall, and slender, and wore her dark hair in a neat bun. She stared thoughtfully at the door of a pink concrete-block building, decorated with metal signs, including one with the establishment's name, Ruby Bee's. Her face reflected curiosity, suspicion, and uneasiness.

Which was the funniest? Well, it depended upon a reader's mood. The fifth book was a raunchy romp, a guaranteed rib-cracker. The first provided wonderful glimpses of the home front during World War II along with a clever mystery. Each was different and hilarious.

The front door bell jangled. "Anybody here? This place open? Where's Annie Laurance Darling?" The staccato male tenor, hurried, demanding, yet not unpleasant, reverberated down the center aisle.

"Here I am," Annie called, turning to face the front of the shop.

Abruptly, the atmosphere was charged with tension. A lean, beak-nosed man in his fifties strode down the center aisle, exuding energy, determination, and impatience. His face was leathery and his forehead looked to be permanently wrinkled in a frown. Questing green eyes of an unusual brightness darted from Annie to the paintings to the collection of mugs behind the coffee bar. His white shirt was tucked haphazardly into tan cotton slacks and his lank brown knit tie was askew.

The newcomer jabbed a nicotine-stained finger at the mugs. "You sell pottery, too? Thought this was a mystery bookstore." His voice had the sharp, nervous quality of a collie's bark.

"Not for sale," she retorted crisply. "We serve coffee, too, and each mug carries a different title."

"Clever." He surged past her, stalking behind the coffee bar. Agatha poked her head from behind the stack of books, narrowed her amber eyes, and headed for the rattan furniture area near the classic mystery section. Wiry brown fingers snatched up a mug. *The Mind of Mr. J. G. Reeder* by Edgar Wallace. Why him? Man was a hack."

"Not fair," she objected. "He did write a lot, but—"

"How many?"

Annie looked at her inquisitor in surprise. One of the problems in serving the G.P. (as Ingrid, her good friend and helpful clerk, described the General Public) was the ever-present danger of confronting a nut. This man didn't look like a nut, but what was the point of his barrage of questions? "Wallace wrote eighty-eight mysteries, six nonmystery novels, sixty-two books of short stories, four collections of verse, twenty-eight plays, and ten screenplays. Once he wrote a book over a weekend. *The Coat of Arms.*"

An approving smile fleetingly creased the tanned, bony face. The parrot-bright eyes moved back to the display. He reshelved the Wallace mug and grabbed another. *"The Glass-Sided Ant's Nest* by Peter Dickinson. What's this about?"

"Murder in a London attic where members of a primitive New Guinea tribe live. Dickinson's one of the most original crime writers alive."

He slapped the mug back in place with a thump that made Annie wince. "Who wrote, 'But down these mean streets a man must go who is not himself mean, who is neither tarnished nor afraid'?"

"Raymond Chandler, of course."

He snapped his fingers. "Who's Selwyn Jepson's clever female series character?"

"Eve Gill. *Man Running, The Golden Dart, The Hungry Spider, The Black Italian, The Laughing Fish,* and *Fear in the Wind.*"

His green eyes shone. Annie had a feeling that she'd passed some kind of test. He stuck out his hand. "I'm R.T. Burke, new chair of the journalism department at CC." A pause. "Chastain College," he amplified.

She took his hand. "Annie Laurance Darling," she offered. His handshake was firm, quick, and hurried.

Chastain was a lovely small town snuggled in a pleasant harbor on the mainland, about 13 miles from the ferry dock that served the island of Broward's Rock and, of course, Death on Demand. Settled in 1730, Chastain had prospered in the heyday of cotton, missed destruction when Sherman passed by, and flowered in recent years as a mecca for tourists appreciative of antebellum homes. Annie vaguely recalled a live oak-rimmed campus and buildings of uniformly Georgian architecture. She had a little trouble picturing R.T. Burke in this milieu.

Either he was very perceptive or he had a keen self-awareness. "Believe it or not, I went to school there. Bright Georgia cracker back from Europe. CC was started in forty-four. Flooded with GI's after the war." He squinted speculatively at her. "World War Two."

"I've heard of it," she said dryly. Why did everyone over forty assume her generation was illiterate?

"You're damn young." He cleared his throat. "You free on Tuesday and Thursday mornings?"

Before she could answer, he barreled ahead. "Damn short notice, I know. Classes start next week, but everybody says you're a whiz. Have you ever taught anything?"

"Taught?" She felt as disoriented as a first-time reader on page 150 of a Craig Rice mystery. "Mr. Burke, I don't—"

"Call me R.T. Don't go with titles and all that crap. I'm a newsman, pure and simple. Never thought I'd be teaching anything. Worked for AP for twenty-five years. Bureau chief the last ten. Had a triple bypass. Doctor ordered me to take it easy."

"And, of course, that's what you're doing," she said mildly.

He gave her a piercing look, those brilliantly green eyes sparking, then laughed. It resembled a hyena's bark. "Damn sharp, young miss. Right. Right. I spew. Sometimes I explode. Simmer the rest of the time. Just as soon go out with a bang as a whimper. Having a hell of a time, actually. Like to stir things up—and believe me, this department needs some fresh blood. Bunch of damn three-toed sloths with tunnel vision. Giving 'em hell. Furious at me, the governing board, and the president. You know Charles August Markham?"

Annie recognized the name of the college president. She'd glimpsed him once at a beach replenishment meeting here on the island. Broward's Rock had taken the lead in working toward improvement of the beach replenishment bill recently passed by the legislature.

"I know him by sight."

"I was in his platoon. Been pals ever since. Asked me to take on the department, see if I could get it up to snuff. Told him I'd be glad to." His bushy black eyebrows bunched. "Thought it'd be easy. The more fool me. But I'll get there. One way or another. Damn academics. Know more ways to obfuscate and delay than a politician in a filibuster."

Annie was beginning to enjoy this truncated conversation. She leaned comfortably against the coffee bar and realized that, for once in her life, she was dealing with someone a good deal more uptight than she. It gave her a sense of cool well-being. Why, she could be as laid back as Max, her new and always relaxed spouse. What a pleasant feeling! She smiled at her visitor. "Do you know what Robert B. Parker said about academics?"

A hyena bark in anticipation.

Encouraged, Annie quoted from John C. Carr's *The Craft of Crime: Conversations with Crime Writers:* " 'Somebody once said that one of the reasons academic infighting is so vicious is that the stakes are so small. There's so little at stake and they are so nasty about it. More than any other group I've ever seen, academics don't seem to know how to act, and there *is* a way to act.' "

R.T. Burke slammed a fist on top of the coffee counter. "Damn right. God, I'd like to set him—or Spenser—loose in my department." There was no glint of humor in those vivid green eyes. "Goddam, wouldn't I like that! There *is* a way to act. First class, that's what we need. First-class teachers. First-class writers. First-class reporters. I won't stand for cheaters and liars." He leaned across the wooden bar. "You know why I went into newspapering? Truth, that's why. Men like Zenger and Pulitzer and White. Decent men trying to tell the truth. And the muckrakers, who went out there and found out how people worked like slaveys. Those writers told the world and got some laws to keep kids from grinding out twelve-hour days in the mills. That's journalism. Not this poking into people's bedrooms that passes for investigative reporting today. Cheap trash." He was breathing heavily. "By God, there *is* a way to act." He glared at her. Slowly, his breathing eased. "Bet you think I'm going to have a heart attack on the spot, huh? Not me. Tougher than a sob sister at a hanging. And I don't put up with fools." The red ebbed from his face, and there was what sounded like a snort of either laughter or embarrassment. "Puts me up a creek sometimes. Like now. Just fired the sorry jerk who was going to teach feature writing. Found out he'd been let go for making a story up. *Making a story up,* can you believe that?" The flush rose again from his neck to his hairline. "Thank God, you can *fire* adjunct faculty. Anyway, I've got a damn big hole in the schedule. Classes start next week for the winter quarter. Heard you put together a mystery program for the annual house-and-garden tours last spring. Occurred to me maybe we could use a course on the mystery."

She blinked in surprise. "In the journalism department?"

"Sure. Why not? That's what I told Charles August. News gives the reader information, fiction gives him emotion. And the mystery provides moral judgments. Damn near the only place in the world we find 'em anymore. Be damn refreshing. What about it?"

Annie felt a quiver of excitement. What fun! But, of course, she wasn't really qualified. "I've never taught—"

"Doesn't matter. You speak right up. Saw you in *Arsenic and Old Lace* last summer. Anybody who can do summer theater can handle a class. How about it? You could start with Poe, of course. And there's Hammett, Chandler—"

Annie held up both hands. "Not that same tired track," she objected. "Mr. Burke—"

"R.T.," he interrupted.

"R.T.," she repeated. "If I teach a class, it's going to be from a different slant. I'm sick of the same old incantation: Poe, Doyle, Hammett, Chandler, and all their derivative brethren. Not that lots of them aren't wonderful. But many of the greatest mystery writers of all time are women and no one ever talks about them!" Her voice rose excitedly. If Max were there, he'd no doubt point out that she'd climbed up on her favorite soapbox. "Do you realize that Agatha Christie outsold almost every writer in the world except the Bible and Shakespeare? Oh, they give lip service to her at mystery writers' meetings today, then make snide remarks about her paper-thin characterizations, her inadequate settings, her reliance on the puzzle. Well, I'm here to tell you—"

That thin wiry hand grabbed hers and began to pump. "You'll do it! Faculty meeting at four Thursday afternoon. Like to make adjunct faculty feel part of the team." He rolled his eyes. "Shit team, but it's all I've got. See you then." He wheeled around and charged up the central aisle.

Annie stared after him. "Mr. Burke. R.T.—Hey, wait—"

The bell jangled as he yanked open the door. "Be a challenge. Counting on you. Do any damn thing you like. Any writers. Women. Men. Pygmies. Academic freedom. All I demand is good work. Have at it."

As the door banged after him, Annie felt like Donald Lam contemplating a Bertha Cool disaster. What had she let herself in for? Teaching. Next week. Next week! Authors and titles swam in her mind. Christie, of course. And three of her best titles, *Murder for Christmas, Murder in Retrospect,* and *A Murder Is Announced.*

But who else?

She turned, her eyes darting from shelf to shelf, then an answer burgeoned in her mind. Humming, she moved down the aisle, looking for titles. Oh, yes, indeed. The three *grande dames* of the mystery: Mary Roberts Rinehart, Agatha Christie, and Dorothy Sayers. As her arms filled with books, the tuneless hum rivaled Agatha's throatiest purr.

Henny Brawley's eyes narrowed in a steely gaze. "I *know* that book. I know that *book.*" Annie's best customer (Henny devoured mysteries the way Agatha Christie had lapped up Devonshire cream) drummed beringed fingers against the counter top and glared at the fourth watercolor. Henny was a fashion plate this afternoon in a black-and-white silk jacquard print with a V-neck and back kick pleat. Her graying brown hair was upswept and gold hoop earrings dangled from her ears. She looked like a clubwoman en route to a board meeting, but Annie knew this deceptively conventional exterior masked an original and formidable personality. (Henny was also quite at home in sweats and sneakers or camouflage fatigues, and she had a sharp, bony nose that wriggled at moments of high stress.) And Annie was getting darned tired of handing out free books and coffee to Henny, who'd won three contests so far this year. Enough was enough. It was someone else's turn. But Henny was preternaturally adept at finagling tidbits of information, especially out of Annie.

Without removing her determined gaze from the figure in painting four, the indolent young man with insolent eyes, Henny remarked conversationally, "That fellow behind the desk has on a coat and tie. But the young guy—a PI?—looks so casual. Almost beachy."

Annie's lips tightened into a thin straight line. Not a word was she going to say. Not a word.

From the front of the store, she heard Ingrid mask a giggle with a very phony cough. So Ingrid thought this was funny! Just wait til Henny left.

Henny's light brown eyes flickered toward her. Annie concentrated on straightening the Phyllis Whitney titles. Annie preferred to arrange an author's work in order of publication date and she noticed in passing that she lacked this mistress of mysteries' first title, *Red Is for Murder.* Of course, it was reissued in 1968 as *Red Carnelian*—

"That style of shirt was popular in the seventies, wasn't it?" Henny mused.

"No comment," Annie replied pleasantly.

Henny's nose twitched, but she too managed a pleasant tone. "How about a little wager, Annie?"

"Wager?" Annie knew full well that a weak repetition shifted the conversational balance of power, but she was determined not to engage in a substantive discourse with Henny. It could be injurious to her mental health.

The champion mystery reader of Broward's Rock smiled with the bloodcurdling enthusiasm of the marine protagonist in *Jaws* upon sighting a swimmer. "Sure." She sauntered past the coffee bar to the shelving filled with classic collectibles. "If I win the contest again this month, you put up a bonus." Her eyes glistened as they fastened on the first editions. "How about Nicholas Blake's *The Beast Must Die.*" She snatched it up and opened it to the title page. "I thought so! This is one he signed with his real name, Cecil Day Lewis." Her voice was reverent.

"Why on earth should I—"

"But if someone beats me to it and wins the contest," Henny swept on majestically, "I'll give you my first edition autographed copy of *The Mysterious Affair at Styles.*"

Annie's heart thumped. There hadn't been a first edition vf (very fine) copy of that book offered in the past forty years! It could be worth ten thousand dollars. Fifteen thousand!

"In the original dust jacket." Henny's tone was dulcet; the devil couldn't have offered the world more seductively. "Perfect condition."

"Perfect condition! Oh my God. Sure. Yes. What a deal!"

Beaming, Henny gave a touchdown wriggle as classy as any in the National Football League and sashayed up the center aisle. "You're on!" She paused at the front door. "I *love* a challenge. You're a sport, Annie."

After the door closed behind her, there was a long silence.

Annie stalked up the aisle and glared at her suspiciously mute clerk. "So you think I shouldn't have done it?"

"I didn't say a word," Ingrid replied innocently, but the corners of her mouth twitched. Hastily, she scooped up the latest issue of *Publishers Weekly*.

"Don't try and hide," Annie snarled. Then, plaintively, "I didn't give her any hints, did I?"

"Oh no, no. Not one." Behind *PW* there was a sound suspiciously like a giggle. "No hints. But you sure made her the odds-on favorite to win again. You know how Henny is with a challenge."

Annie knew.

Ingrid took pity. She reached down and grabbed her purse from the second drawer of her desk. "Look, I've got an idea. I'll go catch her. I'll tell her all about your class—the one on the three great ladies of the mystery—that'll distract her, for sure."

Annie grabbed Ingrid's slim arm with fingers of steel. "God, no. I'll give her *three* Nicholas Blakes. I'll give her that John Dickson Carr title we just got in." (*The Man Who Could Not Shudder.* Scarce. Priced at $45.) "But I don't want Henny in my class. Why, she knows more about mysteries than Carol Brener. Or Bruce Taylor. Or Dilys Winn. Or Kate Mattes. In my class! Ingrid, what a lousy idea!"

"A class on the greatest ladies of the mystery? On Mary Roberts Rinehart?" The rising note of excitement in Laurel's husky voice was the first indication to Max Darling that his idle chatter, his well-meant, *innocuous* report on his and Annie's doings, was of altogether too much interest to his mother. When Laurel got that particular tone in her voice, that vibrato—

Max stiffened. Which wasn't easy when lying almost horizontal in the soft leathery embrace of his reclining desk chair. Not even the soothing warmth of the heater assuaged the sudden chill enveloping his mind.

"I'll write you all about it, Laurel. I'll keep you informed. I'll send you the books on the reading list. Of course, Annie's hoping that no one she knows enrolls. Her first time to teach, you know."

"My dear child, Annie must be *confident.* Maxwell, we must *encourage* Annie."

"That's just it," he said heartily. "We'll be behind the scenes. *Behind the scenes*, Mother."

"A noble thought, Maxwell dear. You do phrase things so beautifully. Just like Rasheesh."

Max pursed his lips and frowned.

Light laughter, reminiscent of leprechauns in the twilight. "My newest link to the Other Side, my dear."

"Of course, Mother. So glad you're all linked up. And I know you're very busy with—with—with linking, and all that."

"Not *too* busy. In fact, I was just thinking how *much* I missed Broward's Rock. And I've quite despaired of finding another mystery bookstore as wonderful as Death on Demand. And dear Ingrid. I had a note from her just the other day with a new shipment of books."

"You're reading mysteries?"

"Of course, my dear. I feel that it is incumbent upon a mother-in-law to create a rapport with her children's spouses. And you know how *hard* I've tried with the girls' husbands."

Max winced at the memories. Laurel taking up skydiving (Diedre's husband Ed's hobby—until an outing with Laurel), moose hunting (the former passion of Gail's husband Kenneth), and crapshooting (of course, Harry, Jen's husband, was better off not gambling. Still—).

"Mother, we all—the girls and I—enormously appreciate the efforts you've made, but you must give time to yourself." He scrambled for a diversion. "After all, there must be so *much* for you and Rasheesh to discuss."

A thoughtful pause. "Rasheesh," Laurel murmured. "Maxwell, what an excellent suggestion. I shall speak to Rasheesh about it."

After he hung up, Max refused to admit to himself that his failure to inquire as to the subject of her talk with Rasheesh was no evidence of moral cowardice.

And there was no point in worrying Annie.

Was there?

The little tickle of warm breath in her left ear was distracting. And the light but lingering kiss on her cheek—

"Max, go away. I can't think when—"

Somehow—Annie was unclear just how—Max insinuated himself beside her on the couch, despite the uneven mound of books with paper markers extruding like lake wind warning flags. And where was that particular passage? The one about the death of Mary Roberts Rinehart's canary Dickie and the indelible mark it had made upon her? More than breath now and the lingering touch of lips—

"Max, I can't think—"

"You don't need to *think.*"

"But the faculty meeting's tomorrow and—"

His lips got in the way.

The books toppled to the floor.

5

ANNIE WAS TOO EXCITED to spend the ferry ride sitting calmly in her aging Volvo. (She'd resisted Max's attempt to substitute a Porsche. Her car worked.) She rested her elbows against the white metal railing, breathed deeply, relishing the salty sea scent, and gazed across the softly green water of Port Royal Sound at the mainland. A ragged V formation of stiff-tailed glossy cormorants skimmed low, seeking their prey, menhaden and minnows. The expert divers were a sure sign of fall, coming south to follow the migrating fish schools. And there, to port, was a bobbing band of lesser scaup, wintering tidewater ducks. Their glossy black heads glistened in the November sunlight.

Fall. To a plains Texan, it evoked memories of cool mornings, wind out of the north, and geese overhead on their way to the Gulf.

And school.

The shrill sound of bells, the scrape of shoes on wooden floors, the clang of lockers between classes. The screech of chalk against a blackboard, the smell of cafeteria food, the pleasure of learning.

She was, of course, en route to Chastain to take her place, if only briefly, as part of a college, not a high school, faculty. But all educational institutions had the same elements. And she'd never surveyed a classroom from the vantage point of that godlike creature, the professor. It should be a new experience.

The ferry horn beeped three times, signaling the approach to the dock. Annie ducked back into her car and impatiently waited her turn to debark. As her Volvo bumped off the ferry, she wheeled to the right onto the blacktop. Seventy-five-foot loblolly pines topped by silvery umbrella crowns towered on both sides of the narrow road. Annie, of course, was soon trapped behind a lopsided pickup proceeding with great dignity at exactly twenty-eight miles per hour. This was SOP on a southern back road. Annie knew it, but still her hands clenched on the steering wheel and her shoulders hunched. An unending series of chicken trucks in the opposite lane kept her from passing. She did have one opportunity and was just about to make her move when a horn blared behind her and a canary-colored Corvette hogged onto the lane to sweep triumphantly past her and the pickup. Annie glimpsed sleek black hair, aviator sunglasses, and a tanned arm negligently draped on the red leather seat. She seethed the rest of the way into Chastain, continuing to inhale the pickup's acrid exhaust fumes through the stop-and-start of town and down Ephraim Street past the elegant old mansions where she had staged a very murderous mystery program during last spring's annual house-and-garden tours. She flicked on her left turn signal as she neared Prince Street. Thank heavens, the pickup chugged on, and she made her turn. The entrance to the campus of Chastain College was just past two more historic homes quite familiar to Annie. The Volvo jumped forward as she pressed the accelerator. She didn't want to meet the owners of either of those homes ever again. She'd read recently in an area newspaper that one of them, Sybil Giacomo, was spending the autumn in Italy. But the other—Annie suppressed a shudder. She sped by Miss Dora's brown brick home with its tabby-covered pillars. With relief, she turned onto the boulevard leading to the campus. Annie looked with admiring eyes at the cool, shadowy grounds. Woolly festoons of gray Spanish moss hung with gossamer grace from the low spreading limbs of the glossy-leaved live oak trees that lined either side of the wide drive. She loved the dangling tendrils of the much-maligned plant, which, contrary to popular belief, does not devour its host, instead receiving its nutrients from the air and rainwater.

As she glimpsed the red brick Georgian buildings, she felt a thrill.

Annie Laurance Darling, Professor. Well, adjunct instructor, actually, but as Shakespeare observed, a rose by any other name—

She glanced at the seat beside her. No doubt professors had a grander title than lesson plan for their projected classwork, but, whatever they called it, Annie was prepared. And it would be interesting to meet the faculty members of the journalism department.

According to Burke, journalism was quartered in Brevard Hall (named for Miss Dora's family?) which was the third building on the right. Most of the parking spaces along the drive were empty and the graveled lots behind the buildings sparsely tenanted except for the lot behind Brevard Hall, which held a clump of cars, several battered coupes, a vintage VW with bright pink paint, and one sleek red Camaro. Annie noted the red-lettered sign that designated student parking. So some students were there even though the new session didn't start until next week. The slots in front of the building, reserved for faculty at all times, held one car, a canary-colored Corvette. Annie coasted to a stop behind it and eyed the car thoughtfully. The road hog? Probably not, although she doubted Chastain teemed with yellow Corvettes. Shrugging, she grabbed her green folder, stepped out of the car, and hurried toward the oyster shell walk. Midway up the walk, she paused to admire the elegant entablature supported by four glistening Ionic columns. The classic frieze depicted a chariot race in ancient Rome. Which was apropos of what? The race goes to the swiftest? As she recalled her Roman history, the chariot races quite soon became the province of professional drivers, hard-bitten, tough men not above filing an adversary's wheel or slipping a mickey to a competing horse. Whatever else under the sun might be new, man's tricky, twisting nature was not.

Whatever symbolism might be intended, and perhaps the architect had intended none, the campus stretched out in placid, late afternoon loveliness. The vivid warm rose of fall flowering camellia japonica shrubs studded the dusty grounds with enchantment. Knobby black cypress brooded over the dark waters of a central pond.

It was a scene of absolute peace and beauty. Idyllic. Smiling, Annie walked briskly on up the path, enjoying the sound of shells crunching underfoot. She pulled open one of the white double doors and stepped inside, then stopped short, her hearing assaulted by a blare of high-decibel synthesizer music. The noise, which sounded like a machine shop gone mad, emanated from the first door to her left, which was, unfortunately, propped wide open by a tattered orange backpack.

A sign above the door, with a few missing letters, identified the offices of THE CHASTAIN COLLEGE CRIER. Suddenly a stocky, broad-faced young woman with improbably long, black braids appeared in the doorway. She wore an Elton John T-shirt, baggy Levi's, and work boots. She paused, looked back into the room, and bellowed (the only possible way to be heard over the din), "Hammermill's a shit, but I'll try to get the story. Listen, you owe me one for this." Head poking forward, horn-rims slipping on her nose, she plunged into the hall and swept toward Annie, then jerked to a halt to stare at a hand-lettered poster on a table by the door to Annie's right. Her long braids quivered like storm-whipped electrical lines as she shook her head irritably. "Oh hell. Double hell," she groused loudly. Stamping one booted foot, she gave Annie a sharp glance and demanded, "So who gives a damn about mysteries? Crap, I've *got* to get two more hours of electives and that's the only time that works for my schedule! Oh, shit," and she swung toward the exit.

Mysteries?

Annie was turning toward the table to see what occasioned that outburst, when the entry door at the far end of the hall banged open. She gave the newcomer scant attention until he began to charge down the hall. For a wild moment, she thought he was bearing down on her.

His appearance wasn't threatening. He had short, curly brown hair, a snub nose, freckles, and a square chin. His dress would have passed muster at any preppie academy—front-pleated khaki slacks, button-down blue shirt, rep tie, and blue blazer. But the scowl on his face was enough to send Annie backpedaling.

When he careened past her to burst through the open door to *The Crier*, she took a deep breath of relief.

Her relief increased when the mind-numbing din of the synthesizer ended abruptly in midchord. Welcome, assuaging silence descended.

But she tensed again when a deep voice roared, "Hey, what the hell, jerk. What're you doing with my tape?"

Stepping nearer the open doorway, she looked into a long room dominated by the glowing green screens of three rows of monitors. Oh, of course. The newsroom for *The Crier*.

But she was only peripherally aware of the variously dressed students behind some of the monitors or clustered near a desk. Because she expected all hell to break loose any minute.

The fellow who'd charged past her into the newsroom had a wiry, compact build but he wasn't big or impressive, and he stared up, confronting an infuriated giant, who stood at least six foot six and had neck and chest muscles that would be the envy of a pro football player. Heavy cranial bones made him look like a Neanderthal survivor. The giant glowered down at his small tormentor. "That's my tape player, Kelly."

"Sure." Kelly's voice quavered just a fraction. "You can play it anywhere you want to—except here. This is a newspaper office. It's going to be run like a newspaper office. Anybody who's here is here to work. No music. No loud stuff. No crap, Bernie."

"So who's gonna make me," the giant taunted, reflecting a lifetime of dependence upon size and meanness to get his way.

"I'm going to make you." The voice was thin, but determined. "I'm the new editor of *The Crier* and what I say goes. If you turn that music on one more time, I'll kick you off the staff. And I mean it, Bernie."

It hung in the balance. Bernie's face reddened, his meaty fists bunched, but his smaller opponent met his angry gaze unbendingly. Finally, Bernie turned back toward his desk. "Sure gonna be fun to work here," he complained, but he settled into his chair and yanked a notepad closer.

The editor waited a moment, then glanced around the room. "Okay, everybody, get busy. We've got a paper to put out." He stepped to the doorway, yanked up the backpack, and looked directly at Annie.

He stared at her blankly for an instant, then asked politely, "Can I help you?"

"Oh no, no thank you. I'm looking for the main office of the journalism department."

"It's directly across the hall," he said, then he turned away and the door closed behind him. But not before Annie had seen the tremor of his chin. She wasn't the only one who'd been scared. And she felt a flash of admiration for a gutsy performance.

But the student newspaper staff was none of her concern. She turned away and looked across the hall. Sure enough, DEPARTMENT OF JOURNAL-ISM was blazoned on the opposite door. But first, she stepped closer to the table with the hand-lettered poster that had excited the wrath of the work-booted young woman with braids.

JOURNALISM 306 (Feature Writing) CANCELED
Scheduled in its place, TTH 10 AM, **JOURNALISM 308,**
a new course by adjunct instructor
Annie Laurance Darling
on **THE THREE GRANDE DAMES OF THE MYSTERY**

Annie beamed at the poster. What a nice ring the course name had.

Cheered, she reached for the main office doorknob, then impulsively paused to study the chock-full bulletin board on the faded beige wall. Substitute drama announcements for these and she could be back in a hallway at Southern Methodist University. Information on contests, fellowships, scholarships, internships, and the usual offers to word process (fifty cents a page) term papers, etc., with the serrated telephone number slips at the bottom of the page. Tucked here and there were the customary thumbtacked cartoons from *The New Yorker,* clips from *Rolling Stone,* requests for roommates (nonsmoker, no cats), and ride queries for the Thanksgiving holiday (requests for Fort Lauderdale predominated).

The office door swung out, and a tall, stooped man in a white suit lurched into her, knocking her folder loose. Annie managed to keep her balance, then turned hastily to scoop up her scattered papers.

"S'sorry, m'dear." He wavered unsteadily and made disjointed motions to help.

"That's all right," she said breathlessly, retrieving the last sheet that was draped over a scuffed wing tip. She rose and smiled.

He gave her a glassy smile in return. A thick shock of snowy hair rose on his bony head like an egret's crest. Pale blue eyes peered emptily from behind heavy horn-rims. "Hope I didn't muss your papers." The words were, with an obvious effort, distinct. An overpowering scent of mouthwash wafted moistly over her. He blinked. "No classes today. 'Rollment—*En*rollment's over."

"Oh, I'm not a student." She couldn't quite suppress the note of satisfaction. "Actually, I'm going to be teaching a class this next quarter."

The glazed eyes blinked again. "Adjunct faculty." He nodded heavily. "Course, course. I'm Josh Norden. Teach advertising." He put out a hand that trembled ever so slightly.

"Annie Laurance Darling." She shook his hand, which was cool, damp, and limp. She nodded toward the office. "I was going to ask where the faculty meetings are held. Do you know?"

Flaccid lips peeled slowly back in a parody of a smile. "Where the faculty meets? Oh yes, indeed. Let me show you the way, Miss Darling." With elaborate courtesy, he took her elbow.

"Mrs. Darling," Annie corrected swiftly.

But her mentor wasn't listening. He was concentrating on negotiating the long hallway. Just as they reached the foot of the stairs, light steps sounded briskly behind them.

"Josh?" a worried voice called.

The frail, gentle-faced woman who caught up with them flashed an apologetic glance at Annie, then turned to Annie's escort, who had one hand firmly fastened on the wooden railing.

Drunk as a skunk, her Uncle Ambrose would have observed.

"Josh, let me drive you home," the woman pleaded. "I have my keys right here. You shouldn't try to go to faculty meetings when—when you aren't yourself."

"I beg your pardon, Charlotte," Josh Norden said with great dignity, enunciating so very carefully. "I am quite all right." He cleared his throat. "Charlotte, my dear, may I introdushe . . . introduce Miss Annie Laurance Darling, who shall be joining our happy faculty family for the quarter." He nodded his snowy head at Annie. "It is a great pleasure to introduce you to Mrs. Charlotte Porter, our dearest and most kindly faculty member." He gave a deep bow and almost lost his balance. "And our loveliest professor."

There was a terrible pathos in the tableau before Annie, the royally drunk faculty member paying homage to a woman who might once have been exquisitely lovely. Traces of past beauty lingered in her wide-spaced blue eyes and fine features, but Charlotte Porter was thin almost to the point of emaciation. Her pale pink chambray blouse gaped at the neck. The lace scarf fastened with a cameo couldn't hide the wrinkled throat. Her too-big blouse drooped over pointed shoulders and only a tightly cinched woven cloth belt held up her sagging gray skirt.

Charlotte Porter shook her head in dismay. "Josh—"

"Time to go," he said robustly, and he started up the stairs, pulling Annie along. Annie tightened her grasp on her folder, managed to keep in step with her wavering guide, and wondered what all of this augured for her first faculty meeting. A sheet poked out of her hastily regrouped folder. Annie glimpsed one line: *Mary Roberts Rinehart is acclaimed for her invention of the Had-I-But-Known school of the mystery.*

Had I but known—

Hmm.

Norden picked up speed on the second floor. Annie tried not to look as though she was running on tiptoe, but Norden was so tall his helpful grip on her elbow lifted her almost from the floor. Charlotte Porter was close behind them, still trying to get Norden's attention.

Outside room 220, a slim and very pretty red-haired young woman stepped forward as the unlikely trio neared. "Mrs. Darling?"

Grateful for an opportunity to break free of her alcoholic companion, Annie nodded eagerly.

The girl lifted a Leica that hung from a leather strap around her neck. "Mr. Burke sent over a notice that you are joining the faculty this next term to teach a mystery class. I'm Georgia Finney, chief photographer for *The Crier,* our student newspaper. May I get a picture of you?"

"Of course you may," Norden intervened. "Good policy, welcoming adjunct faculty."

The young photographer shot him a surprised look, but quickly masked it with another smile. A very self-possessed and perceptive young woman, Annie decided. She was the epitome of the competent professional, her red hair sleekly framing a truly lovely face, her double-blue striped cotton shirt crisp, her brushed cotton blue-and-red plaid skirt wrinkle free.

Charlotte Porter stepped forward. "I'm sure Mrs. Darling will be happy to cooperate." She looked beseechingly at Annie.

"Certainly, certainly," Annie replied quickly and realized she was join-ing in Charlotte Porter's effort to pretend that Professor Norden was all right, quite all right, thank you.

Without seeming to, Charlotte Porter took charge, separating Norden from Georgia and Annie as neatly as a sheepdog cutting out a lamb.

As Georgia used her light meter and focused, Annie listened to the muffled exchange behind her. Charlotte Porter was still attempting to divert Norden from the upcoming meeting.

The Leica clicked three times in succession, Georgia Finney beamed her thanks, and Annie walked into the classroom.

R.T. Burke welcomed her warmly. "Knew you'd come. Counting on you. Bet your class'll knock 'em dead." A hyena cackle. He looked past her, and the laughter cut off abruptly. Irritation flickered in his emerald green eyes. "Tear yourself away from happy hour, Josh?"

"Between quarters," Norden replied distinctly. "Firsh—first time we've ever *had* a faculty—" he swayed perceptibly "—meeting between quarters."

"Sure hope it's not too big a burden," Burke retorted.

Wordlessly, Charlotte Porter stretched out a blue-veined hand.

Burke's face softened. "Hello, Charlotte. You've met Annie?"

At her nod, he took Annie's elbow and turned her toward what seemed to be a crowd of people, introducing her in a staccato burst. "Annie Laurance Darling here is our new adjunct, and a mighty knowledgeable young woman about mysteries. She's going to be a great addition to our staff, no doubt about it." He rattled off names and titles to Annie, then clapped his hands together briskly. "All right, all right, everybody's here. Might as well get underway," and he shooed them to their seats.

Three long tables faced the lectern. Annie grabbed a chair at the far end of the last table and tried to attach names to faces. Sitting at the back right of the room, she had a clear side view of the faculty members.

One name she had no trouble with. She had managed, upon their introduction, not to snarl, "Road hog," but she had no doubt this was the driver of the yellow Corvette. The sleek black hair and aviator sunglasses were unmistakable. Kurt Diggs. His hibiscus-patterned shirt, open at the throat, revealed lots of curly black hair. Diggs had pouty, full lips and a hot, lingering handshake, and he wore his jeans too tight. She wondered if he knew that could be a sperm inhibitor. As she looked at his profile, he turned. He'd removed the sunglasses, and his eyes locked with hers in a knowing, suggestive gaze. Annie tried hard to make it look as though her glance had moved along that table with no interest in him. But he gave a small, satisfied smile and winked languidly.

Asshole.

Casually, she turned her head and hoped that the irritated flush she felt wasn't reflected in her cheeks.

All right. Kurt Diggs, the road hog, taught radio-TV and worked as a newscaster on a local channel.

Charlotte Porter, Professor Norden's champion, sat between Diggs and Norden. She continued to cast worried glances toward a supremely impervious Norden. She taught public relations. Norden slumped a little in his chair, his chin resting on his chest. He breathed so heavily Annie could hear him at the back of the room.

Three men sat at the middle table. The first—yes, that was Professor Garrison. Victor Garrison. Midthirties. Sandy-haired. Baby-faced. Dick Powell as Philip Marlowe in the film version of *Farewell, My Lovely.* Muscular but civilized, though not her picture of the lean, thin-nosed Chandler hero. A sweet autumn wood scent drifted from the pipe cupped in a well-manicured hand. He eyed Burke with scarcely veiled insolence. He taught general editorial classes.

The second occupant of the middle table lounged comfortably with his beefy arms crossed on his chest. He was a big man with curly blond hair, china blue eyes, and a perpetual half-smile that never changed. Which Annie began to find a little unnerving. His name was Malcolm Moss and he taught advertising.

If she weren't a married woman, she would have taken some effort with the last man at that table. Another public relations professor, Frank Crandall. Mmmm, yes. A mop of shaggy brown hair, hazel eyes, a self-deprecating smile, a bony, intelligent face. He wasn't a sexy hunk. No, his appeal was a good deal more subtle than that, though he was definitely a very attractive man. Crandall sort of hunkered over the table as if there weren't quite room enough for his long legs and arms. He wore a white tennis shirt with a ragged collar, and she glimpsed lean legs in khaki trousers rather haphazardly arranged beneath the table. He was the kind of man women like to mother. Though not, of course, all the time. He lifted his left hand to smooth back the droop of hair from his brow, obviously a habitual gesture, and sunlight from the west windows glistened on a golden wedding band.

Not that she was interested. After all, she was a happily married woman of one month and twenty days. Still, she might be married, but she wasn't in a cloister.

An empty chair separated her from a blowsy blonde with vivid brown eyes, an armload of gold jewelry, and bright red lipstick that would surely glisten in the dark should the electricity fail. Sue Tarrant taught general reporting. Annie responded to a friendly grin, and suddenly felt a bit more welcome. At the thought, she realized that she hadn't felt welcome, not until Sue had smiled. Her own smile slipped sideways and she glanced again around the room. Annie didn't go in much for sensing nuances. That was more the preserve of her husband and mother-in-law. But there was an aura—oh God, what had brought that word to mind? She hastily substituted *ambience*, despite its yuppie connotations—an ambience of uneasiness.

Cupping her chin in her hand, she thoughtfully directed her attention to Burke at the lectern. Despite the apparently genial exchange of smiles and nods, Annie decided the atmosphere was decidedly not one of academic bonhomie.

". . . know that you are all looking forward to the beginning of our second quarter together—and all the changes we will be making to improve our department." Burke bared his teeth like a wolf baying at the moon.

Kurt Diggs flicked a silver cigarette lighter and held the flame to a dark brown cigarette. He inhaled deeply, then blew three perfect rings. Charlotte Porter's thin hands clenched spasmodically. Josh Norden hiccoughed once, loudly. Victor Garrison sucked gently on his pipe. Malcolm Moss's perpetual half-smile didn't waver. Frank Crandall shifted in his chair and one knee knocked against a table leg.

Across the empty seat, Sue murmured, "Horse shit."

Annie shot her a quick glance. Surely she hadn't heard correctly—

"I'll open with a call for approval of the minutes of the last meeting."

"I move the minutes be adopted," Charlotte said quickly.

"Second," Norden boomed. Charlotte jumped.

Annie bit her lip to keep from smiling. Norden certainly wasn't worried about his condition, no matter how any of his colleagues might feel.

"Objection." Garrison's voice was mellow, a golden tenor. "Item four is a misrepresentation of the mission of the Curriculum Committee, which I have the honor of serving as chair." He smiled boyishly. "It is my clear understanding that the committee is charged with the responsibility of evaluating current course offerings and considering possible alterations of some substance. You will note that my emphasis is on the adjective *possible*."

Annie glanced down at the mimeographed sheet in front of her.

DEPARTMENT OF JOURNALISM
MINUTES OF FACULTY MEETING OCTOBER 7

Present: Burke (chair), Tarrant, Diggs, Garrison, Crandall, Porter, Moss.

Absent: Norden.

1. Quorum declared.
2. Minutes of meeting September 2 approved.
3. Tarrant moved, Crandall seconded:

The inclusion in internal unit review procedures of guidelines mandating equal consideration of professional attainment with scholarly publications. Objections voiced by Garrison, Moss. Professor Garrison stressed his dismay at according commercial acceptance equality with scholarly publication in a refereed journal. Passed, 5–2.

4. Garrison moved, Moss seconded:

Interim acceptance of Curriculum Committee Advisory Report, pending—

Annie skimmed the headings of the other items, all as laboriously presented as the foregoing. The minutes reminded her why she'd always embraced the dictum of famed jurist Augustus N. Hand: Join no clubs and have no slogans. The consideration of minutes had always struck her as one of life's least interesting exercises. Annie willed away a yawn and felt the beginnings of a letdown. She'd really looked forward to this meeting: her introduction to the world of scholarship and academic excitement. She was eager to share her love of the mystery and her fervent conviction that the mystery serves as the twentieth-century version of the medieval morality play. Surely those involved in transmitting knowledge and values would understand her theme. Instead, it looked as though this meeting was merely another in a long line of sessions dominated by Roberts' Rules of Order and very little else. Who the hell *was* Roberts, anyway? And why did every gathering in the English-speaking world have to degenerate into *Will the chair rule?* and *Someone has to second the motion!*

Garrison's voice rolled on sonorously. The man obviously took great pleasure in hearing it. Even looking like Dick Powell couldn't excuse that. "My objection, of course, as my colleagues will appreciate, is with the unfortunate inclusion of the modifying term *advisory.*" He pointed with his pipe stem at the offending agenda.

The classroom door opened.

Garrison paused.

Every eye swung toward the young man poised on the threshold. Annie recognized the young editor who had faced down the giant. She sat forward, the beginnings of boredom forgotten. As he stood, the moment lengthening, the tension growing, Annie felt a sudden sharp bond, the underdog against insuperable odds, the gladiator facing a snarling, pacing lion. He stood stiffly, facing them, his young face almost stern, his gray eyes determined. But he was pale and the freckles spattered across his face seemed to stand out. Then, like a diver plunging into a cauldron, he strode purposefully toward the back of the room.

Garrison waggled his pipe. "I beg your pardon, Mr. Kelly."

The editor stopped, one hand gripping the back of Annie's chair. "Yes, Professor Garrison?" Once again Annie thought she detected a slight, ever so slight, quaver in his voice.

"Mr. Kelly. This is a faculty meeting." Garrison's measured tone placed it right on a level with a National Security Council conclave.

"Yes, sir. I know." Kelly squeezed behind Annie's chair and slipped into the empty seat between her and Sue. Placing a fresh steno pad on the table, he pulled a ballpoint from a pocket of his blazer.

"Mr. Kelly, faculty meetings are closed to students." Garrison's tone was pleasant, but firm.

Moss nodded in agreement, still with that same half-smile. Annie decided he was creepy. Crandall scratched his cheek and frowned.

Kelly's gray eyes turned attentively toward Garrison. "I understand that, Professor. But I'm not here as a student. I'm here as editor of *The Crier.* We're putting out our first issue tomorrow. I intend to provide the most in-depth coverage of the college that has ever been achieved by a *Crier* staff." As he talked the telltale quaver lessened, though his voice remained thin. "That coverage will include detailed reporting of faculty meetings. As you've pointed out many times in class, South Carolina has an open-meeting law. You've always stressed the importance of this law to the healthy functioning of society. And, of course, as you've taught us, any exception to that rule constitutes a muzzling of the press."

Garrison stiffened. A tiny flush stained his cheeks. "Mr. Kelly, you *must* leave."

"No, sir," Kelly responded respectfully. "Any meeting of any entity receiving at least sixty percent of its funding from the community is open to the public. By law, Professor." He gazed determinedly at the infuriated academic, but the fingers holding the pen were shaking.

Garrison faced the lectern, his face flaming. "Mr. Burke, this is an intolerable and unwarranted intrusion into the private deliberations of the faculty." He had forgotten his posture of geniality, his smooth face twisting with anger.

Burke's raucous laugh exploded. "By God, Kelly's right. Good thinking, young man. Sure. You can cover us. I like for our young people to show initiative. All right, Victor. Back to your complaint with the minutes. Let's get this settled and get underway."

Garrison glared at Burke. "I wish to make clear," he said icily, "that I deeply resent the intrusion of a student into the arena of faculty consultations. I continue participation under duress." He paused. A muscle twitched in his smooth jaw. "I wish forcefully to state my objection to the minutes of the last meeting as they now stand. The Curriculum Committee has never been considered merely an advisory body. Its deliberations have always been accorded full weight." Garrison took a deep breath and modified his tone, once again parading his mellow tenor. "As chair of the Curriculum Committee, I have understood our mission to be the most effective utilization of the department's resources to create course work which will demand the utmost in effort from our students and which most appropriately demonstrates the academic integrity of our institution."

"Academic crap," Sue murmured.

The hand poised over the steno pad started to write. Sue reached out and clasped the young man's wrist. "Down, Geraldo."

Geraldo, Annie thought in confusion. It seemed an unlikely name for a guy named Kelly.

"Furthermore, I feel it imperative once again to remonstrate with my colleagues." Garrison's voice rose, but retained its creamy tone. "Such unseemly haste in approving basic—yes, fundamental—revision of course work merely to curry favor during what I understand to be a temporary shift in leadership surely reflects poorly upon their commitment to academic excellence, which we have long sought in this collegial community, feeling quite strongly that scholarship is not to be solely the function of the major institutions. As a faculty member with some seniority, I find it incumbent upon me to steadfastly reiterate *my* devotion to this commitment." He drew deeply on his pipe.

Kelly scrawled: *G. anti-trade schl. pitch.*

Clearly, Annie thought, deep waters swirled here and she apparently didn't speak the language.

"Objection noted, Victor," Burke said impatiently. "Now, let's vote on the minutes. Charlotte moved—"

Malcolm Moss drawled, "For the record, Professor Garrison is correct. The committee has not heretofore been designated as advisory in its capacity."

A taut silence ensued. Annie glanced from one grim face to another. She reran Moss's innocuous—to her—statement in her mind. Who cared whether a committee was designated as advisory?

A lot of people, apparently. Kurt Diggs's sensuous mouth twisted in a sardonic smile. Charlotte Porter nervously creased and recreased the mimeographed agenda sheet between her thin fingers. Josh Norden swung his head toward Burke and his crest of white hair quivered. Victor Garrison nodded portentously. Malcolm Moss's half-smile never wavered. Frank Crandall sighed. Sue Tarrant's lips tightened in disgust.

Burke's bright green eyes glistened with the joy of battle. "Have to hand it to you boys. Never give up must be carved on your ass."

Garrison drew his breath in sharply, and Moss's smile finally fled. Burke grinned at their discomfiture.

"Semantics aren't going to change one basic reality—the buck stops at *my* desk. I made it clear when I came in August that I intend to reshape the course offerings. I've welcomed everybody's suggestions." He glanced at Garrison. "Input, you call it. Okay. Everybody's inputed. Of course, the Curriculum Committee has backed and filled and insisted that further deliberations are essential. Fine. You deliberate all you want to. But I've finished deliberating. Next week I'm presenting my plans for new course requirements to the academic vice president."

"Next week!" In a woman it would have been a scream. Garrison lunged to his feet. "Next week! That's absurd. We can't possibly have completed our survey and correlated our data—"

"Damn shame," Burke replied.

"So you intend to ignore the faculty's efforts?" Moss said heavily.

Burke feigned surprise. "Who, me? Ignore the faculty? Perish the thought, Malcolm. I have sought faculty input. I have also set a deadline. After all, that's what we are teaching our students, isn't it? To meet

deadlines? If some material isn't available at that time, I scarcely see it as
my fault. Now, the vote on Charlotte's motion."

It was, Annie thought, like coming into a darkened auditorium during
the second act. Although she could hear the words, she couldn't be sure of
their meaning. She was certain of one thing only: nobody liked anybody
very much.

The rest of the meeting didn't alter her conclusion, even though there
were exchanges of exaggerated courtesy. Professor Tarrant reported for
the Library Committee, Professor Moss for the Scholarship Committee,
Professor Garrison for the Personnel and Planning Committee, and Professor Diggs for the Alumni Affairs Committee. Barbed comments flew in
a discussion of a proposed reduction in management theory courses for the
master's program, Burke insisting that the business of writing is writing,
not business, and Garrison vehemently countering that the focus of communications education across the country was on mass media management. "Look at Northwestern!" he exclaimed.

"You look at it!" Burke retorted. Annie's head swung from side to side,
following the verbal sallies. But finally, they reached new business.

"Delighted today to announce the addition of yet another outstanding
adjunct to our faculty, Mrs. Annie Laurance Darling, proprietor of the
famed mystery bookstore, Death on Demand, on Broward's Rock Island."

Annie tried to look modest, intelligent, and mysterious.

Burke smiled. "This young lady knows her mysteries, and she's going to
share her knowledge with our students."

"Mysteries?" Garrison repeated.

A method actor couldn't have freighted the word with more and varied
emotions: astonishment, disdain, incredulity, aversion, and disgust.

Sue's small gasp of pleasure and the student editor's "Good stuff!"
didn't quite compensate.

"Mysteries," Burke repeated firmly.

"When is this class scheduled?" Moss asked. "I thought we had only
one adjunct slated for the next term."

' "That's right. Room two-oh-six. Ten A.M. Tuesdays and Thursdays."

"Bob Puckett was hired for that slot. To teach feature writing." Moss's
face looked like a chunk out of Mount Rushmore.

"I fired him," Burke said crisply. "Sorry bastard faked a story. Supposed
to've interviewed people in a bar on pros-cons death penalty. Made it up!"

Slowly, Moss pushed back his chair and stood. He was damned impos-
ing, topping six feet and built, again as Annie's Uncle Ambrose would
have observed, like a bull moose. A vein pulsed in his temple. "I saw that
story. A good read. He presented all the views."

"Jesus Christ, Moss. Did you hear me? The fucker made it all up! He
sat on his ass in his apartment and created that story. I know it for a fact.
The city editor told me. Now, I'm not going to have a sorry bastard like
that within a mile of this place."

Moss's massive shoulders hunched. "He was one of my best students."

"If that's true," Burke shot back, "this department's in worse shape
than I thought."

"You had no right to fire him." Moss's deep voice was thick in his
throat.

"Oh, yes," Burke replied, "I had the right. I have the right. Remember,
Moss, I'm the S-O-B-I-C." He punctuated this enigmatic pronouncement
with a brusque nod. "Meeting adjourned."

As she picked up her folder, Annie leaned past the student editor, who
was scribbling furiously in his fresh pad. Annie looked inquiringly at Sue
Tarrant. "S-O-B-I-C?"

Sue enunciated very clearly and with evident satisfaction. The words
rolled across the room. "Son of a bitch in charge."

Annie was deeply immersed in the second edition of John M. Reilly's
Twentieth Century Crime and Mystery Writers. Yes, there it was. Christie's
play about the Egyptian pharoah Akhnaton was published in 1973. She
frowned, puzzled. But wasn't it written in 1937 when she was working on
Death on the Nile? She pawed through a stack of books—

"Mrs. Darling?" The accent was familiar, liquid, rolling, genteel South
Carolina, but it took an instant for her to place the woman smiling shyly
at her. Then Annie jumped up. "Hello, Mrs. Porter. How are you?"

The painfully thin woman with the once-beautiful face held out a
folded tabloid. "I just happened to be on your island and I thought I
would take the opportunity to drop by and see your wonderful bookstore
and bring you a copy of Friday's *Crier*. Georgia's picture came out beautifully. Let me show you."

Charlotte Porter opened the paper to page six. The two-column photograph was excellent, showing a smiling Annie. The cutline read: *Annie*

Laurance Darling, mystery expert, visits Brevard Hall. Darling will teach a two-credit course, THE THREE GRANDE DAMES OF THE MYSTERY, *during the winter quarter. Department Director R.T. Burke predicts the class will be very popular.*

"That's terrific publicity," Annie said happily. "It should increase enrollment."

"Oh, I've already heard students talking about it," Mrs. Porter replied. "They are very excited."

There was the slightest of awkward pauses.

The academic looked brightly around the coffee area. "I'm just so excited to have a chance to visit your store."

This was right down Annie's alley. "Let me give you my deluxe tour."

They ended up at the coffee bar, Charlotte Porter clutching two Juanita Sheridan books. ("I just love Janice Cameron and the Hawaiian background.")

Pouring coffee in mugs respectively inscribed *The Silent Bullet* and *The Case of the Sulky Girl,* Annie continued to shine as a hostess and wonder, with more than a little curiosity, what had brought Charlotte Porter to see her. The possibility that she had actually just been in the neighborhood (on an island thirteen miles away by land and two by sea on a misty November Saturday) seemed just a trifle farfetched.

"It was really very nice of you to bring *The Crier,*" Annie said finally, as she took a last sip of her magnificent (if she did say so herself) Colombian coffee.

"Oh, it was no trouble," Mrs. Porter assured her earnestly. She didn't look quite as worn today; her faded blue eyes sparkled as she talked about one of her favorite authors, Kathleen Moore Knight. A spot of color touched her almost cavernous cheeks and the thick weave of her wool cardigan hid the thinness of her upper body. "We do so enjoy the delights of getting to know our adjunct faculty members. Really, our faculty has always, historically, been one to be very proud of, even though we are such a small college. Mr. Burke is a prime example of the college's willingness to go outside the narrowness of academia to seek out wonderfully accomplished professionals. You may know that he has won many awards over the years for his excellence in reporting." She nodded, her gray head bobbing energetically. "And, of course, our regular faculty has had so many, many outstanding members. Joshua Norden, for example." The blue eyes regarded Annie steadily. "Why, for many years he served as an advertising consultant to the Chastain National Bank and to the State Bar Association, and he is a past chairman of the American Academy of Advertising. When he worked in advertising, he was a winner of Addys at four different times."

"I'm sure he is very outstanding," Annie said gently.

There was more, of course—references to other faculty, to their achievements—but, as Annie walked her new friend to the front door of Death on Demand, she knew why Charlotte Porter had come.

Annie watched as the thin figure disappeared into the November mist. What a gallant effort to preserve the reputation of an old friend—and how deeply Charlotte Porter must identify her own life with the needs and objectives of the Chastain College journalism department.

Annie walked slowly back to the coffee area and began to straighten up. She checked the coffee pot, which was almost empty, but decided against brewing more. There wouldn't be many people in today. It was too gray and dank and there weren't any tourists, in November, to clog the aisles with disappointed sun worshippers.

She picked up *The Crier*, thinking she must be sure and thank the young photographer, and closed it, then stared at the boldface announcement at the top left of page one.

A NEW DIRECTION

THE CRIER will offer a new dimension in its coverage of Chastain College with the publication today of the first issue under the editorship of Bradley M. Kelly.

Kelly promises to report all the facts of interest and concern to students, faculty, and administration.

Today's issue contains complete coverage (lead story, page one) of an unannounced meeting of the journalism faculty on Thursday. During that meeting, factions supporting and opposing more professionalism and less academicism in the school clashed.

In next Tuesday's edition, *The Crier* will run the first in a series on the handling of personnel matters in the school that directly affect student welfare.

Kelly, a senior from Columbia, has served as managing editor, sports editor, and news editor.

He has been awarded a Fulbright to Oxford for
the next academic year.

Annie nodded admiringly. A spunky guy, that Kelly.

Ah, shades of Helen Kirkpatrick, Ruth Cowan, and Marguerite Higgins. They rest secure in the history of women war correspondents, but Mary Roberts Rinehart beat them to it. An argument could be made for Nellie Bly (Elizabeth Cochrane Seaman) as the first woman foreign correspondent, but actually Nellie was making news, as well as reporting it. Of course, looking even farther back, Margaret Fuller wrote about Louis Napoleon's siege of Paris in 1849 for the *New York Tribune*. But honors for being one of the first in the trenches should go to MRR, who reached the front in the early days of World War I despite a ban on correspondents, jouncing up a shell-pocked road in an unlit car to the flooded no-man's-land between the German and Allied lines. Bodies bobbed grotesquely in the icy water, and the night smelled of death.

MRR was no stranger to death in many guises. In the 1890s, she had trained as a nurse in a Pittsburgh hospital that served men injured in the great steel mills and on the railroads. One night she agonized over the slow death of a man who had been caught in a flywheel. She stood beside him in the Emergency Room. "I wanted him to die quickly, not to go on breathing. I can't stand it. Die and stop suffering. I can't stand it. I can't."

"Challenges," Annie announced aloud.

Max looked up from his book *(The Amateur Cracksman* by E. W. Hornung). Diverted, Annie wondered what his choice indicated, then decided not to pursue that thought.

"Challenges?"

Annie paused to admire her husband. Really, he *was* a grown-up Joe Hardy, with his thick blond hair and eyes of such a dark blue they rivaled a mountaintop lake. And such a superbly muscled body. A tiny frown drew her brows together. Somehow she couldn't picture the impetuous Joe Hardy quite so relaxed. Max sprawled full length on the sofa, three pillows bunched behind him, and he looked about as muscled as a jelly fish. Was Max getting soft? Was married life blunting his keen edge? Actually, had Max ever *had* a keen edge?

He draped the book across his chest, put his hands behind his head. "Challenges?" he said again.

"Mary Roberts Rinehart," she replied absently. Then, more excitedly, "That's the key to her life, a zest for challenges! Entering a hospital at sixteen in 1893 to train as a nurse (she lied, she lied, Max, and said she was seventeen) when only a few young women of her class were choosing such arduous and unprotected work, beginning to write in earnest some years later when she and her doctor husband owed money because of the market crash of 1904, daring as a novice to write for Broadway, finagling her way to the front lines in 1915, later seeking out the still-challenging American West and traveling the deserts of Egypt and Iran!"

"Always living on the edge," Max said affably, burrowing more comfortably into his pillows.

Annie's frown became more pronounced, then she sighed. She didn't have time now to think about Max's incredible relaxation since marriage. Not certainly that he had ever been uptight. But she must focus her energies on the task at hand, preparation for her first class.

Her first class.

Tomorrow morning.

Annie clutched her Rinehart folder. Should she approach each writer one at a time or perhaps meld together a quick overview of all three?

Rinehart knew the gritty realities of life and death but fashioned a romantic world in her fiction where love always triumphed.

Christie believed in evil. She created puzzles and delighted in sleight of hand.

Sayers was brilliant and erudite, with a boisterous sense of humor and no capacity for tolerating fools.

The Three *Grande Dames* of the Mystery. Annie wondered for just an instant what the topic would be if the three of them came to tea.

Rinehart had great social charm.

Christie was very shy.

Sayers loved to stay up all night, smoke incessantly, and talk voraciously.

It would be quite a gathering.

6

MAX HELD THE FRONT DOOR.

Annie balanced three folders and her purse atop a box crammed with paperbacks. "Do I look all right?" she asked anxiously.

"Adorable," her charming spouse responded with an insufferable grin.

She stamped her foot. "No, no, no. Do I look all *right?*"

Max tilted his head and stroked his chin contemplatively. "You don't think a navy blue suit and plain white blouse with a Peter Pan collar is a little—well, perhaps, a little extreme?"

"Frumpy?" she demanded, peering down at the smooth expanse of offending navy blue gabardine.

"Of course not frumpy," he said loyally. "Just a little . . . understated, perhaps."

"But Max, I don't want to look young!"

"Is there something in the faculty manual about age?" he asked innocently.

"Max, you know what I mean," she wailed.

He bent, kissed her cheek. "Annie, my love, you are, as always, beautiful, desirable, and delectable. Don't worry, your class is going to adore you."

"Not if they think I'm just a kid," she mumbled, starting down the tree house steps. She paused and peered back at him worriedly. "Now, you'll be all right—?"

Lounging against the doorframe, he arched a quizzical blond brow. "Is there some unheralded danger abroad on Broward's Rock of which I am unaware? Fire-snorting dragons? Martian tarantulas?" He paused, grinned. "Truant officers for adults?"

"You *are* going to work?" she shot out sharply.

"Of course. Cross my heart, et cetera. Wouldn't miss a day in the office for the world."

Nodding, still worriedly chewing her lip, she started on down the steps, paused again. "You could go and check on the progress of the house." She looked past him, at the weathered boards of her tree house. She did love it, but their stay had grown longer than anticipated. Not only had their new house not been ready upon their return from their honeymoon, it was still not completed.

So much to think about. The house. The store. Of course, Ingrid was quite capable of handling everything at Death on Demand. Annie paused, balanced her carton atop the mailbox, pulled down the lid, and fished inside. Bills, of course. Only two real letters. One to Max from his sister Diedre. One to her with a Paris postmark. The handwriting, a bold clear script, was familiar. Who could it— She ripped it open, then smiled. How sweet. A note from Emma Clyde, the island's most successful resident writer and creator of that famous fictional sleuth, Marigold Rembrandt.

Annie was all the way to the car and had stowed the box in the trunk when she realized the morning's mail lacked the weekly letter from her esteemed mother-in-law, Laurel. She paused, her hand on the car door, and looked back toward the tree house, but Max had already gone inside. Oh well, it would keep and surely the letter had only been delayed. Perhaps Laurel was busy with— Her mind quailed at the prospect of what might possibly be occupying Laurel's time. But at least she was in Connecticut. Such a lovely, *distant* place, Connecticut.

Annie wheeled into the faculty lot. The Volvo windshield flaunted a newly applied crimson-and-white sticker, FACULTY AND STAFF. How many badges there were in the world, little emblems of belonging. Or not belonging. As she lifted her box of books and materials from the trunk,

Annie sighed happily. To be a part of an academic institution, even if on a lowly level, was thrilling. And she'd already had so much fun preparing for the class and learned so many new facts about her favorite writers. Mary Roberts Rinehart used her own Bar Harbor mansion as the scene of the crime in *The Yellow Room*. Agatha Christie wrote the surname of her husband's mistress when she signed the register of a hotel during her headlined disappearance in 1926. Dorothy L. Sayers, in the opinion of critic Trevor H. Hall, indicated her debt to Arthur Conan Doyle by giving Wimsey the address 110A Piccadilly, which is half of 221B Baker Street plus one (A as the first letter in the alphabet representing one).

Annie was grinning at the last as she stepped inside. It was wonderful what critics could suggest, that Christie developed into one of the world's finest storytellers because her mother kept her home from school and so the lonely child populated her world with imaginary personalities. And the thesis of Rinehart's biographer that the woman who became a national celebrity excused her career on the basis of family need and always pretended to herself that her family came first because her Victorian sense of propriety demanded it. And the suggestion that Sayers's fruitless search for the true love of her life led her to create Lord Peter.

What would those ladies say now, had they the opportunity?

Annie paused just inside the back door. She had a clear view of the central hallway. It didn't take Nurse Adams, Hercule Poirot, or Peter Wimsey to deduce that something was afoot—and that charming redhead who had snapped her photograph was right in the middle of it all.

Body language can shout. Four women stood squarely in front of the student newspaper entrance. Arms tightly folded, faces grim, their heads snapped toward her, then she was dismissed. The front door creaked open, and they swung in unison to face it.

Annie was glad she wasn't the one they were waiting for. Somebody was going to catch hell. It wasn't, of course, any business of hers. She could have gone up the back stairs, but the tableau of anger intrigued her. What was going on? And probably she should check in at the main office anyway, see if there was anything she needed to do before her first class.

She paused at the main office door and gave a quick glance across the hall at the militant group, a pudgy blonde in a wrinkled bright green Mexican shift, a tiny dark girl with elfin features and brilliantly black eyes, a slightly older woman in a replica of Annie's plain blue suit, and the red-haired photographer. Annie was startled by the change in her appearance. Gone was the elegant self-possession of last week. She looked as if she'd tossed on the nearest clothes at hand. The paisley skirt clashed with the plaid blouse, and her hair wasn't sleek and controlled, but looked as though she'd jabbed at it hurriedly, scarcely combing it at all. She didn't even have on any makeup and her face was gaunt and pale.

The pudgy blonde jerked around and grabbed the handle to the closed door of the *Crier* office. She rattled it angrily, then pounded on the wood panel.

The tiny, dark girl tapped her foot impatiently. "Nobody's there, Lizzie. Listen, we're wasting time." Brilliant black eyes crackled. "And I've *got* to go to class. Let's call an emergency meeting, then we'll march on the *Crier* offices this afternoon, when the staff is there."

"I could kill him. I could just *kill* him." Lizzie's voice rose in a furious screech.

"The thing to do is go to Mr. Burke," Blue Suit suggested. She turned toward the photographer. "Don't you think so, Georgia?"

The pale redhead didn't respond.

"Georgia?"

Slowly, troubled green eyes focused on the speaker's face. "It's so sickening. He has to be stopped, Ruth, before he does any more. He has to be stopped."

"Let's talk to Mr. Burke," Ruth said decisively.

Annie followed the four into the departmental office.

Ruth, whether by status of age or force of personality (was it the blue suit?), took charge. Leading the way to the counter, she surveyed the empty office behind it. Without a moment's hesitation, she lifted her voice to a piercing level. "Emily! Emily, where are you?"

The creaking of the floor in an interior office sounded first, then labored breathing.

Slowly, an enormous creature, bulbous with fat, wedged sideways through the doorway. She—it was a woman, perhaps even a young woman —was a mass of flesh almost lacking in definition, a bloated moon face atop a swollen body, chest and girth and hips merging into a mountainous whole that moved and swayed beneath a huge yellow caftan. She clutched a handful of tissues in bratwurst-size fingers. Angry red splotches mottled her face. She snuffled into the tissues as she waddled toward the counter.

Ruth's placid face reflected no repugnance, no recognition of the grotesque. But she did hesitate for an instant, then asked gently, "Emily, are you okay? Are you feeling all right?"

Tears welled in eyes so deeply mired in fat that they stared out at the world through slits. Emily swabbed her huge face with the tissues, then glowered at her inquisitor.

"What's wrong, Emily?" the red-haired photographer asked quickly.

"Nothing," she said harshly. "Got allergies. That's all." The fat woman's voice was high and thin, and her answer was so patently false there was a moment's silence, then Ruth shrugged her blue-suited shoulders and said crisply, "A delegation from the Women's Press Association. To see Mr. Burke. About today's issue of *The Crier.*"

"Can't."

Lizzie bristled and the green Mexican dress quivered with outrage. "Of course we can."

Emily blew her nose. "Not unless you go to Charleston. He's gone to a meeting of the state newspaper editors. Won't be back till tomorrow."

The small dark girl tossed her head angrily. "Tell him—tell him—oh well, never mind. We'll see him in the morning."

And the group swept out.

Annie darted into the faculty women's restroom on the second floor with a sense of reaching sanctuary, even though she knew a restroom could scarcely qualify as such. The Reverend Julian Harmon defines sanctuary quite precisely in the Christie short story of the same name. Annie stared anxiously at the mirror. Actually, she looked fine, even though she felt she'd been through an emotional wringer from the assorted angry vibes ricocheting around the ground floor of Brevard Hall. And that poor, poor secretary. God, how awful to be that fat. But she mustn't let herself be distracted from her own responsibilities. She glanced at her watch. Lordy, just a few more minutes and she would face her first class. Her first *class.* She glanced again at the mirror, then glared at her own image. Darn her hair. She'd pulled it back in a no-nonsense bun, but strands kept straggling loose. A stern application of water temporarily defeated the rebellious sprigs. Satisfied, she applied a fresh coating of pale pink lipstick, straightened her skirt, and headed toward the door.

Almost time now. And she was prepared. That's all it took in life. Preparation. She patted her bulging folders which included a printout of her trio's publications, including plays and films. Interesting that all three were successful playwrights, not a given with novelists. Plain white index cards contained a neat outline of her lecture topics. She began to feel a modest glow of well-being. No need to be tense or worried. Why, this was going to be duck soup. As the restroom door sighed shut behind her, she considered the phrase. What could possibly be its origin? Duck soup sounded complicated to her.

A bell rang and people poured from doorways. The hall filled. Lots of jeans and knit shirts, cotton skirts and pullover blouses, friendly, smiling, cheerful faces, mostly young, but all ages and races represented, a gaggle of hearty, middle-aged women with brown faces, muscular golf arms, and intense expressions, a pretty coed with her head tilted to look up admiringly at the bulky young man beside her, a stylish young black woman reading a TV script as she walked. Annie wormed her way up the hall, relishing the sense of bustle and purpose. She didn't see any of the angry women who had gathered in front of the *Crier* office earlier. What had that been about? Obviously, this morning's edition had ignited some angry responses. She felt a moment's curiosity. But probably nothing quite as momentous had occurred as their behavior had implied. It was fascinating how situations could get blown out of proportion, especially in the closed environment of an institution. Perhaps that was why so many mysteries had academic settings. She thought fondly of three of her favorites, Gwendoline Butler's *Coffin in Oxford,* V. C. Clinton-Baddeley's *Death's Bright Dart,* and Robert Barnard's *Death of an Old Goat.*

But whatever passions embroiled Chastain College, they were of no moment to her, just a curious blip on an otherwise cheerful morning, which had been quite productive. It had been smart of her to arrive early. After the militant quartet departed, the immense departmental secretary had morosely, still sniffling, found Annie a set of keys, directed her to the supply room (what a sense of power to be entrusted with a green-backed grade book), and pointed down the hall to the faculty lounge. Annie had rather shyly stepped in, been relieved to find it empty, and delightedly spotted a hot plate. A motley collection of chairs served two worn tables. Mail slots of old-fashioned varnished brown wood filled one wall. Her name was taped to a slot in the last row. In the remaining time, she had located her classroom (currently in use) and nosed around the second floor. Now, she swung confidently ahead, aiming for room 206.

Smiling timidly and holding open the door for her was a stocky young man with faintly pink hair that poked straight up from his forehead and dangled limply on his neck.

She smiled in return. "Thank you."

Striding briskly to the front of the room, she put her box and her folders down on the desk and studied the lectern. Good, it had just enough tilt for good reading and not enough to dump her index cards on the floor. People (her students!) began to file in. The secretary had sullenly informed her that faculty enrollment cards hadn't been sorted yet. Annie could make up her own roll (send around a sheet of paper for sign-up) for the first few class meetings. To gain admittance, each student must give her a yellow card with her course number and the student's name on it. They would match the purple cards the faculty would receive.

She was skimming her lecture notes when she stiffened, her senses assaulted.

Scent.

Sound.

Sight.

The scent came first. The unmistakable fragrance of lilac, clear and sharp and sweet.

Annie's hands tightened in a death grip on the sides of the lectern. It couldn't be. Surely it couldn't—

It could.

Laurel swept through the doorway, beaming, of course. She was a vision of ethereal loveliness, her golden hair shining like a cap of spun moonlight, her patrician features Grecian in their perfection, her deep blue eyes brimming with good cheer and happiness and a kind of childlike delight that no one (in Annie's experience) had ever been able to resist. She moved, as always, so lightly that she might have been a ballerina in flight. Her costume was fetching in its simplicity, an oversize pink shirt, white cotton trousers, and pink canvas sneakers. A pink-and-green-striped cotton carryall hung from one shoulder. Obviously, this was Laurel's vision of coed stylishness. She could have passed for fourteen.

"Annie, my sweet, it's so *marvelous* to be with you again. My dear, I've *missed* you. Ingrid is a dear, of course, keeping me supplied and offering so many *tips*. But it isn't the same thing as being here at your feet." An impish smile. "Metaphorically speaking. To follow your mind in its dogged path—no, no, that isn't quite what I mean. But you are *so* orderly. First things first; a place for everything, everything in its place; the early bird gets the worm. Though I've always thought a *hurried* breakfast so often causes indigestion. But your passion for order is wonderful, admirable. It will make you such a good instructor."

A waft of lilac and the touch of Laurel's lips on her cheek, swift as a hummingbird.

"Now, I'll just take my place to one side. I won't be in your way. Dear Maxwell thought behind-the-scenes support the very best approach. But I say family is family and where is one's place but beside the family in the midst of new and challenging endeavors." An ecstatic sigh, a gentle wave of pink-tipped fingernails, and Laurel drifted to a seat at the far end of the front row. With a final cheery, *encouraging* smile, she slipped gracefully into the chair, dropping the woven carryall at her feet. It gaped open and was revealed as a book bag, chock-full of crisp new paperbacks: *The Murder of Roger Ackroyd, The Man in Lower Ten,* and *Whose Body?*

Laurel here. Laurel *here!* Annie stared after her. Then the back of her neck prickled. That sound. That thump behind her!

It took every vestige of will to turn her head to face the door to the hallway.

Thump. Thump. Thump.

Quick, purposeful, decisive thumps.

The ebony cane with its black rubber tip poked around the corner, followed by its mistress.

The tiny old lady stood motionless in the doorway for a long moment, staring at the room, the other occupants, and then at Annie. She had raisin-dark eyes luminous with intelligence. They were deeply set in a yellowed, crinkled face that looked like parchment. A tall red velvet hat with a yellow feather perched atop her shaggy silver hair. Her heavy silk dress was red, too, so dark a red it rivaled blood. Tiny feet shod in high-top leather shoes peeked from beneath the full skirt.

"Miss Dora," Annie gasped.

A cold, formal nod and the silver hair shimmered like cirrus clouds across a winter sky. The cane thumped on the wooden floor. Miss Dora Brevard settled, as if to a birthright, in the chair directly in front of the speaker's lectern, sitting straight as a ramrod, feet firmly planted on the floor, wrinkled hands tight on the silver knob of her cane.

"Received the course announcement. It said—" Miss Dora fumbled in a crocheted receptacle, drew out an old-fashioned pair of pince-nez, clipped them to her bony nose, then rustled further to haul out a yellow mimeographed sheet. " 'Mrs. Annie Laurance Darling, proprietor of the Broward's Rock mystery bookstore, Death on Demand, will present at ten A.M. on Tuesdays and Thursdays a course on The Three *Grande Dames* of the Mystery.' " She shoved the sheet into her bag, removed the pince-nez, and demanded, "Who?"

"Who? Who what?" Annie asked faintly.

"The Three *Grande Dames*. Who are they?" Those obsidian eyes glittered with irritation.

Laurel's husky voice, ever-so-slightly chiding, flowed across the room like golden syrup. "Now, now, now. We must all be patient. Dear Annie will share in her own good time. It doesn't do to hurry young people. And emanations of an irritable nature do have *such* a damping effect upon nervous, high-strung creatures."

"Perfectly reasonable question," Miss Dora snapped, eyeing Laurel with the enthusiasm of Chief Inspector Wilfred Dover for his long-suffering assistant, Sergeant MacGregor. "Don't believe in pussyfooting around."

Annie was just ready to intervene (after all, she didn't need Laurel defending her—she was *not* a nervous, high-strung creature—and Miss Dora's question *was* perfectly reasonable) when her glance froze.

Oh God.

The sight framed in the doorway was almost too much for her to accept. Laurel was bad enough. Miss Dora would cast a pall on an Addams Family tea party.

But this—

It wasn't as though she didn't recognize the costume: a large gray flannel skirt with a droopy hem, a full blouse with a lacy panel down the front, a shapeless rust-colored cardigan, lisle stockings, extremely sensible brown shoes, and hair bobbing in springy sausage-roll curls.

"Henny," she moaned.

Henny Brawley gave her a reproachful look and pulled an apple from her skirt pocket. "Dear girl, here!" and tossed it. "Full of nutrition. Just the thing for a woman's intuition."

The latter hint, of course, was to prevent Annie from the embarrassment of not recognizing Christie's irrepressible sleuth and alter ego, Ariadne Oliver.

Annie was too dispirited to reply. She caught the apple, and stared from Henny, dropping happily into the far left front seat, to Miss Dora, just opening her mouth, to Laurel, who gave a *reassuring* nod.

The bell rang.

The boy with the faintly pink hair scooted inside, kicked the wooden chock free, and headed for the back of the room as the door slowly eased shut.

Her class had assembled: Pink Hair, a massive hulk who had to be a football player, three middle-aged women, an elderly man in an orange jogger's warm-up, a woman in her forties.

No surprises there.

The door burst open and a young woman with a dark frown and two improbably long, black braids stamped inside. Oh God. Yes, that was an Elton John T-shirt. Maybe she had a whole closet of them. Her arrival would have been a downer, Annie recalling her outburst about mysteries, but her inclusion in the class faded to insignificance as Annie contemplated three particular students. Never had she envisioned spending a morning discussing the mystery with Laurel, Henny, Miss Dora, and assorted strangers.

She was committed.

She would pretend the front row wasn't there.

Fixing her eyes resolutely on the boy with the faintly pink hair in the back row, Annie cleared her throat. "Good morning. I'm Annie Laurance Darling. I'm not a teacher by trade. I'm a bookseller and a collector. I specialize in mysteries. In this class, we are going to be discussing The Three *Grande Dames* of the Mystery." At her unwavering regard, Pink Hair's ears began to pinken, too.

The black cane thumped imperiously against the floor.

Annie reluctantly looked down. "Miss Dora?"

"Who?"

"Now, I'm sure that Annie, in her very thoughtful way, has prepared this morning's presentation," Laurel began melodiously.

"Ladies, ladies, thank you," Annie said swiftly. "We shall study Mary Roberts Rinehart, Agatha Christie, and Dorothy Sayers."

"L," Miss Dora rumbled.

It was hard to shock Laurel, but her gasp was clearly audible. "Hell? I must say, I *am* surprised at such an unwarranted response, when poor, dear Annie is doing her very *best* to offer writers appealing to almost all readers."

"L! L! L!" Miss Dora screeched. "Dorothy *L.* Sayers. Drove her mad if you left out the initial. Dorothy Leigh Sayers, after her mother's family. Broke a contract once with the BBC because they left the L out of her name. L. L. L," she repeated venomously.

Gesturing vigorously with an apple, Henny demanded, "Good show, but what about P. D. James? Ruth Rendell? Mary Higgins Clark? Elizabeth Peters? Phoebe Atwood Taylor? Charlotte MacLeod? Dorothy Salisbury Davis? Mignon G. Eberhart? Phyllis Whitney? Daphne du Maurier? Christianna Brand? Josephine Tey? Patricia Highsmith? Mary Stewart? Victoria Holt? Helen MacInnes? Margaret Millar? Mabel Seeley? Dorothy B. Hughes? Amanda Cross?"

Miss Dora got into the spirit of Henny's inquiry, punctuating each name with a vigorous thump of her cane.

The boy with the pink hair silently rose and, back to the wall, began to sidle toward the closed door.

"Of the Golden Age," Annie bellowed valiantly. She gripped the lectern. "These three great women mystery writers each contributed substantially to the mystery, and it is upon their foundation that many subsequent great writers have built. But it is they who led the way."

"Footprints in the sands of time," Laurel cooed, approvingly.

"Before I pass out the reading list," Annie said hastily, "and a roll sheet for everyone to sign, I would like to give a brief sketch of the lives and work of our three great—"

The hall door swung in again. Annie flicked a sidelong glance and recognized the square-faced, snub-nosed, wiry new editor of *The Crier.* He ducked his head apologetically, and turned toward the back of the room.

Annie spoke a little louder. "Mary Ella Roberts Rinehart was born August twelfth, 1876 in Allegheny, Pennsylvania, in very modest circumstances. Her father, Tom, was a dreamer and an inventor. Her mother, Cornelia, was an intensely practical woman. Rinehart was destined to become the highest paid author in America."

The editor dropped into an aisle seat midway toward the back.

"Dorothy Leigh Sayers, the only child of a Church of England minister and his wife, was born July thirteenth, 1893 in Oxford, an appropriate beginning for a woman with a brilliant mind and a scholar's quest for truth. When she focused that intelligence upon the detective novel, she created an immortal sleuth, Lord Peter Wimsey, and enhanced the status of the crime book to that of the novel of manners.

"The greatest detective story writer of all time, Agatha Mary Clarissa Miller Christie, was born September fifteenth, 1890 in Torquay, the daughter of an American father of inherited wealth and an English mother. Although all three authors continue to sell very well today, Christie is the reigning queen of the mystery. No one has ever surpassed Christie in brilliance of plotting."

Lordy, how she loved to talk about Agatha Christie. Annie smiled impartially at all the class, forgetting her determination to ignore the first row. Henny smiled back, Miss Dora elevated a sardonic eyebrow, Laurel radiated quiet pride.

The hall door burst open.

Annie knew the ropes. Like a minister with a wailing child in the congregation or an actor with a restless audience, she ignored the interruption. As a drama instructor had once admonished, "Pro*ject,* pro*ject,* pro*ject!*" She raised her voice and continued, "These three women profoundly affected the course of the mystery novel, marking the genre forever afterward with the stamp of their own individual genius. The course of true love marred by murder, an intellectual content that amazed, plotting so brilliant—"

"I'm sorry."

Annie paused.

Georgia Finney, her face even paler than before, hesitated just inside the classroom and looked at Annie imploringly. The red-haired photographer carried a rolled-up newspaper in one hand. "Please forgive me for interrupting." Her voice quivered.

"What's wrong?" Annie's query was instinctive, a response to genuine distress.

The girl swallowed convulsively and her sea green eyes swung from Annie to the student newspaper editor. "Brad, I got your class schedule. I have to talk to you. Now."

Kelly frowned. "I'll be at *The Crier* this afternoon, just as usual. How about three o'clock? That's a pretty good time, before everything gets hairy with our deadline."

Georgia thrust the rolled-up newspaper toward him. "It says there are going to be more articles. Brad, you've got to stop it! Please come out in the hall. We've got to talk."

Kelly's square face looked suddenly implacable. He stared at her solemnly. "It's the duty of a newspaper to report the truth."

"Brad," her voice was low and stricken, "these are people you know. Brad, you're hurting people. Please."

"No," he said shortly, and Annie remembered how he'd faced down the giant with the synthesizer music. "These are people who are being paid with tax dollars. The public has a right to know who they are and what they do. I'm just doing my job."

"Are you?" Anger flushed Georgia's cheeks. "Your job? Or Mr. Burke's? Is he behind this?"

"My source is confidential," Kelly retorted quickly.

Annie had had enough. Whatever quarrel these young people had, it wasn't her quarrel. And this was her classroom. "Wait a minute," she said sharply. "Mr. Kelly, you may go out in the hall for this discussion. If you please."

He shook his head stubbornly. "I don't please."

Georgia's face hardened. "You're going to regret this, Brad." In a swift and violent gesture, she ripped the newspaper in two and flung the pieces on the floor, then turned and plunged out into the hall.

The students, including Laurel, Miss Dora, and Henny, followed her exit with fascinated eyes.

Annie took a deep breath. "Mary Roberts Rinehart grew up on Archer Street and this street would figure—"

Max tried to look supportive, indignant, and apologetic without assuming any faint hint of responsibility. "Sweetheart, of course I didn't know she was coming!" Guessing and knowing were not, of course, synonymous. "This comes as a great shock to me."

Annie paced in front of his desk. She was obviously steamed, but the angry sparkle gave her gray eyes an unforgettable vividness and her tousled blond hair (she'd probably paced on the ferry all the way across the sound) reminded him of rumpled sheets in the morning sunlight. Not that there was anything remotely loving in the glares she was emitting right this moment. Her glances were right on a par with Bertha Cool scanning Donald Lam: suspicious, testy, and decidedly grouchy. Fortunately, the similarity ended there. Annie was still his sexy, sweet (sometimes) wife, though afternoon delight might be temporarily on hold if he couldn't convince her of his noncomplicity in Laurel's unheralded arrival.

Annie stopped, braced her hands palms down on his desk, and stared at him accusingly. "Laurel said you suggested behind-the-scenes support! So what does that mean? You told her about the class? You *told* her?"

"Annie, love, I was so excited at the prospect, so pleased for you. I know how much you enjoy digging out all those fascinating facts about mysteries. The ones you told me about, like Mary Roberts Rinehart basing *The After House* on the famous ax murders that occurred in the 1890s on that lumber schooner, the *Herbert Fuller*, and how her book reopened the case and resulted in freedom for the mate who'd been convicted. And Agatha Christie patterning Louise Leidner in *Murder in Mesopotamia* after Sir Leonard Woolley's imperious wife, Katharine. And all the fun Dorothy Sayers—"

"L," Annie interrupted automatically. "Dorothy L. Sayers."

"—had when writing *Murder Must Advertise,* using her background as a copywriter at the London advertising agency of S. H. Benson's." He paused. Annie was nodding contentedly. "Certainly, I had the best of intentions."

That wasn't the politic remark to make.

"Good intentions!" she fumed. She resumed her pacing. "The road to hell is paved with good intentions."

He received this original pronouncement in respectful silence.

Annie shoved a hand through her sandy hair. "I can't believe this has happened to me. My class—just a nice little class on murder, and now look what's happened!"

Max began to feel a trifle combative. After all, Laurel was a good sort. He banished to a deep recess of his mind the outcome when Laurel had engaged in activities close to the hearts of his brothers-in-law. "Well, now, Annie, really, don't you think you're overreacting? I know Mother can be a bit overwhelming, but she really does mean well."

"It isn't just Laurel. I could cope with one. But not three!"

"Three?"

"Oh Max, it isn't just your mother. Henny's in my class, too. And Miss Dora. You remember her. She has that old house and she runs that town and everybody's scared to death of her. She's in there, too. And every time I really get started, one of them interrupts. Laurel coos something about love and Miss Dora thumps that damn cane, then Henny has a bright aside. Max, they're devouring my class."

Not just Laurel! Max was careful not to let his relief show, but this certainly put a different face on it. "Three of them," he exclaimed happily.

Annie glared, and he promptly assumed a totally sympathetic expression. "Annie, that's a damned shame."

"Isn't it just," she said bitterly. "And if that's not bad enough—a free spirit, an old bat, and a mystery nut—all hell's breaking loose over the college newspaper and I might as well have recited GNP statistics for the rest of the class period. Nobody gave a damn about anything but that damn student newspaper."

Max seized on the diversion. "What student newspaper? What happened?"

"I don't know and I don't care. And I can tell you this, Max Darling, I'm not going to have a single thing to do with any of it!"

7

ANNIE BREATHED DEEPLY of the cool November air. A light breeze stirred the Spanish moss in the live oak limbs and rustled the fronds of the sturdy palmettos. Their footsteps echoed on the wooden verandah. They had the harborside to themselves, it was so early. She squeezed Max's hand, then darted a quick sideways glance. Max looked glum. Which was, of course, so unlike his usual pleasant, equable demeanor.

Was it cruel and unusual punishment to roust him from the comforts of the tree house and deposit him at his office door before eight o'clock in the morning?

Annie almost took pity. After all, they could be home in five minutes, and she knew what would lighten his mood. Turn him effervescent, as a matter of fact.

Then she vanquished temptation. Duty called. She had been so distraught over the unexpected composition of her class that she had thrown up her hands in despair last night and neglected to prepare.

Preparation was paramount. She was determined, at all costs, to hew to the line. Nothing was going to deflect her from the task at hand. Nothing. In such a doughty fashion would Inspector French pursue even the most tedious investigation. (And he was as fond of food as was Annie, though, of course, this had nothing to do with her admiration for him.)

So she smiled encouragingly at her husband. "Max, work is *fun*. Look at it that way."

"At eight o'clock in the morning?" he asked dismally.

"It's for your own good. You haven't been busy enough. I can tell," she said firmly.

"Really? Does my hair turn green? Do my ears droop? What signal do you receive?"

She grinned. "It's much more subtle. You are as languid as a sunning cat. Max, you need to be stirred up. Activated. Energized. Now, I want you to promise me you'll take on a new challenge today."

"Hmmph."

They reached the front door to Confidential Commissions, Max's agency which specialized in solving problems. He had formed it and purposefully kept its nature and function vague, because the sovereign state of South Carolina has quite rigorous requirements for the establishment of private detective agencies. So Max ran a tasteful ad in *The Island Gazette* and *The Chastain Courier:*

> Troubled, puzzled, curious. Whatever your prob-
> lem, contact CONFIDENTIAL COMMISSIONS, 555-
> 1321, 11 Seaview, Broward's Rock.

Annie stood on tiptoe and slipped her arms around his neck.

Max immediately looked much more cheerful, and he caught her up in a vigorous embrace.

"Max! Not here. That's too—"

Annie was trying to make her point, but somehow she lost track of it.

In a moment, he surfaced. "Oh, yeah," he said happily. "Hey, Annie, let's go home. Just for a little while."

Honestly, he was appealing, his thick blond hair, now ruffled, those dark blue eager eyes, and the warmth of his lips.

Annie almost succumbed, then drew herself up—and away—with a stern shake of her head. "Duty, Max. It calls."

"Lunch at home?" he asked hopefully. His vivid eyes took on a look of cunning. "Some R and R, Annie. It does wonders for morale."

One of Max's stepfathers had been a bird colonel in the army, and, taking a fatherly interest in Laurel's son, early explained the efficacy of rest-and-relaxation periods. Laurel had been so pleased at Max's warm response to this military influence.

"Well—" Annie temporized.

Max bent close and his lips traveled from her cheek to her throat.

"Oh Max, you make it so hard to be serious."

"This isn't serious?"

"Lunch," she finally agreed feebly. But it was nice to leave a cheerful Max behind. She turned once to wave, but he was already inside Confidential Commissions.

Annie hummed a little tune. She always enjoyed going to Death on Demand. Her bookstore. Her very special, wonderful lair of mysteries. As she unlocked the front door, she paused to admire the window displays. The south window featured Tony Hillerman's supremely original books, so evocative of the glory and grandeur of New Mexico and its people, *The Blessing Way, The Dark Wind, Dance Hall of the Dead, Listening Woman, The Ghostway, People of Darkness, A Thief of Time,* and his only non-Indian book, *The Fly on the Wall.* (Hillerman wryly recounts how his agent responded to *The Blessing Way,* instructing him, "If you insist on rewriting this, get rid of all that Indian stuff.") The north window contained an exhibit of golf mysteries, *Murder on the Links* by Agatha Christie, *Death on the First Tee* by Herbert Adams, *The Murder on the Sixth Hole* by David Frome, *An Awkward Lie* by Michael Innes, *Lying Three* by Ralph McInery, and *Fer de Lance* by Rex Stout.

As the door swung in and she smelled the particular, exhilarating (to her) fragrance of Death on Demand, a compound of freshly ground roast coffee, ink, paper, and moist Whitmanii ferns, she felt a thrill of happiness. The store to herself for two whole hours and books, books, books. She wanted to find that reference in Christie's autobiography to the breakdown of the touring car in the desert when the young archeologist Max Mallowan was escorting her to Baghdad. It was, Agatha learned later, her unruffled acceptance of that potentially dangerous occurrence which convinced Mallowan that Agatha should be an excellent wife.

Annie paused at the cash counter to see if Ingrid had left any messages from yesterday. A sheaf of slips rested beneath a skull-and-crossbones paperweight. Hmm. A call late in the afternoon from Miss Dora Brevard. No message, would call again. Annie's shoulders tightened. Something to do with the course, no doubt. Had she left out one of Sayers's publications? No, she'd checked and double-checked. The list was complete and included Sayers's Dante translations and her religious writings (especially that brilliant theological exposition, *The Mind of the Maker)*. A call from Henny Brawley, and this dramatic quote: *Double, double, toil and trouble; Fire burn and cauldron bubble.* Annie sighed. The last slip, on pink paper of course, carried a cherubic happy face, the pronouncement, *"One has a duty to love,"* and Ingrid's editorial comment, *"Laurel sounded quite chirpy but very determined. Something's afoot."*

Annie's sense of peace eroded. Dammit, what did all of this mean? She stared down at the messages, then, with a decisive flourish, ripped the slips in half and tossed the scraps at the wastebasket.

She flipped on the lights and strode purposefully down the central aisle. The click of claws on the heart pine flooring announced Agatha's approach. As Annie reached the coffee bar, the sleek black cat jumped atop it. Annie bent down to nuzzle her silky ruff, and Agatha made a guttural demand deep in her throat.

Agatha's breakfast (salmon and fresh water) duly provided, Annie reached for the coffee pot. Colombian or Kona this morning? She opted for Kona and was filling the pot when the telephone rang. Annie reached out for the receiver, tucked it between shoulder and chin, caroled "Death on Demand," and measured the coffee.

"I am a trustee."

Annie's heart sank. The voice, dry and crackly, like the rustle of old newspaper, was unmistakable.

"That's good, Miss Dora."

"My land, you see. Deeded it to the city for the campus. Life member of the Board of Trustees."

"Very generous of you," Annie responded, switching on the coffee maker.

"Don't like controversy."

"Certainly not," soothingly, taking a deep breath of the pungent aroma steaming from the pot.

"Despise people who humor me."

Annie made a face at the mouthpiece.

"You're nosy. I want you to find out what that man's up to."

"What man?" Annie asked blankly.

"Burke. A new broom. Doesn't give him license to sweep out the best and the brightest. Hideous way to treat Charlotte. She won't even answer her phone. I want you to find out who said all these dreadful things about her. Talk to that Burke man first."

What was it about Miss Dora that evoked such a hostile reaction on Annie's part? The arrogant assumption that all the world must do her bidding, because she was Dora Brevard of Chastain, South Carolina?

Despite every good intention, Annie felt herself sizzle. "Miss Dora, I don't know anything at all about Mr. Burke or Charlotte, whoever that is." But, of course, she knew. That nice Charlotte Porter who had made a special trip to Broward's Rock to tell Annie what an outstanding faculty member Josh Norden was. A too-thin woman who had once been beautiful. But she didn't owe this knowledge to Miss Dora. "In fact, I don't have any idea what you're talking about, but I can tell you this, I'm not getting involved in any academic infighting. I've been hired to teach a mystery class and that's what I intend to do. And that's *all* I intend to do."

A long, lethal silence ensued, then a clipped demand. "Your last word?"

"Absolutely."

The line went dead.

Annie replaced the receiver with a troubled frown, then shrugged. The trials and tribulations of faculty, staff, and students at Chastain College were no responsibility of hers. What she needed was coffee. Nodding decisively, she turned to reach for a mug.

The bell on the front door jingled. Annie swung toward the central aisle. Dammit. It was two hours before opening time. Obviously, she'd forgotten to lock the door behind her but what dolt would come inside when the CLOSED sign was prominently—

"Knew you'd be here. Time for a conference. Sometimes the task of a good detective is to *prevent* crime." Henny nodded sagely. "Think of Miss Marple in 'The Affair at the Bungalow.' "

From the collected short stories in *The Tuesday Club Murders*, Annie noted automatically. Then she shook her head and drew up for battle. "Henny, we are *not* detectives. You are *not* Miss Marple. You have to stand on tiptoe to reach five foot four and Miss Marple was tall. Your eyes are brown, hers were blue."

"China blue," Henny said cheerfully.

"She's frail and knits. You're about as frail as a low-country alligator."

Henny cupped her chin thoughtfully in her hand and gazed at the bookstore with a faraway manner. For the first time, Annie realized that her favorite customer wore a hand-knit shawl over the shoulders of a black grosgrain dress. Her hair was no longer sausagey, but was now fluffy and a delicate white. However, the telling transformation, Henny's magic, was in attitude: the sudden sense of penetrating intelligence, modesty, Victorian sensibility, and village acumen.

Damned if she *didn't* look like Miss Marple.

But it would just give her a big head to admit it. And she was impossible enough as it was. Annie picked up the coffee pot. "A cup?" she asked.

Henny became Henny and shot an appraising glance at the collection of white mugs behind Annie. "Sure. I'll take *Death in a Tenured Position* by Amanda Cross." Annie picked out *The Long Goodbye* by Raymond Chandler, and they grinned at each other in mutual appreciation of their exquisite subtlety.

Henny leaned against the counter. "I'll put my cards on the table, Annie. I've never seen a situation so ripe for murder."

Annie gulped the hot, strong coffee. "Wishful thinking."

"Annie," Henny chided, "I do not have blood lust."

Annie raised a sardonic eyebrow.

"My motives are of the purest," Henny insisted. "I scent trouble. We can forestall it."

"No. No. No," Annie said simply, firmly, declaratively.

Henny tipped open her knitting bag and fished out a crumpled newspaper. She spread it out across the coffee bar. Clear tape held the puckered edges of a jagged tear. She nodded at Annie's look of inquiry. "Yes. The very paper that young woman, Georgia Finney, tore up so dramatically in class yesterday."

Annie ostentatiously yawned. Agatha finished her last scrap of salmon, looked up, and yawned, too.

"Listen, this may be one of the few papers still in existence. They disappeared like wildfire. I understand Burke's demanding that they be turned in and destroyed. He's furious."

Annie bent down to retrieve the watering can beneath the coffee bar sink. Agatha meowed inquisitively. The pig. "Time to water the ferns," Annie informed her.

As water gushed from the faucet, Henny lifted her voice another level.

"And talk about trauma! A highly respected professor revealed as an embezzler. Burke accused of a cover-up. Hints of more sensational revelations to come. Who'll be fingered next? And who's dishing out the dirt? A well-placed source—what does that mean?"

Henny was hot on Annie's heels as she toured the reading area, splashing water on the ferns and straightening the red and yellow cushions in the rattan chairs.

"It's dynamite," Henny insisted.

Annie returned to the coffee bar and stored the watering can, then faced her pursuer.

"Henny, love, the passions abroad in the Department of Journalism at Chastain College are of no interest to me. Zero. Zip. Zilch. I do not intend to become involved. I was hired to teach a course in the mystery and—"

The phone rang. Annie reached out, grateful for the interruption. "Death on Demand."

"Annie dearest." The husky, mesmerizing voice dipped and rose. "There is no time to lose."

Annie stiffened. "Laurel. You're up early this morning."

"We must seek out that lovely young woman and offer her succor."

"What lovely young woman?"

"Georgia, of course. Georgia Finney."

Annie's eyes dropped to the coffee bar and the taped-up front page of *The Crier*.

"Laurel, we don't know what's behind that scene yesterday. And it isn't any of our business. And I don't know why she had to use my class to jump on the guy."

"Annie, I am amazed." Laurel's voice quivered with disappointment. "You, of all people. Why, how can you stand before a class and purport to teach us about Mary Roberts Rinehart and yet be oblivious to all that she stood for?"

Annie was bewildered. "What does Mary Roberts Rinehart have to do with Georgia Finney?"

Henny, who was unabashedly eavesdropping, pointed an index finger at her temple and twirled it. Annie ignored her.

"Love," Laurel said simply. "Oh my dear, we must get to the bottom of this before our next class. But, unbeknownst to yourself, you have led the way and I am seeking the truth. Love shall prevail." The connection was abruptly broken.

Annie slowly replaced the receiver and looked at Henny. "Laurel. Love shall prevail."

"Not in this world," Henny retorted. "Now come on, Annie. Admit you're curious. Admit you're dying to know what's happening at the college." She jiggled the newspaper enticingly.

"Not I," said Annie stubbornly. "I'm going to prepare for my next class."

"You're going to miss out on all the fun," Henny warned. She took a last sip of coffee. "Good stuff," and swung toward the center aisle. She did pause for just a moment, to frown fiercely at the fourth watercolor, then she charged briskly toward the door.

Annie glanced at her watch. Good. Still quite a bit of time before the store opened. Time now to check out Christie's autobiography. But she paused at the nonfiction section, her glance lingering on the top of the coffee bar.

Henny had left that newspaper behind.

Annie reached out.

She yanked her hand back. She didn't care! It was no concern of hers.

What was it Henny had said? Embezzlement? A cover-up? More to come?

She picked up the newspaper.

The head to the lead story, one-column in forty-eight-point type, with a twelve-point kicker, read:

Official Cover-Up?

INFORMED SOURCE REVEALS
PORTER MISUSED FUNDS

BY BRAD KELLY

An informed source has told *The Crier* that journalism professor Charlotte Porter has admitted to "borrowing" more than $8,000 from the Student Press Association during the school year 1986–87 and is presently making repayment.

Porter, a member of the Chastain College faculty since 1976, has refused to comment upon the allegation.

The revelation comes amid growing concern among faculty members over the policies of R.T. Burke, who assumed chairmanship of the journalism department in August. Burke, according to this informed source, intends to change the direction of the department and has indicated he would like to see several tenured faculty members leave, including Professors Joshua Norden and Kurt Diggs. However, it was reportedly Burke's decision not to consider prosecution in the case of Porter and not to request her dismissal.

Burke is critical of some faculty members over lack of time spent in class, incidents of purported sexual harassment, and recalcitrance in accepting a new, more professional direction for the department.

The Crier, now under the editorship of Brad Kelly, intends further disclosures revealing behind-the-scenes information about journalism department policies and decisions as information becomes available.

Porter has served as faculty advisor to the Student Press Association since 1978. An audit this past September uncovered the missing funds. A further audit of previous years revealed no other irregularities, and all funds are duly accounted for until the year of 1986–87. According to the highly placed informant, the matter was discussed at several meetings of the Committee on Department Policies and Personnel, which serves in an advisory capacity to the chairman. However, the decision not to prosecute was made solely by Burke.

Porter joined the faculty after working for several years in a local advertising agency. She was a several-time recipient of Addy Awards for excellence in print advertising. She is a graduate of Chastain College and has a background in both print and media advertising.

A sidebar to the main story proclaimed:

SEE FRIDAY'S EDITION
OF *THE CRIER* TO FIND OUT
MORE OF THE INSIDE STORY
ON THE CHASTAIN COLLEGE
JOURNALISM DEPARTMENT

Annie looked again at the lead story. This was journalistic hardball, no doubt about it. If she hadn't met Charlotte Porter and liked her, she would have admired a student editor for breaking a story of malfeasance. But she had met Charlotte Porter. She had liked her. And now she felt confused. But she agreed with Miss Dora; it was an ugly situation for a charming woman.

The phone rang.

"Death on Demand."

"Mrs. Darling?" A high, thin, somewhat unpleasant voice, vaguely familiar.

"Yes."

"This is Emily Everett, the secretary at the journalism department. An emergency faculty meeting has been called for four o'clock."

Stymied.

Until this moment, Annie had never understood to the fullest extent that state of being. She stared wordlessly at Max.

That, of course, was enough to concern him.

"Annie, love, what's the matter? Why does your mouth keep opening and closing? I thought you'd be really pleased. You *did* urge me to accept a new challenge today." His handsome face shone with pride.

But was there a glint of amusement in those dark blue eyes?

Annie took a deep breath, then once again said nothing. What could she say? Certainly she *had* urged him to look for a worthy task.

"A five-hundred-dollar retainer. I will say for Miss Dora, she doesn't stint when she makes a commitment. All expenses paid."

Miss Dora. The old harridan. The clever, manipulating hag! Annie cleared her throat. "And what exactly does Miss Dora want you to do?" Watson himself couldn't have made the inquiry with more naïveté.

"Find out who spilled the beans about the faculty problems to the student newspaper editor. It ought to be a snap. I'll get right to work on it. After lunch." His eyes glistened.

This time Annie had no difficulty in deciphering the message.

Annie's steps lagged. Max gripped her elbow. "Now, sweetheart, remember. You are a helpmeet, furthering me in the pursuit of my profession."

"You *know* I don't want to have anything to do with the mess over here," and she glowered at the lovely rose-colored building, drowsing in the thin November sunlight. She had, of course, been quite unable to resist a bitter diatribe against Miss Dora. Max, naturally, had professed his innocent acceptance—"Just trying to make you proud of me, love"—of a task which he was now, as, of course, she understood, duty-bound to complete.

"A commitment once made," he murmured stalwartly.

Savagely, Annie wondered if a twisted sense of humor was grounds for a divorce.

Annie reluctantly edged inside the room. As expected, she read surprise and disdain on the faces of several faculty members. She didn't blame them. She had no real reason to be at this emergency gathering, despite the notification from the secretary, who obviously was merely following orders to inform everyone on the list of full-time and adjunct faculty of meetings. But this particular meeting Annie would not—out of delicacy— have attended, except for Max's importunings. And she devoutly wished Max were here right this minute to face these hostile glances.

Even Burke looked blank as she stepped inside. Then he nodded abstractedly.

Annie slunk to the back of the room, her face flaming. But, when she settled at the last table and looked around, she realized that she was being overly sensitive. No one was paying attention to her. The air crackled with tension.

The faculty members sorted out into the same seats they had taken last Thursday. There were two exceptions. The road hog, Kurt Diggs, sat alone at the first table. Neither Charlotte Porter nor Josh Norden had arrived. Diggs sprawled ungracefully, one arm balanced on the back of the next chair. A heavy silver identification bracelet edged out from beneath his moss green cable knit sweater. His sensuous face looked sullen, the full lips set in a disagreeable pout. He didn't remove his aviator sunglasses with their deep green tint. At the middle table, Professor Garrison's smooth cheeks had an unhealthy reddish tinge and his pipe jutted from between clenched teeth. The big blond man with the unwavering half-smile, Professor Moss, focused an equally unwavering gaze on Burke. The third occupant of that table, Frank Crandall, shifted uncomfortably in his chair and nervously drummed the fingers of his right hand against the table top.

Sue Tarrant nodded briefly at Annie, but there was no warmth in her greeting today. Her eyes burned with anger when she glanced toward Burke. The cheery color of her bright lipstick was in stark contrast to the grim set of her mouth.

At the front of the room, Burke closed the door, then walked to the lectern. His bristly eyebrows were drawn into a sharp V over his beaked nose, and his green eyes moved searchingly from face to face.

There was no buildup, no marshaling of facts, just the implacable demand.

"Which one of you did it?"

Silence.

Silence so absolute that the restless drumming of Crandall's fingers thudded like the muffled drum roll accompanying a riderless horse until—abruptly—his hand stilled.

Burke clawed savagely at his cheek and left reddened streaks against his leathery skin.

"By God, I'm going to find out." Those green eyes smoldered with fury. "And when I do, I'll make sure—if it's the last thing I ever do—that whoever did it never works for a college or a newspaper or an advertising agency or a television station again. Whoever you are, I'm going to find you. One way or another."

Garrison pursed his mouth judiciously. "I am, of course, appalled at this evidence of a colleague's reprehensible revelations of confidential information to the public. However," he cleared his throat, "I wonder if perhaps we, the faculty, have not benefited from this unfortunate occurrence."

"Benefited?" Sue Tarrant stared at him incredulously. "Victor, how could you possibly say that? I haven't been able to talk to Charlotte, she won't answer her phone, but this is dreadful. Just dreadful. That matter—well, I don't even want to discuss it—but it was just a desperate, one-time act—and she's repaying it, every penny with interest. How could anyone—" and she looked from Garrison's smooth face to the petulant droop of Diggs's lips to Moss's half-smile to Crandall's sympathetic headshake "—find any good in this?"

"Now, Sue," Moss rumbled. "You're like most women. Can't look at any problem without emotion. Next thing we know you'll write a tearjerker on Charlotte for the Sunday supplement. Make all the women cry. And you can pick up five hundred bucks."

"Go to hell, Malcolm," she said fiercely.

That eerie half-smile intensified just a little. "Be glad to, Sue. Might be interesting. But, to the point, if you can manage that. As to any good arising from this situation, I believe I appreciate Victor's appraisal. Although I regret any distress suffered by Charlotte, I'm afraid we all have to admit that there is a question, isn't there, about the propriety of public officials condoning criminal acts because of friendship with the perpetrator? Nonetheless, overlooking Charlotte's probable unhappiness and the distress of any others who might expect to be subjects of this young editor's revelations, I believe Victor's point is that perhaps it is to the good that we, as a faculty, bring out into the open and discuss just exactly what our new chairman has in store for us." His sky blue eyes challenged Burke. "In fact, it has occurred to me that perhaps our chair is transferring his struggle for control of this department from the private domain to the public."

"What the hell do you mean by that?" Burke demanded.

"He means maybe you know bloody damn well who dumped on the faculty," Tarrant accused shrilly. "Maybe you're coming on a little too hot and heavy as the Great Avenger. Maybe we don't buy it, Burke."

Garrison chimed in. "It does look a little odd, to say the least. You are, of course, uniquely situated to provide that kind of information. And we all know who permitted Kelly to attend the faculty meeting last week. Could it be that you're presenting yourself as a hero, as Charlotte's protector? Then the other information critical of the faculty will be revealed and you can bewail this invasion of privacy as you plan farewell luncheons for us and hire new people."

Burke managed a sour smile. "I always knew you had a truly serpentine mind, Victor, and you just proved it." He shook his head. "I don't play games with people. Not with you, not with anybody. And you can believe what you goddamn well want to, but I'm telling you—and everybody else here—I do intend to find out who betrayed a position of trust by feeding confidential information to Kelly. I'll tell you straight out, I despise this kind of journalism. Despise it. News is information that rightly and understand my word, understand it well, *rightly* belongs to the public. This is a public institution, so the public has a right to know whether it is being run as it should. That doesn't mean the public has a right to know every personal fact about every person employed here. I didn't cover up malfeasance in office by Charlotte. I discovered and accepted restitution from

her for one mistake. One. I consider that a judgment call on my part.
Further, I have every intention of righting what I see as several wrongs
and making changes which I believe will benefit the department, but I
have no intention of destroying reputations publicly to do it. So, I'm not
behind the information revealed in *The Crier*. I believe in the public's
right to know—and I believe in the right of privacy. We're supposed to
teach students where one ends and the other begins. We've done a lousy
job with Kelly."

Crandall brushed ineffectually at a droop of shaggy hair across his brow.
"If you didn't give him that information, then it has to be one of the
other committee members who played Deep Throat."

It took Annie a second, then understanding came. Of course. *All The
President's Men*. Deep Throat, the still-unknown source in the executive
branch who met at two A.M. in underground parking garages with Bob
Woodward, the *Washington Post* reporter, during the unfolding of Watergate.

"It sure as hell looks that way," Burke growled. "There are four on the
committee besides me. Professors Garrison, Moss, Norden, and Tarrant."

Kurt Diggs slammed a meaty fist against the table. "Listen, my
friends," and his voice was ugly, "let's get one thing straight. If anybody
jerks me around, they're going to have trouble. And I mean big trouble."

"We've got to get this stopped," Tarrant cried. "Where is Brad? What
does he have to say about all this?"

Burke's face looked like volcanic slag. "The sorry bastard. I haven't
been able to find him yet. But when I do, I intend to tell him what a lousy
newspaperman he is and—"

"Lousy?" Brad Kelly couldn't control the tremor in his voice and his
face was pale, but he stood in the doorway like David facing Goliath. "Is
that why I'm getting calls from AP and UPI and *The Atlanta Constitution*? What's wrong with telling the truth?"

"Punk, tabloid journalism," Burke said levelly. "You know better. You
know you should check with every possible source on a story. Why didn't
you call me as department head? Why did you hide behind 'informed
source'? Because you wanted a sensational exposé, that's why, young man,
and you are willing to sacrifice anybody and everybody to do it."

Kelly breathed deeply, trying to draw air into stress-emptied lungs. He
swallowed jerkily. "I called Mrs. Porter. That's the other side, isn't it? I

asked her why and she"—he paused, looked down at his clenched hands—
"she just kind of sighed and hung up." With an effort of will, he relaxed
his hands, let them hang limp, and faced his accuser. "I'm sorry to dump
on her. I like her. Who doesn't? But it's a story! A big story. And somebody's ox always gets gored. That's what Professor Garrison said in ethics
class. But I got a hell of a story and I ran it. That's what investigative
reporting is all about. Look at *Sixty Minutes*! Look at Geraldo Rivera!
They do *real* stories. That's what I'm going to put in *The Crier*. And you
can't stop me." He took a step into the room, gave each of them a
considering, defiant glance. "And nobody's going to stop me. Nobody *can*
stop me. *The Crier* may be housed with the journalism department, but
it's independent. I'm elected by the students so there's not a thing you
can do about it, Mr. Burke. So you people might as well brace yourselves.
I'm editor. I'm going to stay editor, and I intend to keep on publishing the
real stories, not just the prettied-up handouts you'd like for me to run."

"Who fed you the information?" Burke demanded.

Kelly shook his head. "No." The tremor was gone now. "I'm protecting
my source. That's what you teach us to do. It's in the finest old traditions
of journalism to protect your source. And that's what I intend to do."

"But we may take it that your source *is* a member of the faculty?"
Garrison asked smoothly.

"You may take it any way you want to," Kelly replied gruffly. "Now, I'm
here to cover this unannounced faculty meeting for *The Crier*." He looked
steadily at Burke. "Do you have any statement to make regarding your
plans to redirect the focus of the journalism department?"

"I will speak to you after this meeting is concluded, Mr. Kelly. If you
wish to take your seat—"

"Surely you are not still permitting this young man access to our deliberations," Moss objected.

"I will not close an open meeting," Burke said brusquely.

Kelly nodded in quiet satisfaction and walked toward the back. As he
slipped into the seat between Annie and Sue, who glared at him, the door
to the hall opened again.

Josh Norden wavered unsteadily in the doorway.

"For God's sake, Josh—" Burke began.

Norden gripped the doorjamb with a shaking hand. A tear trickled down his face. "I went to get Charlotte. I wanted her to know we were behind her."

"Of course, we are," Burke said quietly.

"But I was too late."

Sue broke the shocked silence. "Too late?"

Norden's mane of white hair quivered as he nodded and the tears coursed down his cheeks. "Bloody, bloody water. She cut her wrists and sat in the bathtub and all her blood ran out."

8

THE PHONE RANG. "I'll get it." Annie smiled at Max, immersed in papers on the couch. She swept the books from her lap onto the coffee table and popped up.

"Hello."

"Have you found Charlotte's murderer yet?" the crackly voice demanded.

"Miss Dora, it was suicide. The police are quite certain. Her apartment doors were locked and bolted on the inside. And the knife had only her fingerprints. A steak knife. Very sharp." An unwelcome vision arose. "I'm sorry. I know it's hard to accept. But it truly was suicide."

"Hounded to her death. Same thing as murder. I want to know who caused it."

"Perhaps you'd better talk to Max." Annie held out the receiver, mouthed, "Your client," and escaped back to her chair.

"Of course, Miss Dora, I'm working very hard on it." It was his most charming and persuasive voice.

Annie stared pensively at her notepad, then wrote, "Mary Roberts Rinehart's novels often associated death with water: Loon Lake in *The Wall*, the playhouse pool in *The Great Mistake*, and, of course, the pool in

The Swimming Pool, her last full-length novel." Another unwelcome image arose: an older woman, a bathtub, and rose red water. She shivered.

"Certainly I intend to talk to all the faculty members. And Brad Kelly, of course. Yes, as soon as possible." He sounded a little less charming. "I *am* working on it. In fact, I've made some progress."

Almost without volition (the Golden Age writers were so fond of automatic writing), Annie scrawled down the list of faculty who were members of the committee privy to personnel information:

1. Victor Garrison
2. Malcolm Moss
3. Josh Norden (but he cried)
4. Sue Tarrant
5. R.T. Burke

As she studied the names, faces came to mind: Garrison's plump cheeks, Moss's perpetual half-smile, Norden's befuddled blue eyes, Tarrant's too-bright makeup, Burke's hawklike face.

"Of course, I'll report to you as soon as I discover anything concrete." Then Max glared at the receiver. He turned to Annie. "She hung up."

"Miss Dora is not one to waste her time in common civility."

Max replaced the receiver. "You don't like her very much."

"Perceptive of you," Annie remarked.

He shoved a hand through his thick blond hair. "I'm not sure I like her much either." He dropped back onto the couch.

Annie pushed up from her chair, clutching her list, and joined him. "That's all right. I'm glad you're going to investigate it for her."

He looked at her inquiringly. "That's a switch."

Annie squirmed. It wasn't really true that she was stiff-necked and would never admit to making a mistake. After all, the circumstances had changed. "I've been thinking about it. Charlotte Porter—she was such a *nice* person. Like somebody's favorite aunt. Like Miss Silver. Why would anyone humiliate her that way? Whoever it was has to be a rat and deserves a little trouble."

"I agree," Max said firmly.

Annie waggled the list. "So it's one of these? Which one, Max?"

He took the list. "It's not that simple, Annie."

"But these are the people on the committee. That's what Burke said at the meeting. No one else knew. It has to be one of them."

"Maybe. Maybe not. While you were in the faculty meeting, I talked to the department secretary, Emily Everett."

They exchanged understanding glances. It was painful even to see someone as obese as Emily.

"Unlovely and unhappy," Annie murmured.

"Very unhappy. She wouldn't talk about the article in *The Crier*, kept mumbling, 'Awful. Awful. I don't want to think about it.' And this was before we knew about Charlotte Porter's suicide, remember. So I told her I was doing a study on efficiency for the trustees. That got her attention. I told her that her office was considered one of the best run on the campus and I needed some insight on how she arranged everything. She kind of forgot about *The Crier* for a while. People love to talk about themselves and their work, even if they despise it." A look of supreme satisfaction. "I had her explain the filing system."

"The filing system?" Shades of Poirot's Miss Lemon, creator of a filing system beside which all other filing systems faded into insignificance. "What does that have to do with anything?"

"Annie, my sweet, if I have learned one thing from my arduous labors for Confidential Commissions, it is that the world today is inundated with files, records, pieces of paper. Really, criminals didn't know how great they had it fifty years ago. In green or beige filing cabinets or, increasingly, on little black disks, across this great land there repose mounds of records on each and every one of us. I have become expert in unearthing information. But," and a look of great guile slid across his regular features, "I do not reveal this skill. So, I talked to Emily. About the office. How long she'd been there. What she did on a typical day. The immense number of responsibilities upon her bowed shoulders. How—"

"Max, I am truly impressed at this evidence of your devotion to your career. But, back to the point, what did Emily know?"

He looked at Annie with suddenly troubled eyes. "It's funny you should put it like that. Because I'm certain she knows something. I'm not sure what. We were getting along great. She told me all about the color coding of the folders, the use of tabs, the dead files, the arrangement of the filing cabinets. She even took me on a tour of the office and pointed out the locked closet that held the personnel files. So far, so good. No hesitation on her part. Then, as I stood there looking at that locked door, I thought about keys. And I asked her. She stared at that door like she'd never seen it before. I swear her face turned green. And yet, she didn't hesitate at all when I asked who had keys. In fact, she seemed to relax. So maybe she turns green every afternoon about four. I don't know."

"Does the master key open that file closet?"

He looked crestfallen. "How did you know about the master keys?"

"As an adjunct faculty member I was offered the choice of receiving—for a fifty-dollar deposit—a master key, which would open my office, my classroom, the faculty lounge, and all other locked doors, such as the main office, the supply closet, et cetera, or individual keys, at no cost, for each door I would have occasion to unlock."

He eyed her curiously. "What did you choose?"

"Individual keys, of course. Why should I make that kind of deposit?"

Max rolled his eyes heavenward.

"I will not drive you to the poorhouse," she retorted righteously.

"Just bananas," he murmured.

Ignoring that comment, Annie reached across him to retrieve a pen from the side table. Her hand poised over her notepad, she asked, "So, does the master key open the closet with the personnel files?"

"Yes."

"Who has master keys?"

He took the pen and pad and added to her list:

6. Kurt Diggs
7. Frank Crandall

And, after a moment's thought:

8. Charlotte Porter.

Annie shook her head. "Crazy. Why should she?"

Max shrugged. "Who knows? The world's crazy. Anything can happen. Or maybe somebody stole her key."

"Hmm. So anybody on the faculty could have nosed around in those files at some off hour. And of course, Emily has access to those files, too."

"During office hours. She made that *very* clear. Only faculty are allowed to possess master keys. Emily uses a key which hangs in the supply closet."

"And Burke might well have noticed if she spent time browsing through confidential faculty personnel folders. So, we can scratch Emily," Annie concluded.

"Maybe. Maybe not." Max still looked troubled. "I'd swear she knows something. Maybe she saw someone at that closet and since it was a faculty member didn't think much about it, but now she's wondering. . . . I'll talk to her again tomorrow."

Annie tapped the sheet. "Obviously, Brad Kelly's highly placed source is on this list." She sighed. "Seven, not counting Charlotte Porter. You've got your work cut out for you."

"Already done it." He tried to look modest and failed miserably.

Annie was impressed, until he handed her a handful of mimeographed sheets and a blue-backed booklet (state-of-the-art desktop publishing). Each sheet was captioned CURRICULUM VITAE, followed by the name of a faculty member. Annie raised an eyebrow.

"In academese, vitae equals résumé," Max explained. "Has a delicious ring, doesn't it?"

She glanced at the sheets, then opened the blue-backed booklet. The title page read:

CHASTAIN COLLEGE
DEPARTMENT OF JOURNALISM
Annual Report of Faculty Activities, Achievements, Innovations, Publications, Courses Taught, Organization Memberships, Offices Held, Academic Papers Presented, Research Undertaken, Workshops Sponsored.

Below this introductory paean was the list of faculty, their academic ranks, and dates of original appointment.

Annie flipped through the thick (forty-six pages) booklet, which included faculty members' participation in seminars and workshops, speeches given, meetings attended, committee assignments, field trips, courses taught, and papers written (the title of one caught her eye, "The Use of Indefinite Articles in Print Advertising"). She tossed the book back to him. "So what?"

He pointed at the copies of the curricula vitae, topped by R.T. Burke's résumé. "I've got the skeletons of their lives right there." He sounded just a little defensive. "Plus I've added some additional personal information from the College News Service."

The vitae were in alphabetic order.

Annie skimmed Burke's résumé first.

Born in Sandy Springs, Georgia, April 6, 1925, he'd enlisted as a private in the U.S. Army in June 1942, and been part of the First Army offensive through Hurtgen Forest, a campaign that suffered more than fifty percent casualties. He was awarded the Purple Heart, Bronze Star, and Oak Leaf with Cluster, and received an honorable discharge in 1946. He earned a B.A. in journalism in 1950 from Chastain College, and worked as a reporter for several Southern newspapers from 1950 to 1963. He joined the New Orleans bureau of Associated Press in 1963, and assumed directorship of the journalism department at Chastain College in August 1988. He was the recipient of numerous awards for outstanding reporting, including coverage of Hurricane Donna in 1960, a forty-two-fatality fire at Maury County Jail in Columbia, Tennessee June 26, 1977, and a 1986 series on corruption of law enforcement officials involved in a Florida drug ring. He married Beryl Aarons in 1954, was widowed in 1983, and had no children. He is an accomplished rock climber, scuba diver, and spelunker.

"Vigorous," she observed and flipped to the next sheet.

Frank Crandall came across as much less active, much more cerebral:

Born March 6, 1957, in Bowling Green, Kentucky, Crandall received a B.A. in journalism from the University of Kentucky in 1978, and an M.A. from the University of Texas in 1979. After two years with a Kansas City advertising agency, he completed a Ph.D. in communications at Northwestern in 1984, and joined the Chastain faculty in August 1984 as an assistant professor on tenure track. His publications ran two pages. He served as sponsor of two student clubs and was a member of several committees. Annie yawned and skipped to the personal data. Married, no children. President of the Chastain Wildlife Photography Club, the Audubon Society, and local chapter of Ducks Unlimited.

Her eyes glinted when she saw the third sheet. "Professor Kurt Diggs." She waggled the sheet at Max. "I'll bet this doesn't tell the half of it. It would take a plain brown wrapper for this jerk."

Max raised an eyebrow. "He really made an impression on you."

Annie recounted the road-hogging Corvette and Diggs's suggestive look at the faculty meeting.

"Thinks he's a stud, believe me. Macho man with hairy chest, sunglasses, skin-tight Levi's. Has leer, will travel."

Her husband grinned. "Not, in short, your idea of a swell fellow."

"Jerk," she summarized succinctly, scanning the vitae.

Diggs was born February 19, 1951, in Flint, Michigan, and had a B.A. in communications from the University of Michigan, 1972. He worked as a news writer for a Grand Rapids ABC affiliate, 1972–75, and did his M.A. at the University of North Carolina in 1977. He joined the news staff of an NBC affiliate in Chastain in 1977, and Chastain College as assistant professor in 1978. He was granted tenure and promotion to associate professor in 1983. He worked part-time in the news department of a local station. He listed no publications, but had presented two papers at the annual TV Video News Workshop and participated in a local news forum at a meeting of the International Radio and Television Society, Inc. in New York. Two children. No wife listed by the News Service. Divorced? In addition to professional and educational memberships, he was an officer of the Chastain Sports Car Rally.

"And chief honcho of the Good Old Boy Society."

Max spread an arm behind her on the couch. "Can't wait to meet the guy."

Annie looked at the next vitae. "From one extreme to the other." Professor Victor Garrison. Smooth as butter and with a résumé to match.

Garrison was born October 9, 1952, in Long Beach, California. He had a B.A. in journalism from the University of California at Los Angeles, 1973, and an M.A., 1974, ditto. Then followed two years as a general news reporter on a Long Beach daily, three years as political reporter for the *Los Angeles Times,* and a Ph.D. in communications from Rutgers. He joined the faculty at Chastain in 1982 as assistant professor, was promoted to associate professor, and was granted tenure in 1986.

He listed three pages of publications, ranging from "Politics and Journalism, a Symbiotic Relationship" to "The Political Reporter, Crony or Adversary?"

He was married to Joan Kimball, associate professor of economics at Chastain, June 8, 1983, and had two daughters. He was chair of six Chastain committees, a member of the Rotary Club, the Chamber of

Commerce, the State Library Resources Commission, the State News Association, etc.

In a publicity photo taken in a paneled den with two walls of books, he sat behind a glossy mahogany desk, wearing a tweed sports coat, pipe in hand, and looked into the camera with a carefully calibrated mixture of serious inquiry and studious charm.

Annie turned to the next vitae with relief. Sue Tarrant might be volatile, but she seemed like a much more genuine person. Annie wasn't surprised to learn Tarrant was from Little Rock, Arkansas. Born July 19, 1948. Graduate of the University of Arkansas. "No advanced degrees," Annie remarked in surprise.

"No tenure either," Max pointed out.

"But lots of experience. Print advertising for ten years, then videos and public relations for another six. Joined the faculty four years ago. Hmm. No mention of tenure track."

Tarrant was active in the Red Cross, the Community Chest, Big Sisters, the YWCA, and the Allied Arts Foundation. Not married; no children.

Malcolm Moss's vitae was by far the longest. His list of publications ran to six pages. He was a full professor, having been at Chastain since 1976. He was granted tenure in 1982. Previously he had taught at Emory and Louisiana State. His degrees were from the University of Missouri, Columbia, and Stanford. Born April 5, 1942 in Kansas City, Missouri. Married with one son. Active in both professional and social organizations. Golfer.

The man with the mocking smile, the bull-heavy shoulders, and blond hair that covered his head in tight curls.

As she read the next vitae, she kept seeing befuddled blue eyes swimming with tears.

Joshua Norden, professor of advertising, was born September 11, 1924 in Peoria, Illinois. He enlisted in the U.S. Army in 1941, and graduated from Officer Candidate School. He served in the Pacific and received honorable discharge as a captain in 1945. He got a B.A. from the University of Illinois, and an M.A. in communications from Northwestern. After fifteen years with a major advertising agency in New York, he taught at Boston University. He joined the faculty at Chastain in

1972, and was made full professor in 1976. Widower. No children. Artist. Watercolor exhibits throughout the South from 1978 to 1985.

Norden's vitae wasn't as long as Moss's, but it was crammed with honors, most of the awards in recognition of his pioneering work in television advertising. Norden was a part of the revolution spearheaded by Bill Bernbach, when advertising agencies convinced clients that advertising didn't need to be dull or boring and that the best ads involved readers, talking to them instead of at them.

Annie turned to the last vitae, then looked at Max in surprise.

Max inked a thick, black question mark after Charlotte Porter's name on Annie's list. "She may be the crux of the problem or she may be an accidental victim. Look at it this way: Why was Charlotte Porter the focus of the first article? Was that a deliberate choice by Brad Kelly? Or was he just using the information as it was supplied to him? Was the intent to embarrass Burke because he had covered up financial chicanery by a faculty member? Or was the informant trying to damage Charlotte Porter? Who was the intended victim?"

There was nothing in Charlotte Larrimore Porter's vitae or College News Service record that would foretell the sad ending of her life.

Born November 11, 1923, in Chastain, she received her B.A. in 1944 from Sweet Briar. She was married on June 5, 1944 to Lieutenant Albert Porter, who was posted as missing in a bombing raid over Berlin in 1945, three weeks before his daughter, Alberta, was born. Porter received an M.A. from Clemson, and a Ph.D. from the University of Mississippi with intervening stints of work for several major corporations in their public relations departments. She returned to Chastain as an assistant professor in 1972. She had a lengthy list of publications and had three times been elected by the students as Professor of the Year. She had served as treasurer of a number of organizations, including University Women, the Rose Society, the Camellia Society, and the Daughters of the Confederacy.

Annie recalled Charlotte's thin and tired, but very civilized and gentle face.

And faces do tell a story.

Kurt Diggs's sensuous mouth and jaded eyes.

Josh Norden's slack and puffy muscles.

Sue Tarrant's middle-aged wrinkles masked by youthful makeup.

The pugnacious tilt to R.T. Burke's chin.

Frank Crandall's sensitive mouth.

Victor Garrison's confident gaze.

The contemptuous twist to Malcolm Moss's lips.

Annie plumped the curricula vitae with their supplemental information down on the side table. "Bare bones, Max, bare bones."

"An excellent start," he disagreed. Pointing at the Annual Report, he insisted, "There's a lot to be deduced from that thing, boring as it is. For example, Moss was acting chair when Burke was hired. Maybe Moss wanted the job. He could have unleashed this stuff to sabotage Burke."

Annie felt sure that Moss's meaningless smile could mask every sort of base intention. "But Moss accused Burke of leaking the stuff to make it easier to dump some of the faculty."

"Of course he did. Whoever leaked that information will try hard to get someone else blamed." He tapped the cover of the report. "Or maybe Norden did it. He hasn't had a new publication in five years. Maybe he thought a general stink would disrupt the department so much that his lack of production would seem minor."

"So he feeds stuff to the student newspaper that pillories a woman he obviously cares for?"

"Doesn't mean he wouldn't be upset if it caused her suicide. Drunks don't think very straight. Maybe he just looked at his own problem, didn't foresee the consequences."

"Maybe, maybe, maybe," Annie objected.

"I know. But tomorrow we'll get to work, find out everything we can about these people." He grabbed her hand, and grinned. "Welcome aboard." He pulled her close, then closer. A cool November evening, the hiss of rain against the tree house windows, what better way to end an evening— The phone rang.

Annie glanced at the clock. Almost eleven. Hmm. She unlooped her arm from Max's neck, scooped up the receiver, and answered, not quite breathlessly, "Hello."

"I wouldn't have called this late except they only let you have one phone call. And I didn't know if Edward—Edward Sattherlie, you know, my lawyer—would be at home. Plays bridge so often—and besides, he's in

Connecticut and that is rather a distance and I do think it would be nice if someone could come now."

"Laurel?" Annie asked. It was her mother-in-law's voice, but somehow it lacked its usual husky resonance and piquant lilt.

"A misunderstanding, of course. The blood has *nothing* to do with me. I was merely passing through. But they seem to think it a trifle odd I was there. Really, these men have *no* auras at all. They are void."

A deep voice rumbled in the background.

"Blood? What blood?" Annie demanded.

Max leaned closer to the phone.

Obviously turning away from the receiver, Laurel said, "I have not used my three minutes!" An outraged sniff, then her voice came more strongly. "Annie, my dear child, so *sorry* to be a bother, but if you and Max could come and get me—and bring some money, of course, I think they said something about bail—I would appreciate it."

"Laurel, where *are* you?"

"Oh my dear, haven't I told you? The Chastain City Jail."

It wasn't quite that simple. The magistrate wasn't in session at eleven-thirty at night. But Max, who regularly challenged him to tennis matches, made a half dozen phone calls and, finally, at five minutes to one, Laurel was sprung. She stood in the dingy anteroom and smiled winsomely.

Max wasn't having any.

"All right, Laurel, what happened?" He glanced down at the notes in his hand. "Stopped by the campus police at ten-forty tonight running from Brevard Hall. Refused to explain presence. Suspicious, campus police (Sergeant Merrifield) entered Brevard Hall where vandalism was discovered. Upon suspect's repeated refusal to answer questions, an arrest was made for unauthorized entry and malicious destruction of property. Suspect's bloody footprints found in hallway leading away from the door of the campus newspaper office, which had been splashed with blood." He folded his arms. "What happened?"

His mother stared down at her dainty, stockinged feet. "They wouldn't let me keep my shoes. Said they were evidence. And they were *new*. The prettiest pink leather. The most darling little shop in Perugia. I *always* go there when—"

"Bloody footprints, Mother. Your footprints. How? Why? Whose blood, for God's sake?" he demanded irritably.

Her deep blue eyes widened in hurt surprise at his tone. "Maxwell, how should *I* know? I was merely passing by."

"No, no," he said firmly. "That's not good enough. At that hour? Come on, Mother, give."

Laurel smoothed her golden hair, lifted her chin, and stared past her son as if to a far horizon. "Sometimes in this life, to fulfill a noble commitment to the very *highest* principles, it is necessary to endure the calumny of the world." Her mouth closed firmly.

And not another word would she say.

Max sighed and took her arm. "If not here, then elsewhere. If not now, then later."

It was much later, of course, by the time he had arranged for a special run of the ferry (for a hundred and fifty dollars Annie suggested they spend the night in Chastain, but she was overruled).

When Max's Maserati pulled up at the inn where Laurel was staying, he said grimly, "Here or in your room, Ma."

Laurel sighed. "Such a *bristly* aura you have, Max dear. But I do appreciate your and Annie's coming tonight, and I will share with you, though, of course, I expect you both to be absolutely mum, should anyone ask."

"Laurel, those charges are not going to disappear. We must have a defense."

Annie intervened. "Things always seem to work out for Laurel. Don't discourage her, Max." Annie patted her mother-in-law's slim shoulder. "Now, what happened?"

Laurel pressed her fingers gently against her temples. "I have been concerned. Very concerned."

They nodded dutifully.

"I sensed such despair. And you know, despair can spawn such irrevocable action. So I followed her." Those graceful hands came together in a prayerful pose.

"Followed who?" Annie asked gently, pinching Max before he could bellow.

"Georgia Finney. That dear, dear child. In an invidious situation, of course. But I do understand about love. And, of course, he should never have married her."

"Oh God," Max moaned.

His mother looked at him in surprise. She reached out for the door handle. "My sweet, you must be very tired. I do understand. Thank you again for coming." The door opened.

Annie gently barred the way. "Good of you, Laurel, but Max is all right." She gave him another sharp pinch. "Now tell us all about Georgia and who she shouldn't have married." Remembering she was now a teacher, she added quickly, *"Whom."*

A vexed shake of that golden head. "My dears, sometimes I worry about your comprehension. Georgia isn't married. Mr. Crandall is married. But he fell in love with Georgia. And she with him. Absolutely a love match, according to some of the students I talked to. That's how I found out, of course. From the students. It took me no time at all." She couldn't quite suppress her dismay. "Max, I *did* think you were investigating. But I know it's hard for men to be perceptive." She beamed at Annie. "Don't you think, dear?"

"Oh, yes, a real struggle. Now, about Georgia and Mr. Crandall?"

"In love." A sigh. "But, of course, he is a married man. And that is frowned upon, a married professor and one of his students. She's *very* outstanding and worked with him closely on a special project. Travel, you know, and that sort of thing. And, of course, his marriage is unhappy. An older woman. Took advantage of him. He's that kind of man. I do understand about men." A complacent nod. "She was widowed and a *very* strong personality. And he was being kind, but, first thing you know, she had him where she wanted him and he was too much of a gentleman to say no and then she expected marriage and he was lost. Quite lost. So easy to take advantage of some men."

"Mother," Max's voice almost quivered, "what in God's name does all of this have to do with your running out of that damn hall and bloody footprints?"

"Maxwell, you must understand the emanations. That dreadful article and its hint of revelations to come. Of course, Georgia feared the next story would be about her and Mr. Crandall. And he doesn't have tenure. That is such a *precarious* state for a young professor. And if it all came out, that he, a married man, was in love with a student, why, how could he expect to be approved? Oh, a most desperate situation. And Georgia felt it so keenly and she was so disturbed with that stubborn young editor, Brad

Kelly. I didn't know what was going to happen—but I felt strongly, more strongly than I can say, that I mustn't let her out of my sight."

There were a number of side excursions: "Really, it was *such* a dark night, the sort that seethes with spirits, you know." "So interesting, those young men with a telescope in the apartment house next door to the sorority. So quietly devoted to the pursuit of heavenly bodies at such a late hour." "The attitude of the law enforcement gentlemen leaves a great deal to be desired. Such a stultifying atmosphere." But Laurel did finally reveal a few facts: Georgia Finney slipped from a side door of her sorority house about ten-thirty, dressed in dark slacks and a navy sweater and carrying a flashlight. Laurel trailed her down dark alleys and through the shadows of the live oaks to Brevard Hall.

It was at this point that her recital became uncertain.

"You see," she said plaintively, "it was so dark. I lost sight of Georgia. But I knew by then—felt sure—where she was going, so I crept around the side of the building to the back door. It was open. I tiptoed inside and I was perhaps halfway down the hall when several things happened at once. I heard a crash." She clapped her hands. "It was just like the time I launched the USS *Connecticut*. Max, do you remember how the champagne flew in the most glorious pink spray?"

"The crash, Laurel." Max spoke with the patience of a son who had endured years of Laurel's side excursions from the topic at hand.

"Oh, yes. Such a lot of noise. That startled me. Then I heard someone running. Oh, if I'd only had a flashlight."

"Georgia didn't use hers?" Annie asked.

"Oh no, it was as dark as a cave. No light at all."

Max leaned closer to his mother. "Running footsteps? Was it Georgia?"

Laurel didn't answer directly. "I felt someone pass me and so I ran in the opposite direction, toward the front of the building. And *that* door was just closing as I reached it. So that means there were two people, one going out the back, the other out the front."

"You didn't see anyone but Georgia?" Annie demanded.

"It wasn't Georgia who threw that blood. I *know* it," Laurel said determinedly.

Of course, Laurel was committed to the proposition that love must prevail.

"Love must prevail," she said staunchly, echoing Annie's thought. But was there an uncertain quaver in that lovely, husky voice?

9

A FURNISHED APARTMENT with all that implied. Lumpy cushions on the shabby brown couch, a rickety straight chair with a missing rung, a rocker with peeling red paint. No rugs. Mustard yellow linoleum flooring that dipped precariously in the center of the tiny living room. A smell compounded of ingrained dirt, must, and frying oil, with an acrid overlay of something burned.

The whiny-voiced landlady complained, "Who's going to get her stuff out, that's what I want to know."

"She was paid through the month, wasn't she?" Annie asked sharply.

A grudging nod.

It was hard to picture Charlotte Porter in these dispiriting surroundings. The few, very few, lovely pieces in the room were in stark contrast to their setting. An English silver tankard, ornately embossed. A Delft covered jar. A pair of Irish crystal decanters.

Obvious poverty, missing money, the remnants of past glory. The equation didn't figure.

The landlady shuffled impatiently, her laceless scuffed sneakers squeaking against the floor. "This is it. Living room, bedroom, bath, kitchenette. She did it in the bath. You want to see?" She gestured at a closed door with an ill-kept hand, her fingernails cracked and once-red polish peeling. "Nobody's cleaned it up. They let the water out, but the tub's stained. Guess they think I can do it. Shit cops."

"I'm not sure what we want to see," Max replied. "We'd just like to look around."

Unfriendly brown eyes looked Max up and down, spared a brief glance at Annie. Bony shoulders shrugged beneath a dirt-stained sweat shirt. "Look all you want. I got work to do. Bring the key down when you're finished." Her rubber-soled shoes squeaked across the floor. She paused, a hand on the knob. "Don't take nothin'."

As the door closed behind her, Annie looked across the dim room at the bathroom door. "Max, I don't like this."

"I know. But there's something damned funny here. Charlotte Porter sold her house and almost all her belongings last year, moved into this dump, and then she still stole money. Where did it go? What for?"

So she helped him search, except for the bathroom. It didn't take long. The single center drawer in the unpainted wooden desk that sat in a corner of the living room held a checkbook with a balance of two hundred and seventy-three dollars. Recent bills, marked paid. Church envelopes. An address book. An insurance policy. Beneficiary, James Edward Martin, grandson. His name was crossed out and above it, in a shaky handwriting, was inscribed, "Chastain College Department of Journalism." Both the upper and lower drawers on each side were full of personal correspondence, neatly tied packets divided by years. In recent years, the letters were all from Jimmy Martin. There was a gap at the back of the drawer and the last packet carried the date of 1986. In the tiny bedroom, the bed was neatly made, although the thin blue cotton spread was wrinkled at one side. A large red leather photograph album lay propped up against the pillows. As if someone—Charlotte Porter?—had sat on the edge of the bed and looked at the scrapbook. Max thumbed through it in silence, Annie looking over his shoulder. Only a few pictures of Charlotte Porter. As a young woman she had indeed been beautiful, with a fine bone structure and a radiant smile. In her middle years, the radiance was gone but good humor remained. She always appeared very genteel: high-necked blouses with ruffled collars, small pearl earrings, a self-effacing smile. As Max flipped the heavy manila pages, the faces in the other photographs became familiar. A girl with curly brown hair growing to adulthood. Then wedding pictures. A young woman with a toddler, then a little boy, later a teenager. Soon there were no more pictures of the mother but many of the boy. Playing baseball. In a school play. Smiling proudly at high school graduation. On a college campus. Grinning and shading his eyes from bright sunlight on a sunny day at the beach. The inscriptions: *Jimmy in Little League, Jimmy in the senior play, Jimmy graduating from high school, Jimmy at college, Jimmy in California.* The pictures were dated. The last date was October 5, 1986.

No pictures after that—and somewhere around that time Charlotte Porter fell on hard times, sold her house and her belongings, and took money that didn't belong to her.

The bedroom revealed little else, dresses neatly arranged in the tiny closet, cotton gowns and underclothing in the rickety bureau. But in the kitchen, they discovered the source of that smell of burning, a mound, a large mound of ashes in the rust-stained kitchen sink.

Two sets of dried bloody footprints led from the crimson-stained door of the student newspaper offices. Several student desks ranged down the center of the hall, blocking off the vandalized area. Yellow police tape marked the scene.

Henny crouched beside one distinct set of footprints. She looked up at their approach.

"Two women. One in sandals. Estimate size five to five and a half, triple A. The second in Reebok tennis shoes, size seven." She gave Max a commiserating glance. "I understand the Chastain City Jail is holding a pair of women's shoes—pink sandals—in evidence."

"Laurel was—" Max swallowed "—just passing by."

"Of course," Henny said cheerfully. "A ship in the night." She rose, but her glance lingered on the scuffed, splotched, and smeared hall floor. "One interesting point—the sandals overlap several Reebok prints."

Annie nodded sagely, but made no comment. Let Henny pirouette here, if she could.

She could. But she wanted Annie to play the game.

"The deduction is obvious, of course."

Annie wasn't to be drawn, but Max fished.

"What deduction?" he asked immediately.

Henny smiled smugly. "Reebok stepped into the blood first, followed by the sandals. So, Reebok threw the blood."

Max frowned. "Maybe. But the vandal should have known there was a mess and avoided stepping into it at all."

"You're positing a third person in the hall last night?" Henny asked.

"Laurel thought so," Max said.

Annie couldn't resist joining in. "Or the sandals threw the blood but waited to move until passed by the Reeboks."

Max gave her an *"Et tu, Brute"* look.

To divert him, Annie said quickly, "But why blood?" She looked at the sticky door. Blood spatters trailed down the white frosted portion of the door. Slimy dark streaks marked the lower wooden panel. On the cement floor, long, slender slivers of glass lay among clumped pieces. "And whose blood?"

"Don't you suppose it's a warning? A hint to that rather vigorous young editor that the future does not bode well for him if he doesn't desist his rash exposé? As for whose blood—" Henny sighed. "Rabbits, I'm afraid." Her sharp nose wrinkled in distaste. "Animal research is all very well, but it does give you the creeps. Nice fluffy white rabbits injected with viruses, and blood samples taken daily."

Annie hated to boost Henny's already considerable ego, but she had to ask, "Henny, how did you ever discover that?"

"My dear," and her favorite customer was supplanted by Miss Marple, "everything is usually quite simple, if you look at it properly. Blood in vials. So obvious, those long slivers of glass so peculiar to test tubes, you know. And we're on a campus. Research. I checked with the security office and there was another break-in last night, though not reported until this morning. The biology department. Very simple."

Annie nodded slowly.

Max looked thoughtfully at the unmistakable evidence, the long slivers of glass that had shattered on impact with the door. "But that implies pretty specialized knowledge, Henny. To know about research going on and be able to pinpoint the location of the blood."

"Anyone on campus could have known." She reached into the apple-stocked pocket of her baggy cardigan (à la Ariadne Oliver) and drew out a small notebook. Flipping it open, she said briskly, "Series of articles on research into viruses transmitted through blood ran in *The Crier* last month. Written by Brad Kelly. Photographs by Georgia Finney."

The notebook snapped shut with finality.

The wooden stand that was filled twice weekly with copies of *The Crier* stood empty, in mute support of Henny's statement that all the copies of the infamous edition had disappeared. The next issue wouldn't be out until tomorrow, but the students drifting slowly into the building for nine o'clock classes obviously knew of Charlotte Porter's suicide. There were occasional brief and somber exchanges, sidelong glances at the vandalism, and a generally funereal air.

Max held the door of the main office for Annie. She hung back.

"I think we should talk to Georgia Finney first. Of course, she's already had hours to concoct a story and get rid of those Reeboks."

Max smiled kindly. "Naturally, your mind is attracted to the sanguine, but obviously Georgia's the last person we need to talk to." He held the door wider.

Annie nobly resisted the impulse to kick him heartily. "How can you say that? She's in it up to her neck."

"In what up to her neck?" Max inquired blandly.

"Why, the vandalism, of course."

Her spouse gave her an encouraging nod. Unfortunately, it reminded her of Laurel's similar nod during her first class period. Annie's brows drew together in a stormy frown.

He further compounded his problem by saying patronizingly, "But do we care about the vandal?"

"Don't we?" she snapped.

"No. Our task is to discover who spilled the beans to Brad Kelly, boy exposé artist. Obviously, the vandal is wreaking vengeance for the exposé and trying to prevent any further disclosures—ergo, the vandal is not the bean dropper."

Max nudged her gently on into the anteroom of the department office. The lights were on, but the secretary's desk was empty. He glanced around.

Annie considered his explanation. She gave a grudging nod. "Okay, I see your point. But we still have to get those charges dismissed against Laurel."

"No sweat," he said absently, peering over the counter at the door leading into a second office. "Henny's got it figured right. Georgia threw that blood. The fact that Mother's footprints overlap hers makes that clear—and the cops will have to admit it. So we can concentrate on the important problem: Who played Deep Throat to Kelly."

The phone rang. It was cut off in the middle of the third peal.

"Burke must be in his office," Max said, reaching for the swinging gate.

"Do you think it's all right for us to burst in on him unannounced?" Annie asked.

"Miss Dora said we had carte blanche. And she's a trustee." He strode through the inner office to the second door.

Annie followed. She wondered how impressed Burke would be at their commission from Miss Dora. (Max's, actually. Annie considered herself unofficial to the core.)

Max knocked.

It took a moment, but when Burke yanked open the door, the chairman gestured energetically for them to enter. "Take a seat. Be right with you." He returned to his desk and picked up the phone. "So there's no way?"

They settled into the red leatherette chairs facing the desk.

Two framed yellowing front pages hung on the wall behind Burke, *The New York Times* street edition of December 8, 1941, and *The Washington Post* extra on May 7, 1945. Full bookshelves covered three walls. On a window ledge sat a battered shell casing, a bent and twisted bar of iron, and a scorched brick.

Burke hunched over the phone. The sleeves of his green-and-white striped shirt were rolled up to his elbows. Nicotine-stained fingers gripped a pen tightly. He began to write on a white pad. "Yeah, yeah, I got it. So, I can't kick his ass off the paper unless I can get him suspended. What's the school policy? . . . Right. Well, he's no dummy. You can bet he won't do a damn thing that could get him in trouble. Okay. Thanks, Counselor."

Hanging up, he looked at Annie and Max. "What can I—"

The phone rang.

Burke slammed his hand against the desktop in exasperation and his pad slid sideways. "Damn girl. Hell of a lousy morning for her to call in sick. Sure, everybody's upset about Charlotte, but we've got to keep going." He started to reach for the phone, then shook his head irritably, and flicked a switch on the console. "I can't answer the damn phone all morning and get anything done." He grabbed several hard candies from a former ashtray. "Sometimes I think I'll just start smoking again. Candy rots your teeth." He popped some in his mouth, offered the candies to them. They shook their heads. His speech a little impeded, he said, "All right, now, what can I do for you?"

Max stood and held out his hand. "I'm Max Darling. I have an office on Broward's Rock, called Confidential Commissions. People with problems sometimes ask me to help out. Miss Dora Brevard has hired me to find out who's supplying Kelly with his information."

Burke stared at Max for a long moment, then reached out and vigorously pumped his hand. "Sure, you're Annie's husband. The two of you solved that murder during the house-and-garden tours." Wry amusement glinted in his bright eyes. "Made a lifelong friend of our rather heavy-handed chief of police, Harry Wells. Yeah. I know who you are." He waved Max back to his seat. "Miss Dora's got a good idea. And if you find out who the snake in our bosom is, I want to be the first to know."

"If you find out, call a press conference and I'll cover it for *The Crier*." They turned toward the door.

Brad Kelly stepped into Burke's office. His face looked thin and drawn this morning, but he bore Burke's look of disgust without flinching. He jerked his head back toward the front office. "Emily's not out there, so I came on back—and I couldn't help overhearing." He turned to Max. "I'm Brad Kelly, editor of *The Crier*. Are you a private investigator? What's your name?" He pulled a battered notepad from his pocket.

"I'm Max Darling, but I am not a private investigator. I am a consultant. People consult me."

"What's the difference?" Kelly's tone was puzzled.

"A little matter of licensing by the state of South Carolina," Max replied smoothly. "Now, Mr. Kelly—"

"It's Brad. Brad Kelly."

Burke interrupted. "What the hell do you mean, call a press conference if Darling finds out who leaked that stuff to you?"

A flush brightened Kelly's pale face. "I've got calls coming in from all over the state. I had no idea it'd be such a big deal, or I'd have done my best to find out who was doing it."

"You don't know who gave you that confidential information on the faculty?" Max demanded.

"No idea. I never saw him."

"A man?" Annie asked quickly.

Kelly frowned. "I . . . Hell, I just don't know. I *thought* so, but that was because the whisper was low. But it *could* have been a woman."

Burke watched Kelly like he was monitoring a rattler. "Over the telephone?"

Kelly hesitated, then shook his head decisively. "No comment. *No* comment." He turned aggressively on Max. "Now, you've been hired by Miss Brevard, the trustee?"

Max smiled. "I'll be glad to talk to you, Brad, on a quid pro quo basis. How was the contact made with you?"

Kelly's gray eyes narrowed, then he shrugged. "Sorry. I ask questions. I don't answer them." He turned back to Burke. "But I'm going to answer questions this afternoon. Press conference at three o'clock in *The Crier* offices."

Burke's face turned an unhealthy orange-red. "Press conference! What the hell for?"

"*The Crier*—that's me—will announce that despite any and all efforts to suppress the truth, *The Crier* will continue with its investigative series on journalism department practices and policies." The words were brave and forceful, but his tone was an odd mixture of aggression and defensiveness. "I won't be intimidated. It'll take more than blood to stop Brad Kelly." His eyes shifted away from Burke's choleric face. "I've already got acceptances from *The Atlanta Constitution,* CNN, and *The New York Times.*"

"I guess blood *won't* stop you, will it?" Burke said heavily.

For just an instant, Kelly wavered. "Are you saying you threw that stuff?" he asked, clearly surprised.

"Not that blood, Brad. I'm talking about Charlotte Porter's blood. Are you still proud of that article about her? Are you excited about the result?"

Kelly blinked. He swallowed convulsively. Burke's thrust had hit home and hit hard. Slowly, and those watching could feel the effort and the pain, Kelly's young face hardened. When he spoke, his voice was strained. "Yeah, I wrote the story. But you know something, Mr. Burke, I didn't steal that money. I didn't cover up the theft. I just told the truth."

"But not the whole truth," Burke said sharply. "Was Charlotte Porter a thief? Had she consistently over a period of years abused the trust placed in her? No, Kelly. She served this department and this college honorably for many years. In one incident, under tremendous pressure, she 'borrowed' money. She didn't intend to steal it. She was already repaying it, in the tiny sums she could manage, before the shortage was found. So you didn't know all the truth. Just part of it. And part of it was enough to kill Charlotte."

"I called her." The young voice shook. "I called and she could have told me."

"But you stopped there," Burke said heavily.

"I called her." His voice grew shrill. Then, catching his breath, he continued harshly. "I'm not going to keep the problems in this department under wraps just to protect you from criticism, Mr. Burke. I'm going to keep on writing stories. Tomorrow I'm going to tell the truth about Professor Crandall and his 'extracurricular' activities. Do you wish to comment?"

Burke stared at Kelly, his face creased in thought. "Professor Crandall has been an outstanding member of this faculty." He chose his words carefully. "I do not believe that public discussion of a faculty member's private life is justified under any circumstances."

Kelly scrawled in his notebook. "Thank you." He turned to go, then paused in the doorway. "Of course, you are welcome to come to the news conference at three. I don't believe in hiding the news."

Burke's hands bunched into fists. He came halfway out of his chair, his face an angry red, then, slowly, he sank back, but his tone was menacing when he answered. "You can count on it, Kelly, I'll be there. And when I finish talking to those reporters, young man, you can hunt for a job as an ice cream vendor—if you're lucky."

Kelly gave him an uneasy look, then shrugged. "We'll see about that. Those reporters know a story when they see it."

But Burke wasn't finished. "Yeah, I'm coming and I'll talk about you and how you handled your big story and the way big-time journalists write. One thing you forgot, Kelly, there are always two sides to every story. Sometimes there are a hundred sides—and good reporters check every source and give every side, whether they like it or not, whether it makes them puke or inspires them. You didn't come to me and ask any questions. Why did Charlotte Porter steal that money? Why did I—and the personnel committee—accept her promise to make restitution? Why didn't I

call the cops? You didn't ask any questions at all. You took part of the story
—the fact that she took the money and the fact that I chose not to
prosecute—and ran a forty-eight-point head and crucified that woman.
And that's all you did. Why? Because you wanted a BIG story, but not the
whole story. The whole story might not be worth a forty-eight-point head.
So, sure, I'll be there at three."

Kelly's whole body tensed. "So you're going to try and shoot me down."
He thought about it, then shook his head in dismissal. "The bottom line,
Burke, is that I'll still be editor when you finish and I'm going to have a lot
more stories that are going to turn this place on its ear. And there isn't
anything you can do about it."

As the door slammed shut behind Kelly, Burke exploded. "Goddamn
that mother-fucker. I'll get him if it's the last thing I ever do. Him and the
cold-blooded bastard who's using him to get at me."

Max was considering the closed door thoughtfully. "Is that how you
read it? Do you think the objective of the leak is to smear you?"

Burke shot him an irritated glance. "Hell, man, that should be obvious.
You weren't at the emergency faculty meeting, but Annie was. Did she
tell you about it?"

Max nodded.

"Then you know all about that crap Malcolm shoveled out, that I
unloaded to Kelly to get at the faculty because they wouldn't play ball
with me. I don't play those kinds of games with people's lives." There was
an echo of Sam Spade, Annie thought, a man electing honor in a dishon-
orable world. "So there are plenty of things I won't say. But I'll throw out
some home truths this afternoon. For one thing, that will spike Kelly's
guns." He reached for another candy. "Besides, now that my cover's
blown, the best thing to do is lay everything on the line—everything that I
decently can. Then the public—and in my case, the president and the
trustees—can look it over and decide whether I was playing it right." He
popped the candy in his mouth.

"What do you mean?" Annie asked.

Burke picked up a pen and tapped the pad lying in the center of his
desk. "That kid's right on target in one respect. I am trying to make some
changes—some profound changes—in this department. You see, this department has been dominated by academics, people with Ph.D.'s who've
served a few internships here and there, but their practical experience as

journalists is right down on the kindergarten level. So what happens? Their training is as academics. Obviously, they see research and ivory-tower reasoning as paramount. They talk about theories of communications, the society, the individual. They love computers and statistics. Jesus, how they love statistics. They can tell you how many times the typical housewife in Dubuque watches the afternoon soaps and her brand awareness. They're hell on surveys and when they write papers to present to learned groups of other academics, it's six-syllable words all the way. They want to teach kids how to be media managers, not how to write or find out facts or compose ads. Lots of colonels, but no foot soldiers. My job is to change the focus, put the emphasis back on the basics, how to cover a story, how to create ads, how to put forth a client's position most effectively. How to be a professional."

"And you aren't the best-liked kid on the block," Annie summed up.

Burke managed a grin. "Honey, you can say that in spades." It was a fleeting smile. "But nobody hired me to win a popularity contest."

"Who's maddest at you?" Max asked.

"Hard to say," Burke replied wryly. "Maybe Malcolm Moss. He was acting chair when I came. Wanted to be chosen, of course. Hacked him, no doubt about it. He has a lust for power, that SOB. Big guy. They run to it sometimes. Likes to make people squirm. Puts graduate students through hell. And he and Garrison are fighting me tooth and toenail over the curriculum."

Annie leaned forward. "Garrison was furious at that faculty meeting. What was that all about?"

"That?" Burke said softly. "Sweetheart, that was all about the heart and soul of the school—and I'm going to win. You see," and he leaned back in his chair, put his hands behind his head, and squinted dreamily at the acoustic tile ceiling, "there's a little thing called tenure that complicates my life. I can't fire Garrison or Moss because they won't do it my way. The day they were granted tenure, they won the battle to stay in this department. But I can win the war, and here's how I'm going to do it. Next week I'm going to provide the academic vice president with a proposal for a revised curriculum for this department. For example, Garrison has a pet course, Journalism 306, Quantitative Research in Public Policy Reporting. Students spend a goddamn term measuring how many inches the Republicans get, how many inches the Democrats get in a particular newspaper over a three-month period." He blew out an irritated spurt of air. "Jesus, why not count how many times the President gets his name in the paper? It's not seeing the forest for the goddamn trees. It's useless, but you can bet all those numbers get correlated, added, divided, and shined up for some paper he wants to submit to a refereed journal—I mean one where he's got a lot of chums on the editorial board—and whoopee, our professor scores again with a professional publication. Now, I'll admit I'm riding my hobbyhorse. I'm not saying research isn't good, can't be well done or necessary. But let a scholar do research on his own time and use the goddamn class time to teach. So, in my proposed curriculum we'll drop Journalism 306 and substitute Journalism 310, which will be a course on covering elections from the precinct to the national convention with a lot of good, hard, usable information: how each party is structured from the lowest to the highest tier, the names behind the titles, the personalities behind the names, the movers and shakers. I guarantee you that any student who completes that course can handle an election story, plan TV coverage, or create an advertising or public relations campaign for any candidate—and do a hell of a job."

His gaze dropped from the ceiling, focused on a yellow folder. He sat forward, reached for it, and waggled it at them. "The new curriculum is in here—and it's going to rattle some cages around here, all right. But I've got the power, and I don't mind using it. Research is fine. Professional publications are fine. But the primary focus is going to be on a down-to-earth, practical curriculum that will teach students to be first-rate, thinking journalists. And the faculty is goddamn well going to like it or lump it."

Max had been following his torrent of words carefully. "Is everybody on the faculty opposed to you?"

"Over the curriculum?" Burke countered.

"Over anything."

Burke scowled. "You're trying to figure out who might have a grudge against me?"

"Yes, if compromising you was the real point of the leakage."

Burke's eyes narrowed. He absently replaced the yellow folder on his desk. "Interesting possibility you raise. Because there are some other conflicts—but they all relate to private personnel matters."

"I'm not Brad Kelly," Max said quietly. "Annie and I have no ax to grind, no reason to reveal anything we learn from you. But if we're going to find out what really happened, we need to know everything we can about everybody. One of those personnel matters may have triggered this entire episode and caused Charlotte Porter's death."

Burke pulled open his desk drawer, found a stick of gum, unwrapped it, and popped the stick in his mouth. He chewed ruminatively, then gave a decisive nod. "Miss Dora is a trustee. You'll report only to her. Right?"

Max nodded.

"On that basis, I'll tell you what I know. But it's confidential, of course."

"Confidential," Annie promised.

The chairman glared down at his desktop. "Confidential files, too. That's the rub. Either somebody got into the files, or somebody on the personnel committee is behind the leak. But that leaves a wide open field." Those bright green eyes, reflective now, traveled from Annie's face to Max's. "On the committee: myself, Victor Garrison, Malcolm Moss, Josh Norden, Sue Tarrant." His mouth twisted. "Victor's a prick, believe me. Charm you out of your jock while he's inserting a stiletto between the third and fourth ribs. To be fair, he thinks I'm a goddamned boob, an untutored fool, and an ignoramus, and it's his holy duty to protect the academic integrity of the unit from my barbaric ravages. There are no flies on Victor, nothing the least bit derogatory can be said about his actions. Our struggle is for the future of the department, and he'll never give up."

Burke pulled the pad on his desk nearer and glanced down at it. "All the little Indians are listed here." He darted a sardonic look at Annie. "I'd like to turn them over to Mr. Justice Wargrave. That would cook their goose, wouldn't it?"

Annie murmured to Max, *"And Then There Were None* by Agatha Christie."

"If I could put them on an island for a week, I'd get some answers out of them," Burke said confidently, "but I'm going to ask some damn sharp questions this morning and see what turns up. But you want to ask questions, too. Okay." He tapped the list. "Moss. It's power he wants. He doesn't like my coming in and trying to run the department. I presume it's the struggle for power that Kelly intends to write about. But it's the rest of the faculty where it gets stickier."

"Josh Norden?" Annie asked.

Burke shook his head impatiently. "Josh is a drunk. I've given him six months to get in a treatment program. But I don't care how unhappy he might be with me, he would never have done anything to hurt Charlotte. Josh didn't do it."

"Sue Tarrant thought the story in *The Crier* was awful," Annie volunteered.

Burke shrugged. "Sue's emotional. It's hard to read her, hard to know what might trigger an outburst from her."

"Is there anything derogatory in Kurt Diggs's file?" Annie asked, her voice cold.

"What's your guess?" Burke asked.

"I'll bet he trades A's for sex."

"You got it," Burke replied.

Max looked at Annie curiously. "How'd you know?"

"His kind are legion."

"I've had a lot of complaints, but I can't pin anything on him." The chairman added grimly, "But I will."

"If some of the coeds have complained, why can't you bring him before a board on a charge of sexual discrimination?" Max asked.

"Oh, it isn't the ones he's screwed who complain, it's the other students in the class who resent the favoritism. Diggs is too smart to fool with any but cooperative coeds. At least not recently. But I put him on notice. I'm watching and I'm watching closely. Like I told him, one of these days some coed will decide the A wasn't worth it and blow the whistle—or maybe he'll make a mistake and throw a pass at a girl who isn't having any."

"So you're cramping his style," Annie observed with satisfaction.

"Trying my damnedest."

"What's your feeling about Frank Crandall?" Max asked.

Burke sighed. "Jesus Christ, what a fool! I told Frank to cool it with Georgia, and I haven't seen them together lately, but if *The Crier* carries a story indicating his involvement with a student, the trustees will go berserk, and I sure as hell won't be able to recommend him for tenure. Frankly, I'm about to decide against it anyway. Anybody should have better sense than Frank. Look at his damn marriage!"

"What's wrong with his marriage?" Annie heard the stiffness in her voice. After all, she was really all for the institution of matrimony.

Burke shook his head in disgust. "Wrong with it? It should never have happened. The man showed all the intelligence and spunk of a subnormal woodchuck." He ran an impatient hand through thinning gray hair. "Okay, Frank joins the faculty. Adrianne is the chairman's wife. She drives poor Kenneth to a breakdown from all accounts, then when Kenneth dies, she moves in on Frank, who's twenty years younger, and fastens on tighter than a wood tick. Frank, the dumb jerk, is too much of a gentleman to tell her to shove off, so she keeps calling him up. And I'll admit she's pretty sexy, if your taste runs to the front line of a fifties chorus. Anyway, according to Sue, the hungry widow got him in bed, then started making plans for a wedding and the benighted fool let himself be bullied into it." He gnawed at his lower lip. "But if that damn Kelly spills it all in *The Crier*, Frank is through."

"Why doesn't he get a divorce?"

"No guts. Adrianne will give him living hell and people like Frank hate scenes. Plus, he's waited a little late insofar as his career is concerned. The trustees won't have professors screwing coeds. If it comes out publicly, it will be a cold day in hell before Frank gets tenure here. And it could make it damn difficult for him to get a job somewhere else."

"So we can be absolutely certain Crandall didn't supply the information to Kelly," Annie concluded.

"Not unless he's really trying to self-destruct." Burke glanced up at the wall clock. "And that pretty well wraps it up, as far as the faculty's concerned." He stood. "Check back with me this afternoon. Before that damn press conference. We'll compare notes, see what we've found out."

They were almost to the door when Annie paused. "Charlotte Porter. You said Kelly never asked you why she took the money. Do you know?"

"Yeah." He reached out to the windowsill, picked up the twisted bar of steel and turned it in his hands, but automatically, without looking at it, and Annie knew this must be an habitual gesture when he was deep in thought. He gripped the angular bar at both ends. His hands clenched.

The end-of-class bell rang. Ten minutes to ten.

Burke glanced again at the wall clock. He thudded the bar back into place on the windowsill. "Yeah. I know. And that's another decision I have to make before three o'clock. Charlotte died because half her secret was exposed. Do I keep my mouth shut, let people think she was some kind of venal thief, or do I tell why she did it?" A vein throbbed in his forehead. "Kelly's a sorry little shit. I hate to see him getting away with his pose as a great investigative reporter uncovering malfeasance in office, braving the hostility of the department to unmask wrongdoing. Jesus, I'd like to have people understand about Charlotte." He opened the door for them. "All right, you two find out what you can. I'll do the same. We'll huddle just before three."

The first bell for ten o'clock classes sounded as they stepped into the hall, into a swirl of hurrying students.

Annie and Max parted company at the top of the stairs on the second floor, he turning toward the faculty wing, she heading for her classroom. She regretted a little that she couldn't accompany Max on his rounds, but she didn't really envy him, poking and prodding into strained relationships. She walked with a bounce, despite her fatigue (only three hours' sleep after their late-night foray to rescue Laurel), because she was eager to get started with her class. Her surge of happiness was, of course, slightly tempered by the knowledge of the class's composition. However, even Henny, Laurel, and Miss Dora couldn't squelch her joy in holding forth about three of the greatest practitioners of all time. She began to review in her mind today's topic, the contributions of Mary Roberts Rinehart to the genre in addition to her gift of the Had-I-But-Known technique, which had through overuse by less skillful writers fallen into bad repute.

Mentally making a list of some of those offending less skillful writers, she rounded the corner and stopped short. It was a scene guaranteed to strike terror to her heart, those three unmistakable figures deep in earnest conversation.

10

MISS DORA'S SHAGGY WHITE HAIR rippled as she nodded forcefully, thumping her rubber-tipped cane for added emphasis. Today she
wore a green velveteen dress with puffed sleeves and surely, from the
circumference of the paneled skirt, at least two crinoline petticoats. A
matching green pillbox hat topped her flyaway hair. She looked like an
ancient but decidedly determined frog.

Henny gnawed on an apple. (Annie hoped to God she *liked* apples.)
Gray hair spilled untidily to her shoulders from a lopsided, collapsing
beehive hairdo. Somehow (was it the way she stood, the bulkiness of her
sweater, the triple pleats of her gray wool skirt?) she gave the impression
of bulk, because, of course, Sven Hjerson's creator and Christie's wry self-
portrait, Ariadne Oliver, was a good-sized woman.

Not a line of fatigue marred Laurel's magnolia-smooth complexion. Her
shining golden hair was drawn back in a ponytail tied with a saucy laven-
der bow (anyone else her age would have had a crepey neck). She smiled
winningly at Miss Dora and Henny, who appeared to be utterly capti-
vated.

Dear God, what was Laurel putting them up to?

Annie broke into a trot.

Her mother-in-law spotted her and gave a coo of delight, as high, sweet, and endearing as doves calling on a Carolina morning.

Annie steeled herself against the expected blandishments and was totally surprised and not a little unnerved when the trio exchanged brief, conspiratorial glances, proffered brisk good mornings as she approached, and, in tandem, turned to enter the classroom.

In growing dismay, Annie stared at the receding backs, at Miss Dora's sheen of green velvet, Henny's thick woven brown sweater, and Laurel's fetching pink blouse. She *hadn't* imagined it. The three of them—her own version of the conniving three sisters—had clearly been conferring upon some matter of substance and, just as clearly, had reached an understanding.

Annie paused in the doorway.

Miss Dora had reclaimed her seat in the middle of the front row, directly opposite the lectern. She might have been a queen at a state funeral, her posture was so regal. High-buttoned black leather shoes, planted firmly together, peeked from beneath the full skirt. Tiny gloved hands clasped the silver knob of the upright ebony cane. Black currant eyes fastened unwinkingly on Annie.

Henny didn't take the seat she'd occupied during the first class. Instead, she dropped into the chair to Miss Dora's immediate left and began to rummage in a capacious, dark purple knitted bag. Apparently, it served as a repository of aids for any and all roles Henny might play. In addition to a mound of apples and a paperback copy of *The Body in the Library*, a title Ariadne Oliver shared with Agatha Christie (Ariadne was the author of at least forty-six best-selling mysteries featuring her gangling, vegetarian Finnish detective), a perfect rainbow of pastel yarn and shiny ivory knitting needles poked out of one side. It seemed to Annie that the rearrangement was taking ordinarily nimble-fingered Henny quite a while. Could it be that Death on Demand's most industrious fan was avoiding Annie's glance?

In further proof of the newfound and unsettling chumminess on the part of these three students, Laurel darted to the seat on Miss Dora's right. But instead of sitting down, she dropped her canvas carryall, lavender-and-cream striped this morning, then swung about to approach Annie, her dark blue eyes alight with pleasure and satisfaction.

Annie braced herself.

The delicate scent of lilac, the gentle brush of lips against her cheek.

"My sweet, so pleased our little excursion last night wasn't *too* tiring for you and dear Maxwell. Although, you do look just a *tiny* bit weary. That's why I thought I would try to lift some of the burden."

"Oh, Laurel, how thoughtful of you," Annie cried insincerely, and, dammit, she was tired. There was the beginning of a dull ache at her temples. How could Laurel keep right on looking like an ever-younger Grace Kelly? "But I do have a full morning planned for us." She gripped Laurel's elbow and tried to maneuver her toward her chair. "It's a help just knowing you are in place."

With no effort at all, her mother-in-law slipped free of her grasp and wafted gracefully toward a large portfolio balanced against the lectern.

Annie followed, trying to avoid the appearance of a frantic lunge.

The other students were drifting into place. Class minimum was ten. Annie, as a last-minute replacement, had an enrollment of twelve: the young man with pink hair (Tim Wallis? Annie was still attempting to match names to faces); the *Crier* reporter with the long black braids, wound round her head today, and a Grateful Dead T-shirt (Mitzi Morrison?); the massive dark-haired fellow who *had* to play football (Mike Swenson?); the three middle-aged women with blue-white hair and patterned polyester dresses (Mrs. Goodrich, Mrs. Thompson, and Mrs. Fielding?); the stocky elderly gentleman with a scraggly white mustache and darting brown eyes (Fred Jones? Jessup?); and the slim woman in her forties with a tanned face, laugh lines, and a charm bracelet that jingled (Wilma Phillips?). The department's least favorite student, Brad Kelly, hadn't arrived. Annie devoutly hoped he wouldn't.

She reached Laurel as she opened the portfolio. Lifting out five familiar watercolors, Laurel displayed them proudly.

"Ingrid helped, of course. Annie, they are so wonderful!"

Annie rarely found herself speechless. She felt a sudden prick of tears behind her tired eyes. How *thoughtful* of Laurel. Perhaps not in the best of taste. It could be considered self-advertisement, but, really, what harm could it do to display this month's mystery book contest paintings from *Death on Demand*?

Not waiting for a response, Laurel was busy affixing them to the stippled plaster wall with masking tape. Fred—Jones? Jessup? smoothed his mustache and leapt to her aid. Annie felt sure that should Laurel be transported to the Sahara, to the *middle* of the Sahara, and left in lonely exile, a half dozen sheiks would undoubtedly charge up astride their camels within the hour.

The class members watched with interest, including Miss Dora, whose reptilian eyes digested each painting with awesome thoroughness. Henny, of course, was concentrating on the fourth one, with the beachy young man so out of place in the luxurious library. She had that look of teetering on the brink of recognition. Annie held her breath (God, what had she wagered?) then tried to hide a sigh of relief at her customer's vexed headshake.

"Oh, thank you so much. How lovely that there are always strong handsome men to the rescue," Laurel trilled as one of the watercolors almost slithered to the floor. Jones or Jessup, of course, caught it immediately and manfully slapped it against the wall, basking in the warmth of her approval.

It wasn't, Annie almost pointed out acerbically, quite on a level with a rim shot in the last two seconds. But she restrained herself. After all, Laurel was certainly doing her best to make her daughter-in-law happy and the least Annie could do was to be a gracious recipient.

Laurel didn't even hog the limelight as Annie made her thanks. In fact, with uncharacteristic demureness, she brushed aside Annie's expressions of appreciation and focused class attention upon the instructor.

"Oh, Annie dear, you know so *much* about mysteries. Now explain to everyone about the paintings," she murmured as she slipped to her seat.

A fascinated Jessup—Annie was *sure* his name was Jessup—followed right behind her and sat down on her other side.

Miss Dora looked at Jessup sardonically. Henny was again rearranging the contents of her bag.

Annie felt a rush of affection. The three of them had planned it, obviously. Really, she took back everything she'd ever thought (and wisely left unsaid, except, of course, to Max, and that was privileged) about Laurel, Miss Dora, and Henny.

Annie cleared her throat. The class members obediently stopped rustling and whispering.

"As I told all of you at our first meeting, I am a bookseller and a collector of mysteries and I enjoy posing mysteries for mystery lovers to solve." She tried not to sound too full of herself. After all, just because the paintings were one of the best marketing ideas of the century, she had to remember that modest is as modest does. Or something like that. "At my mystery bookstore, Death on Demand on Broward's Rock, I run a contest every month. Five paintings representing five famous mysteries are hung on the back wall near our coffee bar." (It didn't hurt to make clear all the attractions. She didn't cite the kinds of coffee available. That would have been crass. Maybe someone would ask.) "The first person to correctly give me the titles and authors represented wins a free new mystery or non-fiction title and a month of free coffee."

Annie beamed at the class.

Ten agreeable faces beamed back.

All except Jessup. Managing at last to remove his soulful gaze from Laurel's patrician profile, he looked toward the paintings. "Oh, hey, sure. Who doesn't know? Especially that fourth one. It's fuh—"

That he didn't strangle, but emitted not a syllable more, was due both to the speed and to the effectiveness of Laurel's response. And maybe, too, he liked having her palm against his lips.

"No, no, no, no," she cried playfully. "That's against the rules. Every-one must do his own searching. This is an individual quest." Her hand moved, and she gave his pinkening cheek a gentle tweak. "But if you figure them out, we will all celebrate at your victory."

Annie didn't like the way Henny was eyeing Jessup, something on the order of an anaconda spying a particularly plump swamp rat.

"Absolutely," Annie affirmed. "No consultations permitted." She stared hard at Henny. "It's up to each mystery lover to meet the challenge alone."

Laurel sighed in admiration, her blue eyes fervent with approval and respect. "Truly, Annie, you are an inspiration to generations of mystery readers. You epitomize the greatest virtues of the great detectives."

Although the praise seemed a little extreme, Annie gave a modest nod.

"Devotion to the chase," Laurel extolled in her husky voice. "Keeping one's own counsel until all is revealed at the denouement. Refusal to be dissuaded or deflected from pursuing the truth."

Enough was enough. Laurel was perhaps ladling it on a bit too thick.

"In any event," Annie interrupted briskly, "it will be fun for class members to study the watercolors and to join this month's competition at

Death on Demand. Now," she glanced down at the lectern, "let me call the roll."

The door opened and Brad Kelly slipped in. Giving her an apologetic nod, he took a seat in the second row beside the football player.

"Brawley. Brevard."

Annie paused for just an instant. Henny, Miss Dora, and Laurel were all regarding Brad Kelly with an intensity that was staggering. Henny's sharp nose twitched aggressively; Miss Dora's dark eyes brooded. Even Laurel's usually kindly demeanor was touched with disapproval.

Oh, dear. But, after all, what could they do? Annie was in charge of this class.

Briskly, she continued the roll call. "Fielding. Goodrich. Jessup. Kelly. Morrison. Phillips." A withering glare from Mitzi Morrison, but a warm and eager smile from Wilma Phillips. Obviously, a woman impatient to learn more of the three great women mystery writers. "Roethke." Laurel's unblinking gaze never left Brad's face. He moved restively and frowned. "Swenson. Thompson. Wallis."

Tucking the roll back beneath her lecture notes, Annie took a deep breath.

Laurel's hand shot up.

Annie's warm feelings for her mother-in-law's generous gesture began to erode. She gave an acknowledging nod.

"Before we get started—and I know this morning will be full of surprises for all of us—" Despite the bonhomie oozing from Laurel's husky voice, Annie abruptly tingled with foreboding. "But I do just have a few tiny questions about our class work."

Annie's tense shoulders relaxed. "Of course, Laurel."

Her mother-in-law fished the reading list from her carryall.

Miss Dora poked her pince-nez to her nose and snapped, "Not the best selections, by any means."

Henny pulled another apple from her pocket, gave it a queasy look, and replaced it. "Some additions wouldn't do any harm."

Annie's adrenaline began to flow.

Wilma Phillips spoke up, a little apologetically. "I do wish we had a Tommy and Tuppence on the list."

Her comment opened the floodgates. Annie looked out at her class in dismay as the clamor rose. Could twelve people make this much noise?

• • •

Max felt cosy and warm, part of the in crowd, accepted, approved, damn near anointed. It was a curious sensation and one worthy of analyzing. It wasn't that Victor Garrison was obsequious. Not at all. In fact, Garrison exuded self-confidence and aplomb as he sat at ease behind his blond wood desk. The professor was the picture of sartorial splendor in a rust-and-brown Donegal silk tweed sport coat and a paisley tie. His desk was orderly, with several opened books and a yellow legal pad filled with neat, precise handwriting.

"I am, of course," Garrison went on smoothly, "impressed with Miss Dora's continuing and generous support of our college. And this department. Her brother once owned several newspapers in this area. This building is, in fact, named in his honor. A substantial family. I would like to do anything I can to help you in your inquiries." He drew deeply on his pipe, and a woodsy, autumnal smoke encircled Max. "Perhaps I can be most helpful by giving you some background on our department." He quirked an eyebrow and smiled genially.

Max wondered how his mother would describe Garrison's karma. Creamy. A hot tub with the Jacuzzi on low. Satin sheets. Silk jockey shorts. Melted caramel on French vanilla.

Garrison gestured benignly to the window on his right which looked out on glossy-leaved live oaks and a portion of a cypress-rimmed pond. "A small community, but dear to those of us who have devoted our lives to its nurture." Pale blue eyes studied Max dispassionately.

To see how it was playing in Poughkeepsie?

"A community apparently suffering some strains," Max observed.

The professor puffed pensively on his pipe. "I'm not sure just how to explain us to an outsider." This time the grin was engaging.

"One word at a time," Max suggested gently.

A sharp glance, but Max too could maintain a bland expression.

"I'm sure you've already talked to our chairman." The pale eyes glittered coldly, but the voice remained suave.

"Yes, I had an interesting session with Mr. Burke."

"An old-time newsman." The faintest hint of derision. "Brusque. Combative. Aggressive. Well suited to chasing down stories on the police beat. Up front about his convictions." Pipe smoke spiraled lazily up. "Very open. As he makes clear at every opportunity, he has no patience with the use of personal information that is not germane to a story. Strong sense of the importance of the right to privacy. So, of course, I am sure, Mr. Darling, that you are convinced that Mr. Burke could have had nothing to do with those unfortunate revelations in *The Crier*. And further, true to his principles, Mr. Burke hasn't provided you with any personal, truly personal, information about his colleagues." A slightly raised eyebrow underlined his skepticism.

Max frowned uncomfortably. Actually, he had dismissed the possibility that Burke might have engineered the leaks. The chairman's fury at Brad Kelly and his reiteration that he would never play games with people's lives had rung true. And Burke had initially resisted talking about the members of his department.

Satisfaction flickered in Garrison's eyes. "Yes, our chairman is very open with his feelings. Almost," he added silkily, "amazingly so. But I wonder, Mr. Darling, just as a point of information, did you inquire as to reasons the faculty might have for being unhappy with Mr. Burke?"

"Yes."

"And, being an able investigator, I imagine you inquired further about the kinds of personnel problems that might soon be appearing on page one of *The Crier*."

Max nodded reluctantly. "Burke told me in confidence on the understanding that the information would go no further than Miss Dora."

"Of course, of course." A pitying smile.

Max felt a vein begin to throb in his neck. "He didn't unload all the faculty dirt. In fact, he refused to go into the reasons for Mrs. Porter's misusing those monies."

"Oh, really. Noble fellow. Determined to protect her memory at all costs, no doubt."

Max frowned. "But he hates having people think she was venal."

"So?" Garrison prodded.

"There's a press conference this afternoon. Kelly's called it to announce that nothing will stop his exposé. He dared Burke to show up."

"Our stalwart chair will be there, I feel confident," the professor observed with a dry smile.

Max said thoughtfully, "Burke intends to decide by then whether to reveal Porter's reasons."

Garrison laughed wholeheartedly, a man who'd heard a really marvelous joke. "Sounds as though you had a very informative session with our chair. Do you know what, Mr. Darling? If I were a betting man, I'd wager the world will learn the truth about Charlotte Porter this afternoon."

Annie could feel the beads of sweat above her mouth. A 10K road race would have been easier, but she felt confident she was now back in control.

Of course, she had found it necessary to agree to a few changes in the reading list.

It never paid to be stiff-necked.

Henny made a final addition to her mimeographed sheet with a flourish. "Perhaps it would be well, if you don't mind, Annie, to review it. Let's see, for Mary Roberts Rinehart—"

Annie interrupted. "I'll put it on the board."

She turned, grabbed up chalk, and began to write:

> MARY ROBERTS RINEHART—*The Circular Staircase*
> *The Red Lamp*
> *The Swimming Pool*

"So very pleased," Laurel murmured, "at the substitution of *The Red Lamp* for *The Door*. Although it does seem to me that we can scarcely do justice to her light touch if we don't read any of the Tish stories."

The chalk in Annie's fingers broke in half. "The Tish stories were not mysteries," she said through clenched teeth.

"Might as well spend the semester reading Sayers's Dante translations. Have as much application," Miss Dora snapped.

Annie hated to be in her debt, but she flashed an appreciative glance.

"Wrong, wrong, wrong," Henny countered. "Sayers's nonmystery works are terribly important in understanding her. *Mind of the Maker* brilliantly examines the fundamentals of Christianity, and I feel it's fair to say that we can never claim to have any insight into Sayers if we've not read any of her religious writings."

"Wait a minute, wait a minute," Mitzi cried, looking from one to another in dismay, her braids beginning to slip sideways. "Look, I got scratches all over my reading list. Mind of the what? What're we 'spose' to read, for Pete's sake?"

Annie pointed at the board. "These three Rinehart titles and—" She wrote decisively, because it was over the Christie titles that the bloodiest battles had erupted.

> AGATHA CHRISTIE—*A Murder Is Announced*
> *The A.B.C. Murders*
> *Appointment with Death*
> *Crooked House*
> *Murder for Christmas*
> *Murder in Retrospect*

The big jock next to Kelly gave a howl of distress. "Six books? Six? Plus three for Rinehart and three for Sayers?" His tone put the imposition of a twelve-book reading list right on a level with the kind of mayhem so routinely meted out in Mike Hammer novels.

Miss Dora thumped her cane resoundingly. Jessup flinched. "Young man, reading is one of life's greatest pleasures. Try it."

Swenson's mouth opened, then closed soundlessly.

Annie ignored them all and listed the Sayers titles:

> *Murder Must Advertise*
> *The Nine Tailors*
> *Gaudy Night*

She swung around, lips compressed, and snatched up her notes before anyone else could interrupt. "Now, everyone has the correct reading list." The substitution of *The Nine Tailors* for *The Unpleasantness at the Bellona Club* infuriated her, but Miss Dora obviously would have thrown up a barricade and mounted it had Annie resisted, despite Annie's bone-deep conviction that *The Nine Tailors* was one of the most boring books ever written. She swept the room with her gaze. Only Max Carrados would not have seen that she had reached her limit of endurance. (But the blind detective's other senses were so well developed he likely wouldn't have missed it.) "This morning, we shall discuss briefly the original and enduring contributions each author has made to the mystery field, beginning with Mary Roberts Rinehart. As everyone knows, Rinehart is credited with creating the Had-I-But-Known school of the mystery." Affirmative headshakes from everyone but Morrison, who looked bewildered, then at her watch. "In these, the protagonist is recounting for the reader's pleasure and mystification the occurrence of murders which have been solved but the reader receives the story as it happened with occasional comments by the protagonist on the order of 'Then Maud appeared, and I remember waving them off and going back to my office, totally unaware that the first happy phase of my life at the Cloisters was over.'"

"Ohh," Laurel cried, "oh yes, of course. Dear Pat Abbott in *The Great Mistake.* Such a *lovely* girl and in such straitened circumstances."

What could Annie say? Wouldn't any instructor be delighted at such recognition of and enthusiasm about the material by a student? She gritted her teeth. "Very good, Laurel."

Laurel half turned to face her classmates. "Of course, Pat falls in love with Tony—he's Maud's son—but there's more to the story than that. He's still married, for one thing, and there are hidden identities and such complicated relationships and greed, of course, all of which are often Rinehart themes."

"Laurel, Laurel. We'll get into all of that later. Right now I'd like to discuss with the class Rinehart's other contributions."

Laurel nodded agreeably. "Oh, certainly, my dear. Such a good idea." And she watched brightly, as if she were the authority generously approving a neophyte's performance. The middle-aged ladies with blue-white hair gazed at Laurel admiringly.

Annie controlled her fury and managed to speak evenly. "Rinehart contributed four new elements to the field: one, the Had-I-But-Known technique; two, a strong love interest; three, humor; and four, the intertwining of two stories, that of the narrator who observes and reacts to the inexplicable happenings and that of the criminal who is actively engaged in a course of action, often one deliberately intended to destroy the protagonist."

"Two stories!" Morrison bleated. "You mean each one of those Rinehart books has *two* stories?"

Henny took up the cudgels. "The story behind the story. Think of the apparent story as a straight line and the second story as a series of peaks and valleys. The peaks protrude above the horizontal plane when the criminal's activities are apparent."

"Well posited," Miss Dora said grudgingly. "However, Rinehart's works never attain the brilliance and symmetry of Sayers's."

Morrison's gaze moved from Henny to Miss Dora with a look of sheer stupefaction tinged with panic.

Responding to Miss Dora's attack on her flank, Annie said sweetly, "Our novelists are not in competition with one another, Miss Dora. Rather, as a class we will come to appreciate the individual genius of each."

"Only Agatha Christie can be termed a genius," Henny trumpeted intemperately.

Annie clutched the lectern as the class exploded in acrimony.

Max rattled the knob to Malcolm Moss's office door. Despite the posted sheet giving office hours that included ten to twelve on Tuesdays and Thursdays, no light shone behind the frosted glass upper panel and the door was locked.

The faculty offices filled the northwest quadrant of the second floor. A narrow corridor bisected the area and four offices were on each side. Garrison's office was at the far end next to a rear corridor leading to the central west stairway.

On the north side were offices for Garrison, Moss, Porter, and Tarrant. Across the hall were Norden, Diggs, Crandall, and one vacant office.

Whom should he talk to next? He needed a clearer perception of the department and its members. Had Burke played Max and Annie like a drum? Could Garrison's suggestions be trusted? Was he likely to find an unbiased observer among this lot?

Max surveyed the closed doors, tossed a mental coin, and turned toward Josh Norden's office.

Annie felt as stressed as Christie's appealing detective, Mr. Satterthwaite, upon being plunged into the middle of a mystery by the enigmatic Harley Quin. She shot a covert glance at the wall clock. The hour—thank God that really meant fifty minutes—was almost over. At least she'd made most of the points she'd intended: Christie's brilliance with plot, her delight in turning the reader's assumptions against him, her clever use of clichés, her unsurpassed skill at sleight of hand, her Victorian conviction that evil exists everywhere, and, finally, to Miss Dora's satisfaction, a description of Sayers's great gift of language and her introduction into the mystery of finely drawn characters and plots concerned with intellectual integrity which Sayers saw as "the one great permanent value in an emotionally unstable world."

"So," Annie said in conclusion, "we have before us in the next few weeks the pleasure of discussing in more detail the works and attitudes of three superb and sharply differentiated mystery writers. Now, for next week, I'd like for everyone to have read the three Rinehart titles."

"Three books by next *Tuesday?"* Swenson's voice rose in panic. He must have known instinctively that Cliffs Notes would be no help here.

Miss Dora thumped her cane. "A philosophic inquiry."

The other class members were learning. They looked at her in respectful silence. Even Swenson subsided quietly into a lump of misery.

"Knowledge for the sake of knowledge is, of course, a respectable intellectual equation." The wrinkled parchment face was benign. "However, I should be quite pleased if the instructor would deign in our remaining minutes to give us a personal expression of her views on the usefulness of our study."

"Usefulness?" Annie parroted.

"Practical application to the problems of life," Henny proffered. But she didn't look at Annie, and her voice was a mumble.

Unease prickled the back of Annie's neck. She looked from Miss Dora, as bland as Charlie Chan, to Laurel, nodding expectantly, to Henny, assiduously avoiding her eye.

Later, she would ascribe the outcome to her fatigue (very little sleep and a class filled with unexpected pitfalls and challenges) and to her beleaguered status (one against three was never fair).

At the moment, she took a deep breath and committed herself to, she would soon realize unhappily, the very worst position she could have taken.

"Practicality? Certainly. This is a very practical course."

"How about another foot-long?" Max urged. "Be glad to go get it. With double chili?" He leaned forward, poised to hurry back to the Student Union to the fast food carryout window.

Annie considered his offer as she took the last bite of her hot dog (pretty good but not enough onions) and sucked the final suds from her root beer. Max, of course, was trying to make her feel better. Usually he was pressing her to eat broiled scrod or baked halibut. But not even her favorite foods could dispel her current outrage.

She didn't bother to lower her voice because there was no one nearby to hear, unless you counted the alligator who'd arisen from his fall slumber to find a lone patch of toasty sunlight on the west bank. "My class," she cried. "My *class!*"

Max slid closer and patted her shoulder. They had the gazebo to themselves. Although they were probably no more than one hundred yards from the journalism building, they might have been one hundred miles from habitation. The live oak avenue split to circle around this enormous lagoon, leaving a huge, dim pocket of greenery in the center of the campus. Actually, she wasn't surprised at their privacy. It sounded charming, of course, a gazebo constructed upon an artificial island in the middle of a cypress-rimmed lagoon with masses of blooming japonica and hibiscus affording total privacy. But this place would never make it as a passion pit, not with dorm rooms and car backseats so readily available. Secluded, yes. Remote, yes. Gloomy, in spades. Although it was a sunny, mild day, the temperature in the sixties, the tall, dark, knobby trees, nuzzled by weeping willows and shrubs, blocked away almost all of the sunlight, so the gazebo was chilly, damp, and dim, but not, fortunately, a murder site as in *The Gazebo* by Patricia Wentworth.

Annie glared impartially at the dark water, the alligator, and the two wooden bridges that arched to the shore.

"Friggin' school," she muttered.

"Now, Annie, love, you can't blame it on the college."

She transferred her glare to him. What a loathsome, avuncular tone.

"Maybe some fried okra," he suggested hastily.

"I don't want anything else to eat," she snapped. "What I want—I'd like to get—" Her hands twitched.

He couldn't help being defensive. "It sounds to me like it's Miss Dora's fault. If it's anybody's."

"Laurel set me up." It was a simple statement, laden with rancor. "Oh, I know," she said impatiently, "it was Miss Dora who asked the question, got it all started, this nonsense about how practical the class was. My God, I didn't know what they were leading up to. I want to tell you, this damn thing was orchestrated. And I know by who. *Whom.*" Drat, was it 'who'?

She continued to glare at the culprit's son. My God, he looked more like
Laurel every day, the same dark blue eyes, such ingenuous damn blue eyes.

"A banana split? Double chocolate?"

"No."

"But, honey, it's really not such a bad deal. Everyone will learn a lot
about mysteries."

"They could have learned a lot listening to my lectures." She quivered
on the bench. "Do you know what it's like to lecture to a room with those
three in it? It would be easier to teach physics to a Montessori class. No,
they have to horn in. And what could I say, after I'd said the damn thing
was practical. There was Laurel all wide-eyed and sugary." She mimicked
her mother-in-law's husky voice. " 'Annie dearest, how wonderful that you
are urging us to become involved in the mystery of life around us and here
is Chastain College with *such* a mystery. *Who* is behind the revelation of
faculty secrets? *Who* is spreading misery and unrest among both students
and faculty? *Who* is Chastain College's very own Deep Throat?' "

"Wait a minute. Wait a *minute*," Max demanded. "It can't all be
Mother's idea. Annie, I assure you she was oblivious to Watergate. She
was living in an ashram in New Delhi at the time." He paused, frowning
thoughtfully. "Or was it a casbah?"

"I didn't say the three of them didn't connive," Annie admitted grudgingly. "But Laurel was the motivating force, I'm certain of it. Why,
Henny was positively embarrassed about the whole thing."

"Bet she wins, anyway."

"Making it a contest!" Annie exploded. "Whoever turns in the most
clues to Deep Throat's identity gets extra credit. What does that have to
do with the Three *Grande Dames* of the Mystery?" she demanded wildly.
"But they came at me from every direction and then the rest of the damn
class got into the act, beside themselves with excitement at their 'opportunity to rival the detective exploits of some of the greatest sleuths of all
time'!" Her fists clenched. "You know who said that, don't you?"

Max avoided her eyes.

"Laurel Darling Roethke," Annie intoned bitterly. "My *class!* I'll never
get it under control again until we find out who leaked that stuff." She
tried to slow her breathing, bring her heartbeat down to an acceptable
level. "All right. They think they've got me outsmarted. They think I'll
just fall down and lie doggo while they grab my class in their teeth and run

away with it. But that's not true. We're going to put a stop to it by beating them at their own game." She fixed Max with a demanding stare. "Who did it?" When he didn't answer immediately, she said—even she realized a bit unfairly—"Well, you've had all morning to find out. Who did it?"

But Max never had a chance to answer, if answer he could. The mind-numbing roar of an enormous explosion shattered the gloomy quiet of the lagoon.

They stared at each other in shocked silence for an instant, then flung themselves toward the steps and began to run.

It stuck in Annie's mind, as odd details will in the midst of an emergency, that the alligator had responded more quickly than they, shooting back into the dark water before she and Max took a step.

They burst out from the dimness of the canopied trail among the cypresses and stumbled to a halt. Smoke and dust billowed out from the shattered side of the journalism building.

11

A CHALKY BILLOW of masonry grit eddied from the doorway to the *Crier* offices. The door hung crazily from one hinge.

"Emily!"

Brad Kelly pelted up the central hall through the roiling dust. The gritty particles clung to him, coating his clothes and face with gray. He stumbled to a stop by the dangling door, his face slack with shock. "Oh God, I just went to the john—" He reached out, grabbed Max's arm. "I just went to the john. If I hadn't, I'd have been in—" Frantically, he began to pull on the sagging door. "Emily! Emily! Where are you? Emily, answer, for Christ's sake!"

The door came loose in his hands. He heaved it into the hallway and plunged into the newsroom. Glass from imploded video display terminal screens covered the floor, crunched beneath his steps. Desks and terminals leaned at precarious, unnatural angles. Broken joists and splintered lathes protruded from the shattered plaster walls. There was an acrid smell of smoke, dust, plaster, and singed plastic.

Max yelled after the frantic editor as he careened across the room. "Is somebody in there? Where?"

Kelly pointed at the far corner, now a tangle of construction rods and sagging ceiling tiles and mounds of bricks. The exterior wall was gone, and the remains of the office lay exposed to outside. "My office. Emily. Emily Everett. Oh God, look!"

Choking from the dust, straining to see through the milky cloud, Annie and Max stared at the debris and at a bloated hand, gunpowder singed, sticking through a sheet of beaverboard. As they looked, blood seeped from the puckered edges of the wood.

Max gripped Annie's elbow. "Quick. Go for help. We'll see if we can get her free," and he hurried after Kelly.

Annie darted a frantic glance at the unstable wall tilted over the corner office. But Max and the editor had to try. Whirling around, she bolted across the hall into the departmental office.

"Mr. Burke," she shouted. "Mr. Burke!"

Even as she called, her mind was admonishing her for reacting so slowly. Obviously, Burke wasn't in the building. If he had been in his office, the explosion would have brought him immediately to the scene.

Pushing through the swinging gate at the counter, Annie grabbed the telephone receiver and started to dial, then slammed it down. No sound. No tone. Nothing. The explosion must have blown out the lines. Then strong and high came the keen of a siren. It was one of the most welcome sounds she'd ever heard. Help was on the way. Of course it would be. It was a small campus, and the response to an explosion would be immediate and swift.

She was turning, ready to hurry back to help Max and Brad, praying the walls wouldn't tumble down on them, when she saw the smear of red on the floor by the swinging gate.

Blood.

Odd how unmistakable it was.

Even the dried, dark splotches that had disfigured the *Crier* door the morning after the vandal's attack had been immediately, unmistakably identifiable.

This, too, was blood.

But it wasn't old and dried.

Fresh, bright, crimson blood.

The trail was irregular, the smudges growing larger as she walked from the first office into the middle room past the filing cabinets and the table with the mimeograph machine toward the chairman's office.

The siren shrilled to a peak, then cut off.

Annie looked at the open door to Burke's office and the light spilling out, marking an oblong path across the floor, framing the smudges.

One full bloody footprint at the threshold.

A woman's shoe.

"Mr. Burke?" Her voice quavered. "Mr. Burke?"

In the distance, muffled shouts.

Annie moved to her right, avoiding that bloody print.

Then she could see through the open door.

Some sights the mind cannot easily accept.

So much blood.

It was Burke. She recognized the awning-stripe cotton shirt, soft green and white, even though it was sodden with blood. He slumped forward, battered head face down on the desk, arms bent. It looked as though he'd tried to protect himself from his assailant—his arms and hands bloodied— until he was beaten to death.

Annie and Max were herded into an empty classroom, along with the faculty members who'd rushed downstairs from their offices. She saw their covert glances and realized she and Max looked as ghostly as the young editor from the clouds of grit. But the explosion hadn't slowed Brad Kelly. Resolutely clutching his notepad, Kelly confronted the moon-faced sergeant, whose undented full crown hat was too big and rested on neat pink ears.

"Officer, I have to get to a telephone. Two people dead, one blown up, one bludgeoned, *The Crier* destroyed. This is the biggest story in Chastain's history."

The sergeant casually rested a plump, pink hand on the butt of his service revolver. "All occupants of the building are to remain here so as not to interfere with getting those bodies out. Besides, you'll all have to be interviewed."

Bodies. Annie hadn't held much hope that Emily Everett, poor obese Emily, could still be alive, but the sergeant's words made it clear. 'Bodies' was plural. Both Emily and Burke were dead. She and Max needed to talk to someone in authority.

"For how long?" Annie demanded. "Who's in charge? Listen, we've got information about Mr. Burke! We've got to talk to somebody. Quick!"

Ignoring her, the sergeant genially waved them toward the seats. "Might as well get comfortable, folks. It may take a while. Chief Wells is real busy right now, getting everything sorted out. Now, first thing, everybody write down their name on this sheet of paper and where you was when the bomb went off. . . ."

Annie stood frozen by the door. Chief Wells. Chief Wells! Oh God, of course it would be. But at least this time, unlike that horrible period during the house-and-garden troubles, he couldn't possibly think she had anything to do with the murder.

It was a standoff. They glared at each other with equal enmity.

Finally, Chief Harry Wells jerked his head toward the straight chairs in front of the desk. "Sit."

Annie felt herself flush. Did he think she was a dog? And why had she and Max been left, cooling their heels for hours, stuck in a classroom with all the other hapless persons who'd been in the building near the time of the explosion and, presumably, of the murder, and, moreover, not only stuck there, but enjoined to silence. That was the unkindest cut of all. Even Victor Garrison had refrained from exercising his smooth tenor. Malcolm Moss for once hadn't smiled. In fact, his heavy face had looked both grim and wary. Sue Tarrant had paced nervously, her high heels clicking on the floor until the sergeant frowningly insisted she sit down. Kurt Diggs had nervously fingered the heavy silver bracelet on one wrist, glancing again and again toward the door. Only Josh Norden had sat as if oblivious to his surroundings and the circumstances. And Frank Crandall, she had realized at one point, was nowhere to be seen.

So there they'd been, cooped up with some, if not all, of the possible perpetrators, and they'd been muzzled! Annie put her hands on her hips. "Chief Wells, when did free speech go out of style?"

Max whispered warningly, "Annie, shh."

Chief Wells had a face like the side of a weathered granite mountain, gray, pocked, slab-hard. He moved one massive jaw, masticating the lump of tobacco pouching out that cheek. His watery blue eyes glinted with dislike.

"We could've found out a lot, in the hours we sat in that stupid room," Annie said acidly. "Burke was busy this morning talking to the faculty about the leak to the student newspaper. Do you even know about that?

And Emily called in sick this morning. Why was she in the building? And almost everybody who was mad at Burke was cooped up with us, Moss, Garrison, Tarrant, Diggs, Norden, but your little pink gestapo agent—and you ought to get him a hat that fits—wouldn't let us say a word to each other!"

Or to anyone on the outside. But she didn't even want to think about Laurel's brief appearance an hour ago at one of the open windows at the back of the room and her caroled reassurances, "My dears, do bear this enforced idleness with as much grace as you can. So sorry to see you sequestered. But rest assured, Henny, Miss Dora, and I are nose to the trail, nothing daunted, no stone too small to turn. We shall carry the banner unfurled. Tallyho!"

It didn't bear thinking about, what those three might be doing. She and Max must round them up, forestall this investigative nonsense. The stakes in the Who's-Deep-Throat Contest were now too high.

Wells's heavy lips moved. It took Annie a shocked moment to recognize a smile.

Not a nice smile. And a deep rumble that had to be his version of laughter.

"So you got all stewed up, huh? Sorry about that. You just fretted when you didn't need to, Miss Laurance."

"Mrs. Darling," Max said quickly.

"You *married* her?" Wells's voice rose. He shook his head in disbelief. The look he gave Max was one of profound sympathy.

Annie's eyes slitted.

The chief's heavy laughter subsided. "Little lady, you get too het up. Now, married life ought to settle you down some."

"If we can get back to the point," she said icily, "we've got information about Mr. Burke and all the problems here in the department and we can—"

Wells held up a meaty palm. "Right, right. Got to get to business. Wrapping this all up. Now, I understand you found the body, Miss—*Mrs.* Darling."

"Yes, yes. But the point is—"

"The point is, what time was that exactly? Got to get the record right." He held a pencil stub over a small notepad. "Now, we got the call about the explosion at eleven forty-three. Exactly. So," he licked the tip of the pencil, "when did you find Mr. Burke?"

Annie was exasperated. Still, Wells obviously would never get to the substance of the investigation—Burke's relations with the people around him—until she'd satisfied him on this point. She frowned, trying to be accurate. "Okay. If the call came in at eleven forty-three, the explosion had probably just happened. Say, eleven forty-one. We ran right over to the building. We probably got there at eleven forty-two. We talked to the editor, Brad Kelly, went into the newsroom, then I ran to the main office and tried to call for help. The phones were out. That's when I heard the siren, so I guess I found Mr. Burke about eleven forty-four."

Wells scrawled in his notebook. When had he become as concerned with timetables as Inspector French? "Now, for the record, what were you doing on the campus?"

Annie wriggled impatiently. What a waste of time! "Teaching."

Thick iron gray eyebrows rose in astonishment. "You? What would you be teaching?"

"A little class on murder," Max interjected proudly.

Wells's face congealed in disdain, like Hamilton Burger dealing with Perry Mason.

"The Three *Grande Dames* of the Mystery," Annie explained. She knew very well what he was thinking.

Wells, mouthing the words, wrote down, "A little class on murder," then snapped shut his notebook. "All right. That completes the record. That's all we need—"

"All you need? Look, we've got lots to tell you, important—"

"Mrs. Darling." His heavy head swung toward Max. "Mr. Darling. You two amateurs can relax. This investigation's already closed—and the murderer's in jail right now."

For once, Annie was too stunned to speak.

But Max saved the day.

"Who?" he demanded.

A satisfied smile creased Wells's weathered face. "Like most police work, a lot of it depends on bein' a noticin' kind of man. One of my officers, Davis, was off duty, fishin' from the pier down there off Ephraim Street. He saw this girl run out to the end and look around. Said he knew that kind of look, makin' sure there wasn't a cop close. So he ran up and stopped her just as she tried to heave that bar into the river—and it still had blood on it. She tried to run away. He arrested her for litterin', but he knew it was lots more serious. The blood. Said he wasn't surprised when the call came in from the college. Knew he'd caught him a live one."

"A girl?" Annie gasped, then she thought of that bloody footprint.

"Young woman. Student here. Name of Georgia Finney."

They had taken over the top floor of the Palmetto Inn. Three communicating conference rooms had been opened, a bank of telephones installed, a large-scale map of Chastain College pinned to a paneled wall, a chalkboard set up in the middle room. Along one wall was a hospitality table featuring a coffee urn, tea pitcher, cups, glasses, and ice.

Laurel saw them in the doorway. Henny looked up briefly from a mound of papers and waved abstractedly. Miss Dora never turned from her contemplation of a sketch on the blackboard.

"Annie, Max, no time to fill you in. Just pitch in. Perhaps, if you could answer this phone, Maxwell darling, and Annie, do add your order to ours for dinner. Here's the chef now." Laurel thrust a receiver each at Max and Annie.

"Hello," Max managed. "What did you say? Sorry, I can't seem—"

"Another ordair from suite B?" an irate, accented voice demanded in Annie's ear.

"You'll have to speak up, stop whispering," Max urged. "What? Oh? Okay. Miss Dora?" He looked toward the blackboard. "Miss Dora, he wants to talk to you." He looked doubtfully at the receiver. "I think it's a he. Tiny little whispery voice."

"Look, anything will do," Annie said irritably. "A grilled cheese, a hamburger—"

"Grilled sheess? Hamburgair? This is Henri. Of what 'orrors do you speak? I am Henri of La Maison d'Henri, ze only five-star restaurant upon zis coast."

"All right, all right, all right. Two more of anything you're fixing. Chef's choice."

"Barbarians," the chef of the only five-star restaurant on the coast muttered. "Clods. *Primitifs.*"

Annie slammed down the receiver. A sleuth can only take so much.

"My dear," Laurel chided, "Henri is so sensitive. And we must fortify ourselves. We face a long night."

Here was her opening. Annie opened her mouth to attack.

Miss Dora said brusquely, in her crackly voice, "Stop whining, Emmett. I know exactly how Harry will react if he discovers that you are giving me information from his office. So avoid that possibility. Lock your door."

Annie closed her mouth and listened. Max stared at Miss Dora.

The wrinkled parchment face settled in implacable lines. "Door locked now?" A pause. "Emmett, you've always been a fool. If he tries to come in, tell him it's jammed. Now, give the information to this young man, my inquiry agent—and don't leave anything out." She thrust the receiver toward Max.

With a bemused expression, Max dropped into the nearest chair and accepted a pad and pen also proffered by Miss Dora. He tilted his head toward another phone and mouthed at Annie, "Get on an extension."

Extension three glowed. Annie found a free phone, poked extension three, and picked up the receiver.

The voice at the other end cut off in midword. Then a frantic, breathless cry, "Somebody came on the line."

"My secretary," Max said soothingly. "Absolutely trustworthy."

Annie bristled, then decided it would do no harm, for the moment, to join that long line of stalwart ladies to whom generations of private investigators owed so much. Memorable women like Effie Perrine, Della Street, Nikki Porter, Lucy Hamilton, Mary Huston, Miranda Foxworth, Giselle Marc, Rose Corsa, and, of course, the incomparable Miss Lemon.

A piteous moan. "You don't understand. Harry'll kill me if he finds out."

"We won't tell him," Annie said firmly. "We don't like him at all."

Max clapped his hand to his temple. Dark blue eyes glared at her meaningfully.

Annie shrugged. So she didn't have a secretary's temperament.

"You know him?" Hysteria.

It took Max two minutes of soft, calm, soothing reassurance. "And the sooner you tell us, the quicker you'll be off the line."

"Yes. Yes. Yes. All right. I have almost everything they asked for, Miss Dora and the other two ladies. Not much, really, but here it is. You understand, there was a great deal of blood, so some of the material is in the lab. I don't know whether they'll be able to come up with anything there. In Mr. Burke's appointment book for today, Thursday, November ten, the following lines were filled: ten o'clock, Moss; ten-fifteen, Tarrant; ten-thirty, Garrison; ten forty-five, Diggs; eleven o'clock, Norden; eleven-fifteen, Crandall."

Their informant, absorbed now in his recital, was talking in a more nearly normal tone and his voice was precise and just a little didactic.

Annie pictured a pouter pigeon wearing bifocals and suspenders.

"A legal pad knocked to the floor in the attack contained a number of abbreviated notes which I will summarize as well as I can. The faculty was listed with these comments following: 'Moss—chair? Tarrant—jealousy? Garrison—department focus? Diggs—revenge? Norden—drunk? Crandall —stupidity?' There were three question marks after that last one. And scrawled across the bottom of the pad is the name of that unfortunate victim of the blast, Emily Everett. It was written in large block letters and circled a number of times, with three exclamation marks."

"Emily Everett," Annie exclaimed. "Had he talked to her?"

"You must understand," the tone was damping, "the department has no way of knowing just how Mr. Burke spent his final moments and the appointment book does not list Miss Everett. As the chief suggested, Burke may have thought of something he wished for her to do in her capacity as secretary or—"

"Bull feathers," Annie interrupted. "So she gets blown away just before —or after—he's murdered. What kind of coincidence does Wells believe in?"

"She certainly *was* his secretary, that cannot be denied," the speaker admonished. "Now, the circumstances of the explosion are being very carefully considered, but at the moment, Miss Everett is believed to be an accidental victim in that she was merely most unfortunate to be an occupant of that office at the time a bomb exploded. It is Chief Wells's opinion that the subject of the attack was the editor, Mr. Bradley Kelly, and that he escaped through chance, as is often the case in bombings. Homemade bombs are notoriously unreliable.

"Now, the chief has talked to all the persons listed on the legal pad." A dry cough. "Professor Crandall claims he had a very civil talk with Mr. Burke, left his office at shortly after eleven-fifteen, and proceeded to the

Student Union for lunch. Insists he had nothing to do with Burke's murder."

"What does Georgia say?" Annie asked.

"Young woman, Miss Finney has been charged with murder in regard to the death of Mr. Burke. On advice of counsel, she has said nothing whatsoever."

"That's quick work," Max said. "Who hired a lawyer for her?"

A rustle of papers. "A Mrs. Roethke, I believe. A lawyer by the name of McClanahan."

Max sighed.

Annie had become acquainted with Jed McClanahan, the world's greatest trial lawyer, during the difficulties in the *Arsenic and Old Lace* production the previous summer. In fact, she'd hired him to represent Max. She didn't think Max had ever quite forgiven her. So McClanahan wasn't top drawer. He *meant* well. Perhaps he wasn't quite on the level of Rebecca Schwartz, Jesse Falkenstein, or Arthur Crook, but he certainly did his best for his clients.

"Is something wrong?" the informant demanded worriedly.

"Nothing that a bar committee couldn't solve," Max groused.

"Was anything in the office disturbed?" Annie asked.

"Not insofar as the investigators could determine. The desk drawers and filing cabinets were closed. It was only subsequently, of course, upon the impoundment of the iron bar carried by Miss Finney, that it was identified as the memento which normally resided upon Mr. Burke's windowsill."

That iron bar.

The dry voice continued, affirming her recollection, "Three items normally rested there, a shell casing that he brought home from Germany, the bar which had been a part of a luxury hotel destroyed by Hurricane Donna, and the brick from the 1977 jail fire in Tennessee. The shell casing and brick were untouched.

"Several other points are of great interest to the investigators." A touch of excitement lifted the prim voice. "In particular, the bloodied condition of a raincoat found crumpled beside the desk."

Annie frowned. She didn't remember a raincoat—but then, of course, she hadn't looked at the floor in Burke's office. She'd followed those smears of blood from the front office and observed that one clear, woman's print in his doorway, but when she looked into his office, her horrified gaze had been drawn immediately to the body slumped on the desk. She suppressed a shudder.

"The raincoat, of a tweedy material which will not retain fingerprints, belonged to the murdered man and normally hung from a rack in the corner of this office."

Swiftly, Annie made a sketch of Burke's office, combining what she remembered and what she had heard.

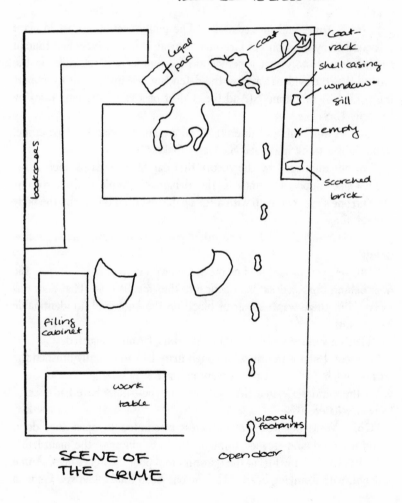

locked door to cross hall

legal pad

coat

coat rack

shell casing

window sill

x — empty

scorched brick

bookcases

filing cabinet

work table

bloody footprints

open door

SCENE OF THE CRIME

"Quite fascinating, actually," their informant burbled. "The killer apparently slipped the raincoat on backwards, gripped the bar with a portion of the sleeve, and thus protected, proceeded to attack the unfortunate Mr. Burke. The back of the coat is quite stained. Somewhat reminiscent of the famous Julia Wallace murder. The murderer, whether her husband or another, wore Wallace's own mackintosh when battering her to death, likely with a poker. The prosecution suggested that Wallace wore the mackintosh while nude then dashed back upstairs to wash up and remove any stains not caught by the coat. Of course, that crime was long before your time."

"1931," Annie said immediately. "The guilty verdict against Wallace was quashed by the Court of Criminal Appeal. It was the very first time in English legal history that a conviction for murder was set aside on the ground that the evidence against the defendant was insufficient to support the verdict. A milestone." (And the subject of a very intriguing essay by Dorothy L. Sayers.)

"Oh." A quickening of interest. "You are an aficionado of true crime. Who do *you* think murdered Sir Harry Oakes?"

"I'm not impressed by the theory that gambling lords planned it because Oakes opposed casinos in the Bahamas," Annie said caustically, "but no one's ever come up with a reasonable explanation of why the body was set afire."

Max cleared his throat. "The other points of interest," he suggested mildly.

"Oh, yes, yes, of course. Let me see, now. The coat . . . oh yes, the door behind Burke's desk that opens into the cross hallway. That door was locked. But there was a smear of blood on the knob and no identifiable fingerprints."

"That's a surface which would hold prints," Annie objected.

"Correct. But apparently some rough material had recently brushed the area, smudging whatever prints were in place."

"If the murderer exited that way, he—or she—must have had a key," Max concluded.

"Chief Wells believes the murderess attempted to open that door, found it locked, and escaped through the outer offices to the main hall."

Wells was certainly fitting the noose around poor Georgia's neck, Annie thought, with a sinking heart. "Has anyone been found who saw Georgia leave the department after Crandall's departure and before the explosion?" she asked.

"Not yet, but the chief made a public appeal which will be carried in the newspaper tomorrow. Someone will have seen her. Besides, that really isn't necessary. The lab reports are conclusive. That bar was the murder weapon. The girl was found trying to dispose of it in the Broad River." Unexpectedly, he added, *"Credo quia absurdum est."*

Annie looked at Max, who mouthed, " 'I believe it because it is absurd,' " then frowned thoughtfully at the receiver and announced, *"Fronti nulla fides."*

What a talented husband she had! She again looked at him inquiringly.

"No reliance," he translated, "can be placed on appearance."

A sudden drawn breath on the line. "The door, the door. I think it's Harry."

The line went dead.

"Huzzah," Laurel cheered from the doorway. "Our repast has arrived. Gather around, laborers in the vineyard of justice."

Annie wished her life were more simple and she just had six impossible things to believe before breakfast. That would be child's play in comparison to the reality. But she was not one to admit to discouragement. And she even dredged from a years-ago French class a lovely aphorism of her own. *"Nous verrons ce que nous verrons."*

Miss Dora was undaunted and stole the spotlight, of course. "We shall see what we shall see. Quite appropriate upon the arrival of dinner."

12

IT WAS THE KIND OF MEAL which, upon completion, left Annie
with a hearty craving for barbecued ribs, cole slaw, baked beans, and fried
peach pie. With a heaping side dish of lamb fries.

Not that it wasn't good. Six courses, beginning with vichyssoise, which
had about as much charm for Annie as melted Jell-O. Admittedly, however, the smoked salmon was good, the ricotta-provolone stuffed chicken
breasts with apricot sauce tasty, the spinach-lamb salad challenging, and
the kiwi mousse light enough to fly.

But was it satisfying?

And it didn't help her indigestion, her appetite, or her disposition when
Laurel forestalled Annie's attempt to get to the heart of the matter (or
one of the hearts, this ridiculous and now perhaps dangerous search by her
class members for the identity of Deep Throat). Laurel decreed with a
gentle, kindly smile that, of course, there could be no conversation of a
criminal nature at the dinner table. Had she been reading Rex Stout on
the sly?

Laurel and Max discussed fly fishing.

Miss Dora embarked on a monologue on the Brevard family, with copi-
ous cross-references to the antecedents of Lord Peter and the interesting

parallels between the Brevards (originally a Norfolk family, too) and the
Wimseys and did Annie know that engaging story about the Wimsey coat
of arms with the crouching cat atop a black shield bearing three mice?
Before Annie could manage a nod, Miss Dora droned on, "Capital story,
really. In Alzina Stone Dale's biography. Shows how clever Sayers was.
When asked by that fellow—you know, Wilfred Scott-Giles—who ulti-
mately wrote the definitive history of the Wimsey family, Sayers told him
the shield originally bore three silver plates but they were changed to mice
when Gerald de Wimsey served as a confidant to King Edward I. Gerald
suggested that the king besiege a castle just as a cat tracks mice, very
persistently." A husky cackle of amusement.

"One thing I've always admired about Dame Agatha is her simplicity,"
Henny observed tartly.

Fortunately, Miss Dora was too busy chuckling to hear her.

Finally, however, dinner was at an end. Laurel, ever and always the
hostess, shepherded them gracefully to a next-door sitting room and
poured the after-dinner coffees. "Perhaps a sorbet?" she inquired.

Annie bounced to her feet from a low-slung love seat. Hot coffee
sloshed over the rim of her cup and sprayed her hand. "Ouch!"

"Festina lente," Miss Dora suggested slyly.

"Not bad advice," Max said cheerfully. At Annie's glare, he added
quickly, "Make haste slowly."

Carefully, Annie placed her cup and saucer on a fake Adam mantel.
Sometimes it didn't do to dignify absurdity with an answer. She addressed
her mother-in-law. "Laurel, we're wasting time. Max and I have a lot to
do. That idiot, Chief Wells, didn't even take time to listen to us about the
department and all its problems. Now, we appreciate the information
you've rounded up." It took an enormous amount of character but she
managed a grateful nod to Miss Dora. "Especially the information about
Burke's office. But it's time for this charade to stop."

"The class project?" Laurel inquired. "Oh, Annie, we've taken care of
that."

"I called everyone," Henny said briskly.

"Only thing to do," Miss Dora seconded.

It was rather like pumping up to face the class bully and discovering he
was a block away and disappearing into a cloud of dust.

"Certainly, my sweet. We couldn't possibly have Chastain students undertaking a *perilous* assignment," Laurel said equably.

"Not the thing at all," Henny agreed.

"The trustees would have objected," Miss Dora explained.

"So it's off? The project?" Annie asked.

Three genial faces. Annie looked from the fox-sharp nose that quivered just a little to the suddenly bland parchment brow to deeply blue, ingenuous eyes.

"But all this—" Annie spread her hand to encompass the connecting rooms with their paraphernalia of investigative tools.

Shocked surprise in triplicate.

"Why, Annie, nothing ever kept Hercule Poirot from his duty!" Henny exclaimed. "Once engaged, he could not be deflected. Remember *Peril at End House.*"

Miss Dora thumped her cane once. "More like *Strong Poison.* In the finest tradition of Lord Peter, I shall pursue truth."

Laurel sighed dreamily. "Mary Roberts Rinehart saw most truly that love is the beginning and the end and shall evermore be triumphant. I should abandon my very soul were I to abandon her ideals."

Annie carefully measured the coffee, chocolate raspberry Colombian decaffeinated.

Max stood with his hands jammed in his khaki slacks, his face drawn in a worried frown.

"Relax," Annie said lightly. "What kind of trouble can they get into on the top floor of the Palmetto Inn?"

He paced into the kitchen. "Will they stay there?"

Annie recalled the trio upon their departure. They had been much too engaged in what was rapidly approaching a shouting match over the virtues and superiority of their respective sleuths to do more than nod an absent good night as Annie and Max slipped out the door.

"It should be really hot by now. Henny will have exploded, saying Lord Peter was a foppish, snobbish ass, Miss Dora will be banging away with her cane and demanding sarcastically to know how anyone could defend the superficial characterizations of Christie and Laurel will be humming 'Always.' "

Max began to laugh. He leaned against the doorjamb and accepted a mug of coffee. "I guess we don't have to worry about them right now." Then his smile slipped away.

Neither said it, but tomorrow, as it inevitably does, would come.

Annie led the way to the living room. "All right. It's time for some real thought."

Max rustled in the desk, brought them each a scratch pad and pen. They settled companionably on the wicker couch. Annie glanced at the clock. Almost ten. And only a few hours' sleep last night.

But, as her three most irritating students would enjoin, duty called.

Annie poised a pen over her pad, then looked at Max, bewildered. "Now I know how Captain Hastings feels—totally at a loss."

"Obviously," her sometimes charming husband suggested, "let's begin at the beginning. The first question is: Do we need to investigate at all?"

Annie's eyes widened. "Max, of course. Wells didn't listen to a word we had to say—"

He held up a cautioning hand. "Annie, maybe Wells is right. Maybe the murderer is already in jail."

Laurel would have hooted it down, the suggestion that lovely Georgia Finney had battered out Burke's brains.

But Henny would have countered that neither youth nor beauty nor romance guarantees innocence, and suggested a thoughtful perusal of *Crooked House, Death on the Nile, Endless Night, Evil Under the Sun,* and *Death in the Air.* And why else had Georgia tried to get rid of the murder weapon?

Miss Dora would have dismissed that solution as boring and pedestrian, two cardinal sins in the Wimsey salon.

But Annie had to consider it.

"She *was* very upset about the article in *The Crier,*" Annie mused. "If Kelly published a story on her relationship with Frank Crandall, Crandall's career could certainly be damaged—if not destroyed. So, I can see why she might have planted the bomb in the *Crier* offices. But why would she kill Burke?"

Max sipped at his coffee. "Maybe Burke told her he was going to recommend against tenure for Crandall because of their relationship. Or, how about this—Georgia thinks Burke leaked the information to Kelly?"

Burke as the betrayer of the faculty.

It could be.

He had denied it. Emphatically.

But whoever had engineered that leak would surely deny any accusation.

"Okay. Okay," Annie said energetically. "Look, we've *got* to find out who planned this. Who pulled Kelly's string. And why." Mrs. Dane Calthrop, in her clear-eyed fashion, put it best in *The Moving Finger* when she called in Miss Marple to help, because Miss Marple was an expert in wickedness. And that was what they faced, wasn't it? "Wickedness," Annie murmured. Her face was stern. "Whoever is behind this is wicked, Max, don't you think?"

He looked at her inquiringly.

She slowly formulated her thoughts. "What kind of person would do this? Someone intelligent enough to know how Kelly would respond? Someone filled with anger? Or at the least, with jealousy? Or was it colder than that? An overweening determination to prevail?"

Max shrugged. "These are brainy people. Subtle people, accustomed to leading others, if not manipulating them. On that standard, it could be any one of them."

"Even Burke," she said solemnly. He had been, to her, likable. But he had also been a determined, angry man.

"Right," Max agreed. "If so, he may have been killed *because* he leaked all the untidy secrets of the department."

"But if he wasn't behind it, could he have discovered who did it and have to be silenced?"

Max brooded. "Murder? Was it worth murder to hide the source of the leaks?"

Annie shrugged. "That depends, doesn't it, on how much someone had to lose."

Max shoved a hand through his thick blond curls, disarranging them in what Annie considered to be a most attractive fashion. Really, rumpled became Max, especially that endearing twig poking up from the back of his head.

"Look at this thing logically," he implored.

Annie tried hard to concentrate, although she yearned for sleep. Or, at the very least, for a good slug of endorphins à la Harry Colderwood. Sleep was almost as important to her as food, and it seemed eons since she'd curled up comfortably in their very cozy bed.

"Logically," she repeated dutifully.

"You see, there could be a number of different reasons for R.T. Burke to be killed." Max didn't even seem tired. He hunched over his notepad and wrote:

1. Burke discovered the identity of leak. Possible Deep Throats: a. Victor Garrison, b. Malcolm Moss, c. Kurt Diggs, d. Frank Crandall.

He studied the list with satisfaction.

Annie rubbed grainy eyes. How did Holmes manage to track criminals for days on end? "Why would Kurt Diggs or, for God's sake, Frank Crandall want all the dirt out in public? Both of them had awfully good reasons to hope those personnel files stayed confidential."

"A gamble. A hope that there would be such a stink, especially focusing on Porter's misuse of funds, that Burke would be discredited. A backlash kind of thing."

"I'd say they'd have to be pretty stupid to unplug the hornet's nest."

Maybe Max was tired, too. Without any comment, he scratched through Diggs's and Crandall's names.

Annie nodded. "So really, on any logical basis, there are only two faculty members who might reasonably be guilty of the leak, Garrison or Moss." She nodded with such enthusiasm she spilled coffee on the blank page of her notebook. "Sure. Look at it! They are the only two who don't have anything discreditable that could come out. They're just crossways about academic matters."

"So far as we know," Max cautioned.

"Damn. We need to see those files."

"We sure do." Max began to smile. He reached for the phone. It took a moment to be connected to the top floor of the Palmetto Inn.

"Hi, Ma. No. We're fine. Drinking raspberry chocolate coffee." A pause. "Something romantic before bedtime?" He sounded puzzled. Then the tips of his ears flamed. "That's all right. We're fine. I mean, don't worry about—Look, Ma, I need to talk to Miss Dora for a minute." He avoided Annie's piercing gaze. "Miss Dora, would you have access to a set of master keys for the journalism building?" He grinned. "Great! We'll pick them up in the morning. Thanks a—Oh no, no, I don't need to talk to her again. Good night," and he thrust the receiver away from him as if it might bite his hand.

Annie opened her mouth, then firmly closed it. Some questions were better left unasked.

Besides, Max was rushing into speech. "Okay, so we've got Moss and Garrison as possibilities. Now, let's turn it around, make Burke responsible. Who might have killed him?"

"The same person who tried to blow up *The Crier*," Annie offered. "Somebody who was determined that nothing more should be leaked."

Max briskly added:

2. Burke betrays faculty. Possible killers: Crandall, Diggs, Norden, Finney.

Annie rubbed her eyes again and blearily tried to focus. Okay, he didn't bother to list Moss and Garrison this time. Obviously, Max didn't believe anybody would kill just to hide an academic firestorm. As for Crandall and Diggs, they made sense. Each had a personnel problem that would look damn awful in cold print. One involved with a coed, the other suspected of trading A's for sex. But she couldn't buy Norden. Alcoholism is a disease and although Norden could be pressured to take a leave of absence for treatment, surely he wouldn't face summary dismissal from a job he'd held for so long and previously done with distinction, according to Charlotte Porter. Besides, and she remembered his tears when he brought news of Charlotte's death, this was a good-hearted man.

"I can't believe Norden would kill Burke to prevent public discussion of his problem. He doesn't seem like that kind of man."

But Max's face was grim. "I know," he said heavily. "That isn't why I listed him." He sighed. "Funny. Now we'll never know whether Burke would have revealed the reason behind Charlotte Porter's theft."

Annie concentrated. Oh yes, the ill-starred press conference scheduled for three P.M., prevented by murder and explosion.

"Max, nobody would do all that just to keep the truth—whatever it is— from coming out about poor Charlotte Porter!"

"I know that. But if we'd had the press conference, it might have gone a long way toward telling us whether Burke was behind Kelly's exposé. Think about it! He kept insisting that he'd never reveal personnel information publicly—but he gave it to us. Everything but the background on Charlotte Porter." Pensively, he underlined Josh Norden's name. "Norden told me." His eyes narrowed. "I'd like to know how much Brad Kelly knows. Because if that kid knows the real story, he's a bastard for sure. Charlotte Porter took the money because her only grandson, the son of her dead daughter, was dying with AIDS, and he didn't have any health insurance. And he'd heard about a treatment down in Mexico. Desperate people try desperate remedies, and those always cost a lot."

"Oh God," Annie said simply. She didn't need anyone to tell her what it would have meant to Charlotte Porter if the truth came out. If her friends knew. She could bear only so much.

"Josh Norden told you?" she asked quietly.

"Yes. And he was sober this morning. Sober and white hot with anger. He said, 'If I ever find out who did this to Charlotte, I'll kill him.'"

Once again, he underlined Norden's name.

Then, he made a final notation:

3. Or, none of the above, and Burke was killed because he was chair and either thwarting or threatening someone. Possible killers: Moss, Garrison, Diggs, maybe Norden, unknown.

"We can't do much until we know for sure about Burke," Annie concluded. "Was he the louse behind Kelly? Or did he discover who did it? Or did he pose some other serious threat to someone?"

"You're right," Max agreed. "First we have to establish whether Burke was or wasn't behind the leak." Again, he shoved a hand impatiently through his hair. "All right, by God, let's find out. Brad Kelly claims he doesn't know Deep Throat's identity, but is he really telling the truth?" Dropping his notepad, he grabbed the telephone.

Brad Kelly. Annie wondered if the shaken young editor had managed to get free of the authorities long enough to contact the news services. Well, they'd know tomorrow. If he had, he would be in the news coast to coast.

What did Brad Kelly know?

If he had any brains, he would've unloaded every fact at his command and any suppositions to Chief Wells. Annie sure would have, if someone had tried to blow her away.

That had to be the point of the bomb, of course. It had been planted in Brad's office.

Was the objective to stop the publication of *The Crier* or to stop ambitious Brad Kelly—permanently?

And why was Emily Everett there?

Was Emily an accidental victim?

Well, surely so. How could anyone have known she would choose that critical moment to come to *The Crier*?

Annie scrawled: *Emily Everett.* She and Max needed to find out a lot more about the dead girl. A lot more. Why was she at the *Crier* office? Why had Burke, in one of the final acts of his life, written her name and circled it?

Was it coincidental or deliberate that Burke was killed and *The Crier* bombed within the space of half an hour?

Was Burke's murderer also the bomber?

Did it make any sense to imagine two separate perpetrators of such violent deeds? Wouldn't that indeed be an incredible coincidence?

But weren't these two acts entirely separate and different?

A bomb presupposed planning.

Careful, detailed, premeditative planning.

And Burke's murder appeared to be exactly the opposite, a spur-of-the-moment, unplanned attack, Burke's own memento snatched up for use as a weapon, Burke's own coat donned as a protective shield.

A hurried, desperate murder.

A thought, nebulous and unformed as the ectoplasm so beloved of Rinehart mediums, wriggled in the recesses of Annie's tired mind.

Hurry. No time. Quick—

Max whistled and looked at the receiver.

Annie blinked and looked at him. "Yes?"

"Wait till you hear this!" He redialed and handed her the phone.

The prerecorded message began to roll after the second ring. "This is Brad Kelly, editor of *The Crier*. In cooperation with the authorities, I have agreed to accept protection because there is a reasonable assumption that the blast which killed Chastain student Emily Everett and destroyed my office at *The Crier* was aimed at me. However, the blast may have been intended to hinder publication of *The Crier* and/or serve as a warning to me to desist with my exposé of personnel and planning problems within the journalism department. Or the blast may have been intended to prevent the news conference which had been scheduled for three P.M. today. Whatever the intent of the blast, I refuse to be silenced in my role as a journalist and I am scheduling a news conference for nine A.M. Friday morning in the Blue Auditorium in Nelson Hall. I wish to make it clear to any and all interested parties that I have communicated fully with the police department of Chastain in regard to the information afforded me as the background of the planned exposé." A long pause and the whistle of tape. Then, gruffly, *"The Crier* shall do everything in its power to see that the murderers of R.T. Burke and Emily Everett are brought to justice."

The wicker squeaked as Annie leaned across Max to replace the receiver. She frowned at her mystery collection, seeking inspiration. Anything there on recorded messages? Nope. There was a small silence. "Well. What do you think?"

"I think Kelly's not stupid. He doesn't want his ass peppered with explosive."

"Or his cranium squashed," Annie added. After all, Frankie Derwent (Lady Frances) had never minced words.

"Pretty smart. He's telling the world that the cops know everything he knows."

"And he has a nice touch for the dramatic," Annie added dryly. "Everybody and his dog'll be at that news conference."

"Yes," Max agreed. "Including us."

13

THE FIRST CALL Friday morning came at shortly after five.

Max thrashed wildly against the sheet and made a guttural noise in his throat which Annie understood to mean, "Tear that instrument out of the wall and fling it into the marsh."

At five A.M., however, Annie's little gray cells were not only colorless but nonfunctioning. She rolled groggily out of bed and stumbled into the living room to answer.

"My sweet, there is an exquisite stillness abroad at this early hour before dawn speaks."

"Not quite still enough," Annie retorted bitterly.

An instant's pause, then a trill of forgiving laughter. "Why, Annie, I sprang from my couch with vigor and cheer. I was so sure you and dear Maxwell would be up and about and already keenly engaged in the hunt."

Max appeared in the bedroom doorway, sleepily pawing at his eyes. He looked like Joe Hardy with a stubble of beard. Irresistible.

Annie began to wake up. Early mornings *could* be fun.

"Annie, my sweet?" her mother-in-law prodded gently.

Stifling a yawn, the distracted newlywed managed, "Hmm?"

A tiny sigh of dismay. "My dear, I *am* counting on you and Maxwell. Certainly, I believe the two of you have wit and sagacity enough to appreciate the importance of emotion in crime detection. Though, to tell the truth, your contributions to this point haven't—But, then, each must give according to his ability. Now, I've been thinking."

Max scratched at his chin. "Anything wrong?"

Annie shook her head. "Yes, Laurel?"

"It's clear to me—" Annie tucked the receiver under her chin and pantomimed turning on water, filling a pot. Max nodded and padded off to the kitchen— "dear Georgia is protecting that young professor."

Frank Crandall. A man with a self-deprecating smile, tousled chestnut hair, and attractively knobby knees in loose-fitting, pleated khakis. The kind of man that women noticed and instinctively wanted to help.

"Surely he wouldn't be rat enough to let her do that." She was wide awake now and unconvinced.

"Annie, what a horrid thought! Professor Crandall is a *gentleman.*"

Annie arched a skeptical brow. Sure. But he was also running around on his wife and romantically involved with a student. Not exactly modes of behavior smiled upon by Miss Manners, kindly and understanding as she is, though such actions would come as no surprise to Miss Marple, conversant as she was with sexual peccadilloes in St. Mary Mead, ranging from those of the choirmaster to cottage weekenders.

"No, no, no," Laurel continued, a tsk of dismay at this evidence of Annie's obtuseness. "Obviously, this is what transpired. Professor Crandall talked to Mr. Burke. You remember, Miss Dora's friend—" Annie thought about that one and wisely translated 'friend' to 'subordinate,' 'lackey,' 'serf,' or 'vassal'— "reported that Crandall said he had a very civil talk with Burke and left him in excellent health. Well, obviously, Georgia, in the manner of young women pining after a beloved yet proscribed from public contact, must have been following Mr. Crandall. Don't you agree?"

Only the rich heavy aroma of brewing coffee gave Annie the strength to reply civilly. "Of course. No doubt about it. Georgia was following Crandall." She looked anxiously toward the kitchen.

"Yes. She saw him leave the journalism office." A pause. "I don't know through which door. Oh, but I do, I do. He must have departed through the main office door, because that is the door one normally enters and if he hadn't departed as he entered, Georgia wouldn't have seen him at all!"

Annie had a sudden vision of a maze and a white rat (in khaki pants) flashing this way and that.

"But, of course," the husky voice continued thoughtfully, "if she didn't see him come out, perhaps she crept into the main office because she was so concerned about the course of this interview and, hearing no sound, slipped closer and closer to the director's open office door and then espied that dreadful sight. . . ." A vexed sigh. "Dear me, it's so complex. I do wish I could talk to that young woman. Oh, they've charged her with defacing the *Crier* office, too, with that rabbit blood. And I understand it's only a matter of time before they tack on the bombing. But we'll find out the truth before then. Poor, dear child. Such a mistake to try and hide things from the police, even to protect a loved one. Just like dear Judy Shepard."

She paused expectantly.

It took Annie just an instant longer than it should have.

Laurel said with only a hint of triumph, "Oh, I thought you would remem—"

"Judy Shepard. *Episode of the Wandering Knife.* But she was trying to protect her brother, not her lover," Annie objected.

"A parallel nonetheless. And it is a recurring pattern in Rinehart's works, the efforts of women, young and old, to protect a loved one. Carol Spencer in *The Yellow Room*, Janice Garrison in *The Haunted Lady*—"

"So Georgia Finney's protecting Crandall," Annie said agreeably, reaching out for the pink pottery mug, filled with Colombian coffee *not* decaffeinated and a generous dollop of milk. Whole milk. (Cream was better but Max had a thing about cholesterol. You'd think it was alive and swarmed.) She smiled her thanks and took a deep gulp and even Laurel's husky voice buzzing in her ear suddenly had a mellow ring.

"—but the point is obvious, I think."

"The point?" Another luscious, blood-warming gulp and another.

"Assuming Georgia to be innocent and, of course, Professor Crandall, the time for the murder to occur is limited. Very limited. Obviously, Georgia did not see anyone else enter or leave the office after Mr. Crandall's departure—if she saw that—but I believe we can all imagine

the various possibilities—or she would not assume he was the murderer."
Annie stopped trying to make sense of it. That way lay madness. "Which
suggests to me that the murderer may have secreted himself—or herself—
somewhere in the office *before* Professor Crandall engaged in his interview
with Burke."

Annie was tilting the nearly empty mug. She wasn't sure whether it was
the caffeine or Laurel's nattering but, abruptly, she did see the point.

"Laurel, that's brilliant."

"Of course, my love. Sometimes I realize that one's perceptions shine
just like crystal. Don't you—"

But Annie had no desire to discuss crystals, their attributes, properties,
or miraculous qualities.

"Laurel, you just stay there and keep on thinking. That's the ticket.
And we'll get back to you as soon as we've checked out some of these
possibilities. Bye, now."

She replaced the receiver and watched it warily for a moment, then,
slowly, her shoulder muscles relaxed. Good. Laurel was no doubt basking
in a glow of self-congratulation and might possibly be occupied for several
more hours.

Annie hurried into the kitchen. Max was eating his oat bran sprinkled
with extra wheat fiber. Was he trying to scour his intestines? She flipped
up the bread box and tried to choose between a chocolate long john or a
croissant, decided it was going to be a long day, and picked one of each.

Max raised an eyebrow at her selection, but sagely made no comment.

Annie poured fresh coffee for them, retrieved her pastries from the
microwave, and spread honey liberally on her croissant. After all, she
would need her strength. "Actually, Laurel may be onto something."

When she'd finished recounting his mother's hypothesis, Max said irritably, "Damsels in distress cause more damn trouble."

Annie had fond memories of many wonderful books of that ilk by
Kathleen Moore Knight, Mary Collins, Leslie Ford, Anne Maybury, Victoria Holt, Barbara Michaels, *et al.* She focused an icy stare on Max.
"That's sexist! The problems are created when the authorities are short-
sighted, stubborn, and/or incompetent."

"What's incompetent about arresting someone who's caught trying to
dump a murder weapon in the river?"

Annie finished her croissant and concentrated on her long john. It was indecent to expect her to contribute intelligently to any discussion until she'd finished her breakfast.

Displaying largeness of character, an altogether disgusting trait, Max chose to smile cheerfully at her. "Hungry? How about another long john?"

She would never admit she'd been thinking about it.

"No, thanks." Clipped response. "Quite full."

"Of course, you're right." Max did prefer peace in the family. "Laurel has made a very good point, although I'm not persuaded as to the innocence of Georgia Finney and/or Frank Crandall."

Annie licked a vagrant swipe of chocolate from her thumb. "You think they might have done it together? Oh, come on, Max. What kind of creep do you think he is? Would he foist the weapon off on her?"

Max's eyes gleamed. "Who's sexist?" he demanded slyly. He didn't press his advantage. "But Laurel's absolutely right about one thing. There *was* very little time. That seems to me the critical point. We know that Frank Crandall saw Burke. He's admitted that to the police. His appointment was at eleven-fifteen. How long did they talk? Five minutes? Crandall leaves and claims Burke was alive when he did so. Okay, the bomb explodes in Brad Kelly's office at approximately eleven forty-one. You found Burke's body at approximately eleven forty-four. Obviously, since Georgia was caught trying to get rid of the murder weapon, she had the weapon in hand and was out of the building before the bomb went off. Also, it makes sense to assume Burke was dead by at least eleven forty-one because he didn't come out of his office when the blast occurred."

Annie poured fresh coffee and began to sip. She was beginning to have that familiar khaki-clad-white-rat-in-a-maze sensation.

"So, let's put the murder between eleven-twenty and eleven forty-one—" Max figured happily with a pencil stub on his napkin. Which was another good argument for paper as opposed to cloth napkins. "We have a period of about twenty-one minutes during which the murder must have occurred."

"Who was in the building then? Who *could* have done it? That's what we need to know," Annie said eagerly.

She reached out for his pencil and spread open her own napkin, ignoring a spot of honey. Quickly, she drew a sketch of the first floor.

First Floor

Back entrance

Front entrance

She tapped the outline of the editor's office. "We know Brad Kelly and Emily Everett were in the building. We need to find out how long they'd been there when the bomb went off. Kelly says he went to the bathroom. When? Again, how long? Was there time for him to have murdered Burke before Georgia found him dead, if that's what happened? Was there time for Emily to have killed Burke and returned to the *Crier* office?"

"Why Kelly?" Max asked. "Why Emily?"

Annie shook her head impatiently. "I'm not worrying about motives here, I'm figuring out opportunity. We need to find out who was in the building from eleven-fifteen on. We know that all the faculty members had been in the building earlier in the morning, because Burke talked to them. But where were Garrison, Norden, Tarrant, Diggs, Moss, and Crandall during the critical time period? Let's see, we don't need to be concerned with any classes that were in session because Burke was alive when eleven o'clock classes started and dead before they finished. But we do need to check on the press area and, of course, the faculty upstairs."

Max took the pencil and her napkin, flipped it over, and drew a layout of the second floor. "There're the faculty offices. And look, they open onto a back corridor that leads to the stairs."

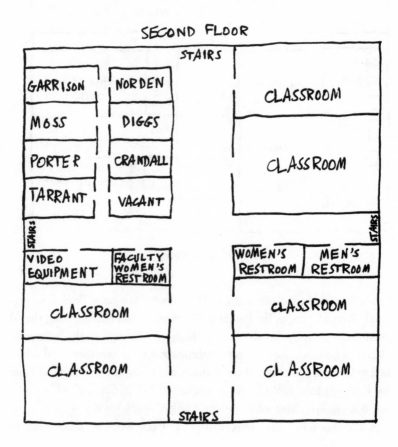

"You know, this isn't going to be so hard. It should be pretty easy to pick out the names of those who might have wanted Burke dead from among the people rounded up after the blast," Annie suggested.

"Unless," Max cautioned, "Georgia really did the deed. After all, isn't it more likely for a murderer to flee than to remain near the scene of the crime?"

Annie had no strong feelings on that. Murderers, both fictional and real, had a long history of staying and an equally long history of fleeing.

"Maybe not. I'd think a faculty member might easily return upstairs to an office and take time to regain composure."

"I'd think so, too," Max agreed. "Unfortunately everyone in the building had an excellent excuse to appear upset. Explosions can reasonably produce symptoms of extreme stress."

"God, that's a poser," Annie said unhappily. "Was the explosion timed to coincide with the murder? Were they independent of each other? Did the murderer plant the bomb? Max, how can we know what to investigate first?"

As if on cue, the telephone rang.

Annie glanced at the clock. Five-thirty. Who else would call at such an unappetizing hour?

"Hello."

"Certainly it's apparent to me the direction this investigation needs to take," the dry, crackly, impatient voice announced.

"Good morning, Miss Dora. How are you at this *early* hour."

"Light-minded women are the bane of society. Rarely been subjected to such idiocy."

Obviously, someone had dared to disagree with her.

"Laurel? Henny?" Annie inquired sweetly. "Are the three of you progressing?"

A snort of outrage. "Told that chattering nincompoop to keep her silly notions to herself. Poor young man. Like being mothered by a firefly."

This was such an enchanting picture that Annie lost the thread of conversation for a moment.

". . . advise you to keep a close watch on *him* through the years. And that woman who's besotted by Christie. Doesn't even *care* about probabilities, has no appreciation of subtleties. Think of how Wimsey built from that single piece of burned rope that he discovered at the campground in

Hinks's Lane in *Have His Carcase*. But he had to be concerned with probabilities. He had to go and look. No detail was too small for his attention. Have you established the customary ebb and flow of people in the building?"

"The what?" Annie knew it hardly ranked as a scintillating rejoinder, but she didn't have the faintest idea what the old bat was talking about.

"Who was where when?" Each word dropped like an icy pellet.

"We're working on that."

"Why did the explosive device go off at that precise moment? I have ascertained that normally the *Crier* offices are empty and locked at that hour. Students begin to gather for work about three in the afternoon. It is, as you should know, a twice-weekly morning paper. What was that young man doing there? Why was that unfortunate young woman there? Lord Peter always found meaning to events that were out of the ordinary. In contrast, the pressroom was locked and untenanted, as it should have been. A pressrun was not scheduled until that evening. The only other occupants of the building on the first floor at that time, insofar as is known, were members of a Russian history class meeting in room one-oh-one and the members of a class on Keats in room one-oh-three. We may dismiss these individuals as their instructors report that no one entered or left those classes after eleven-ten A.M. Moreover, the instructors led their students out the back door to safety immediately after the explosion. Now, what were the effects of the bombing? Study the terrain. Look, just as Wimsey did. That's what you young people need to do. Go and look."

The line went dead.

Max looked at her inquiringly.

"Miss Dora. We are to go and look."

"Where?"

"The journalism building. I think."

A sharp piercing ring.

It was the first time it ever occurred to Annie that her phone actually had a rather unpleasant tone to it. Jangling.

She lifted the receiver. "Hello."

"Been sucking lemons?" Miss Dora's laughter sounded unnervingly like the slither of a snake through dry leaves. "As they said when I was young, missy, you'd better be careful or your mouth might stick like that!" A flood of husky cackles that ended abruptly. "Key'll be in the postbox. Atop the stone pillar, end of the drive."

The line went dead.

Annie wrestled with the temptation to rip out the phone and toss it into the marsh. Max had assuredly had the best idea of the morning. Instead, she replaced the receiver in the cradle with exaggerated care, much as Grace Latham kept her temper when dealing with Sergeant Buck.

Max waited.

"The old monster again. Key's in her mailbox. Do you know, if it weren't for the fact that we'd better figure this out—I mean, we can't let Laurel waft unprotected around that place, it's too dangerous. But I swear, if it weren't for that, I wouldn't lift a finger to do *anything* Miss Dora wanted—"

The phone rang.

"Now, Annie," Max began. "Don't lose your temper. Wait. I'll get it."

But Annie had already yanked up the receiver. "Hello!"

A pause. "Spot of bother, old chap? You sound like Inspector Japp when Poirot's at his most maddening!"

Annie's heartbeat began to slow. She could feel the flush receding from her face. "Henny—"

"Old chap!"

"Oh yes, of course. Captain Hastings." Her turn to pause. "Why do you want to be that ass Hastings?"

"It is my pleasure to be associated intimately with the greatest detective of all time!"

"Thought that was Lord Peter Wimsey."

Henny dismissed the Hastings persona with a bleat. "That woman! That impossible old harridan! Told me Christie's books had all the readability of a Sears, Roebuck catalog. Can you believe that?"

"Now, Henny, everyone likes different—"

"And to champion that overwritten tripe that Sayers produced is absolutely the last straw, and I enjoyed telling her so. Now, I want you to know that I was nice to your mother-in-law. I agreed that we should each pursue our own investigations. I was *kind* about her approach. Max is a dear fellow, so I was charming even though his mother's thought patterns are unreal. As in totally unreal."

Annie made no answer. There scarcely seemed to be a suitable response.

"However," gradually Henny's voice was calming, "I do not intend to permit any distractions to deflect me from my goals: Who is—or perhaps was—behind the faculty revelations, who murdered R.T. Burke, and who killed Emily Everett by putting that bomb in Brad Kelly's office? Now, as Hercule Poirot made absolutely clear, the answer to murder always lies in the victim. We need to know everything—*everything*—about the late Burke. And about Emily Everett. What kind of man was Burke? Who was Emily Everett? Why was she in the *Crier* office? When we know the answers to these questions, we shall know the name of the murderer. Or, possibly, murderers. *C'est vrai.*"

Max had cleared the table by the time Henny rang off. Annie joined him in the kitchen and dutifully reported on Henny's call. In a moment, the dishes were done, the kitchen tidied.

"So the three old dears are espousing opportunity, means, and motive," Annie concluded.

Max tossed a dish towel over the rack. "It looks," he said cheerfully, "as though we're going to have a busy morning." He glanced at the kitchen clock. "But it's just barely after six. We have lots of time before we catch the ferry. Come on, Annie, let's shower."

Annie forgot all about those irritating phone calls. She washed them right out of her mind.

They decided against parking in the lot behind Brevard Hall. For one thing, there were no other cars there. For another, police tape circled the entire building and street barricades barred each entryway. Freshly painted signs gleamed in the headlights of Max's Maserati:

BUILDING CLOSED
DANGER
UNSTABLE

A chilly wind out of the north rattled the limbs of the live oaks, shook the palmetto palms like castanets. The sun wouldn't rise for another few minutes; it was still gray and ghostly. Although gorgeous days in the sixties and low seventies often shine in November, occasional damp and cloudy days remind one that even the low country must have its brief taste of winter.

They stopped among a line of evergreens and studied the dismal scene in the lamplight, the gaping wound in the side of the building, the shattered windows and jumbled contents of the newsroom.

Annie turned up the collar of her windbreaker.

"Do you think we dare go inside?"

"Sure." Max was decisive. "We'll avoid the section with the most blast damage. I want a close look at Burke's office and the rest of the department offices."

Annie wasn't sure she relished a close look at Burke's office.

But at least the blood would be dried by now.

An early-rising student shuffled by. Waiting until he disappeared into the dark and silent math building—God, this early?—they held hands and dashed the thirty feet across the sandy ground to the back door of the damaged building, slipping around the barricade. He released her hand and pulled from his pocket the key they'd retrieved from Miss Dora's mailbox. Using the flashlight from his car, he opened the door and they hurried inside.

The hall was dark. Very, very dark.

Max led the way, the beam of the flashlight dimly illuminating the welter of footprints in the dust. The smell of plaster dust mingled with the deeper odor of explosives. Annie wished Max still held her hand in a reassuring grip. She immediately brushed away the thought. The intrepid Harriet Vane would surely never have felt such a longing.

They stopped by the open entry to the newsroom. It remained as it had when they'd seen it yesterday, only moments after the explosion.

"All right," Annie said briskly, matter-of-factly, keeping Wimsey's Harriet in mind. "The effects of the explosion: One, death of Emily Everett; two, no Friday morning *Crier,* i.e., no further embarrassing revelations about the faculty; three, student editor scared, as well he might be." She looked at Max.

He picked up the refrain. "Four, yesterday's three o'clock press conference canceled; five, young editor in protective seclusion; six, new press conference set for nine A.M. today."

Annie took the flash from him, and skimmed the beam over the wreckage. "God, what a mess. It will cost a fortune to replace all those terminals."

"Yeah," Max agreed soberly. "We can add that to the list. Seven, severe economic stress on the journalism department."

"I always hated multiple-choice tests," Annie complained.

"All, some, or none of the above," Max mused.

She scuffed the gritty floor. "The problem is, we can't figure out who did it if we don't know why. And if we knew why, we'd know who."

"So, that's why we're here."

"Of course, Lord Peter," she murmured.

"It ought to be apparent. It's such a damn drastic move. People don't blow up buildings on a whim. Why isn't it clear to us?"

"It seems obvious to me." (Annie heard her own confident tone in horror. Lord, was she starting to sound like Miss Dora? Edgar Allan Poe preserve her.) She hastily amended, "I mean, it looks to me like it's pretty obvious. Somebody either wanted to kill Kelly or scare the hell out of him."

"Yeah." His tone was dubious. "But was there any real likelihood that Kelly would be in his office? Shouldn't the entire *Crier* suite of offices have been empty at eleven-forty in the morning? Didn't Miss Dora say the staff usually started drifting in around three? So why was he there?"

"We'll ask him." Annie was looking forward to that press conference. She had a lot of questions for Brad Kelly.

She swung the flashlight beam up at the exposed girders in the ceiling, where ruptured acoustical tiles hung on a slant. A crackle, a shifting, and masonry dust showered down in the area near the printer. "I wonder how long it will take before *The Crier* can be published again."

Max shrugged. "I suppose at least a couple of weeks. More likely, a month or two."

Annie turned off the flash. The lighter gray visible through the bombed-out wall signaled the coming dawn. "Any exposé about faculty members will be pretty old hat by then."

"Exposure is exposure," Max objected. "Whether it's in the school newspaper or announced to the world in general this morning at the news conference."

That hadn't occurred to her. "Do you think that's what Kelly has in mind?"

"It seems logical to me."

"So it's nutty to think somebody tried to blow *The Crier* away to *stop* the revelations," Annie concluded.

"Who thinks that?" he inquired.

Annie certainly had no intention of admitting the thought had crossed her mind. Max was being as smug as Lord Peter. Next time she did a little class on murder, she wasn't going to include Sayers. Ruth Rendell would do just fine. (Detective Chief Inspector Reginald Wexford, though a bit old for her taste, was a much more charming companion.)

Their footsteps gritted noisily as they crossed the hall to the front office of the journalism department.

The door was ajar, just as it had been yesterday, Annie recalled with sudden clarity, when she made her frantic dash to call for help. "I don't think the police have moved anything."

She flicked the flashlight on again. A counter separated the office proper from the entrance area. A gate afforded access to the office. Emily Everett had sat at a desk behind the counter.

They pushed through the gate.

Max stopped beside the desk. "Of course, Emily wasn't here yesterday morning. So Burke had to answer all the calls."

"Until he turned off the phone," Annie said.

"She'd called in sick," Max recalled.

But she'd been well enough to come to the *Crier* offices later that morning.

Her desk had an "In" box. Max picked up a couple of pencils and expertly used them as pincers to look through the sheets. Annie focused the light. Obviously, Emily had served as a personal secretary to Burke and also to the faculty in general. An editing test which Garrison wanted mimeographed. An announcement to be distributed to the faculty from Burke regarding department policy for support of research and creative activities. A request from Norden for faculty attendance at the Advertising Club banquet, scheduled next Friday in the Student Union. A memo from Burke to Moss rejecting a proposed course on the functions of mass media managers.

"Emily must have been lazy," Annie said quickly. "Most of those things had to have been in place before Tuesday."

For once, the great detective (in his own mind, she was certain) looked to her for an explanation.

Annie enjoyed it, quite as much as Captain Hastings would have on the rare occasion when he felt that he was informing Poirot and not the other way around. "This is all business-as-usual stuff. You can bet Norden didn't compose that boring little invitation for everybody to come to the Advertising Club banquet after Tuesday's *Crier* came out. He was distraught about Charlotte Porter, trying to get in touch with her. Then he found her dead on Wednesday. Same thing with Burke. Those memos had to've been written before the Tuesday *Crier* came out."

Max's ears were just a trifle pink. It was, of course, obvious when you thought about it.

Annie smiled kindly.

Max let the papers fall back into place.

A mimeographed sheet of faculty and staff addresses and phone numbers lay in the center of the desk. There was a check by every name. It even included Annie's number.

"I'll bet this was Emily's list when she called to tell everyone about the emergency faculty meeting that Burke had called Wednesday," Max reasoned.

Annie held out her hand for his pencils and used them to pull open the shallow center desk drawer.

Paper clips. Rubber bands. Fifteen or so pens and pencils. Tissues. Lipstick (Sensuous Coral). A comb with several broken teeth. A half-full package of Rolaids. An economy-size package of Hershey's Kisses, with four or five left. Juicy Fruit gum. An unopened Baby Ruth. Four Harlequin and three Silhouette paperback romances with brightly colored covers of couples entwined in anatomically impossible positions. A loosely wrapped stick of black licorice. The crumpled remains of a Twinkies package.

Max shook his head.

"Don't worry. They won't reach out and grab you," Annie assured him.

The two full-size side drawers contained files with information handouts for students on major requirements, course syllabi, and job listings. Annie found a folder which held copies of the list of faculty and staff addresses. She fished one out and tucked it in her purse.

They could move now without the aid of the flashlight. Although it was a gray day, enough light glimmered through the ceiling-tall windows to dimly illuminate the rooms.

They looked over the filing cabinets, but everything appeared in order, then stepped into the small room between the first office and Burke's. Max grabbed her arm and pointed.

Annie looked to her left.

"That door's open! That's the closet where the confidential files are kept. And it's supposed to be locked at all times!"

"Are you sure?"

"Yes. Absolutely. I told you how Emily took me on a tour of the filing systems. That's the closet, all right. Think back. Was it open yesterday, when you found Burke?"

But she hadn't looked in that direction. She'd seen the smear of blood on the floor near the swinging gate and she'd turned and followed the trail to Burke's office.

"I don't know," she said slowly. "But can't we almost count on it? Nothing's been changed since the murder. The police have left everything as is. Max, what do you think it means?"

"A lot. For one thing," and there was a touch of awe in his voice, "it means Mother's idea about someone hiding until Burke was alone may not be so far out."

"I don't quite follow that."

Max pulled his notebook from his pocket and flipped through several pages. "Okay, here we have the list of people Burke intended to see."

Annie flicked on the flash and looked at the appointment list: Brad Kelly, Malcolm Moss, Sue Tarrant, Victor Garrison, Kurt Diggs, Josh Norden, Frank Crandall.

"We know that he was alive at least to the point where Crandall saw him," Max asserted.

"According to Crandall," Annie reminded.

"The important thing about that open door to the files is that it indicates someone with a key was in here yesterday morning and that person *could* have hidden and waited until Burke had finished with his appointments," Max proposed. "That really throws it wide open. It means that none of the earlier visitors can be dismissed from consideration."

Annie felt a prickle down her back. Dammit, how had Laurel come up with that idea?

Because, quite simply, she was determined that Georgia and Crandall were innocent.

"A key," Max muttered. "The door in Burke's office." He loped across the room and into the chairman's office. "Sure. Look. A smear of blood on the handle of the hall door. The murderer must have left that way and if he did, he had to have a key."

Annie hated to discourage Max's foray into detection. But— "The murderer could have knocked on the door."

He looked at her blankly.

She nodded impatiently. "Why not? What if Brad Kelly or Emily Everett knocked on the door and Burke let them in? Maybe the door was left ajar. Either one could have beaned him and gone out that way again."

Max wasn't impressed. "Why come in that door? They were both in the *Crier* office. Why not just go across the hall?"

"I don't know," she replied irritably. "I'm just pointing out that the killer didn't *have* to have a key to get in and out of the door from Burke's office into the cross hall."

"But obviously the killer had a key. Why else is the confidential file closet open?"

Annie opened her mouth.

"All right, all right," he said quickly to forestall her. "We don't know that the killer opened the file closet. But it sure seems perfectly reasonable to me."

Annie realized that her spouse was more than a little huffy. "Even if we don't know for certain about the door or whether it was the killer who opened the closet, we have at least established that someone could have hidden and waited until Crandall left, then killed Burke." She scowled, concentrating fiercely. "Okay, if Crandall left and the murderer popped out of the file closet and clobbered Burke, the murderer either did escape into the cross hall from Burke's office or heard Georgia coming and hid again until she left."

They both turned and looked toward the closet.

It was possible.

Annie paced to the window, glancing at the open area on the sill where the bent iron bar had rested. All right. The visitor is talking to Burke and decides—why?—that Burke must die. That moment. Without delay. There is the bar. She looked at the coat rack. And there was the spot where the raincoat had hung. It must have been decided upon so quickly and the visitor moved so fast, too fast for Burke to comprehend his danger and cry out.

Quick. Reach up. Yank down the coat. Slip it on, backward. Grab up the bar in a hand protected by the sleeve. Whirl around. Lift the weapon and strike.

There must have been an instant's awareness by Burke. Perhaps it began as puzzlement, then exploded into horror and pain. Then nothingness.

"Here's why Emily didn't have anything current," Max said triumphantly. "Burke had an 'Out' box. Probably other faculty brought stuff and dropped it into her 'In' box, but since he was chair, he had an 'Out' box that she cleared."

Annie pulled her mind away from the horrible picture she had imagined.

"And you're right, Annie. This is all stuff he'd done after Tuesday. A letter to the college president, outlining Burke's hope that the trustees would reconsider the independent position of the student newspaper, asking that it be brought up at the next meeting and a new policy be put into effect by next fall."

"That wouldn't affect Brad Kelly," Annie said. "His term would be up by then."

Max flipped open a green folder on top of the 'Out' box. "Look, here's Kelly's student folder. It has a note from Burke to refile it."

"Burke must have checked it before he called the college legal counsel. Remember, when we came in yesterday morning he was on the phone, trying to figure out a way to dump Kelly. I don't suppose he found anything in his file that would help."

Max bent closer to the folder. "Doesn't look like it. Good grades. Very good. No record of any rules violations. In good standing." He used a pencil, flipped the top page. "Oh, wow. I'll say he's in good standing. He's been awarded a Fulbright."

"That must have made Burke gnash his teeth." Annie looked at Burke's 'In' box. "So Burke put Kelly's folder up there. He was finished with it and ready to talk to the faculty members. He wanted to know who had leaked the confidential information to Kelly."

Max rubbed thoughtfully at his chin. "Do you suppose somebody gave himself away, that something was said in those conversations that tipped Burke off? And that's why the murder had to happen so quickly, without any preparation?"

They stared at the desk, but if it held any secrets to Burke's murder, they didn't divine them.

The not-too-far-distant chimes of St. Edward's sounded the hour.

Max was reluctant to depart. In fact, he kept them in the building for another few minutes as he timed how long it would take to sprint from Burke's office door to the end of the main hall and up the stairs to the faculty wing.

"Forty-eight seconds," he panted, after several tries.

But Annie's mind was already set on their next task. They had come and they had looked, as Miss Dora exhorted them. They had proved tenable Laurel's defense of the lovers. Now it was time to delve into the characters of the victims, à la Henny (a/k/a Ariadne Oliver, Miss Marple, *et al.*).

14

THE CAVERNOUS OLD HALL hadn't been painted in years, but it was sparkling clean and the shiny leaves of the rubber tree in a brass planter glistened from a recent sprinkle. The house smelled of polished floors, potpourri, the warm aroma of baking, and age. It was post-Revolutionary but old, nonetheless, and built in the familiar manner: a high foundation of tabby covered with stucco, two stories, with piazzas extending from the front around two sides. A bronze marker on the iron gate gave its history: Brooker House, built in 1817 by a plantation family at the flowering of a fortune based on Santee cotton and long before the tragic war which would bring ruin to Chastain and to South Carolina.

Their hostess, a trim middle-aged woman in gray fleece sweatpants, a worn Chastain T-shirt, Nikes, and a calico sweatband, led the way into the front parlor which had gilded cornice ceilings, a fine Adam mantel, ferns in hanging baskets, and shabby wicker furniture with brown and yellow cushions. She waved them to a seat on a comfortable brown wicker couch. "Would you like some coffee?"

"We don't want to impose," Annie said quickly. "It's so early. You're very kind to agree to talk to us at all."

Peggy Simpson pulled off her sweatband and shook out her short brown hair. "I suppose," she said abruptly, "it's because I feel guilty. Of all the kids who've lived here, I guess I saw less of Emily than anyone." She had a frank, no-nonsense gaze. "Not that I'm supposed to be a counselor or anything like that. I'm just a landlady, listed by the college as approved. That means I don't have roaches and there are plenty of fire exits." A wry smile. "When you have a three-quarter piazza, you've got plenty of fire exits."

She looked at them with suddenly pain-filled eyes. "A boardinghouse. I never thought I'd run a boardinghouse." She glanced at the mantel and its jumble of pictures. "But there aren't many options open to a widow with six kids who wanted to be at home to see them grow up. And a lot of it's been fun. My youngest is at Chastain now, and the house is full of kids going to school here. Most college students live in dorms or apartments, but there are still a bunch who can't afford that and someplace like this is the answer."

"It looks like a swell answer," Max said quickly.

Peggy Simpson flashed him a grateful smile. "Not bad. Almost like home, too, for the ones who find it tough to be away for the first time."

"Did Emily?" Annie asked.

"Emily." A sudden frown. "Emily was—" She looked at them inquiringly. "Did you know her?"

"Not really," Max explained. "We'd both met her. That's all."

"But you'd seen her." Outrage glistened in Peggy's eyes. "Why does appearance have to count for so much? Why? Why can't we see the miracle of life and be glad and not demand so much?" She shook her head impatiently. "But I know the answers, as well as you. There's something in us that loves beauty. That would be all right, but do we have to penalize the ugly?" She bit her lip. "That's the truth, you know. Poor Emily was ugly. She was not only fat—so fat that she had to stop at least a couple of times when she climbed the stairs—well, you've seen her. She *was* ugly, with greasy, stringy hair and a bad complexion and watery little eyes almost hidden by folds of fat." Peggy Simpson tightened her hand into a small fist and struck the arm of her chair. "Dammit, that's what I remember. And I didn't really try with Emily. Maybe I thought it was too late. Kids have to have love, you know. Right from the start. They have to believe that somebody thinks they're great, just the way they are, scrawny or nearsighted or clumsy or shy. Or fat." A tear glistened in her eye. She brushed it away. "And I'm not even crying for Emily. I guess I'm crying for all the kids out there that nobody ever loved. And believe me, nobody ever loved Emily. She was self-pitying, self-centered, grumpy, sarcastic, jealous, mean-spirited, spiteful, everything you don't want to be around. And yet—" Mrs. Simpson's eyes widened in remembered surprise "—it just about killed her when that stuff came out about her professor. And I realized I hadn't given Emily any benefit of the doubt. Emily could care about other people too, despite how she acted. She didn't come down for dinner Tuesday night. You can imagine how unusual that was! Never happened before. I went up to her room and knocked. She finally came to the door and her face was all red and puffy from crying. I asked if I could help and she said no, that nobody could help, that it was awful, that all this ugly stuff had come out about Mrs. Porter and Mrs. Porter had been nicer to her than anyone ever had. I told her it wouldn't help for her to make herself sick crying about it, that the nicest thing she could do would be to tell Mrs. Porter that she cared, that she supported her."

"I didn't realize Emily felt that close to Mrs. Porter," Annie said.

"The suicide must have really shaken her," Max surmised.

Peggy pressed her fingertips briefly against her temples. "She was distraught when she came home Wednesday afternoon, there's no other word for it. And I feel dreadful. I should have been more understanding. But her room is—was—just above mine. All night long, she paced, up and down, up and down, and the floor creaked. You can imagine. She was *so* heavy. I went up there once and banged on the door and told her, for God's sake, to stop making all that noise. But she wouldn't come to the door." She swallowed jerkily. "I never saw her again. She didn't come down for breakfast Thursday morning, but I was still furious with her. After I'd finished the morning dishes, I worked in the garden, then went on errands. When I came back, just before noon, she was gone."

"So you don't know what time she left the house Thursday morning?" Annie asked.

"No." The landlady looked at her anxiously. "Do you think it matters?"

"It might." Annie wasn't sure of it. But the more they knew, the more likely they were finally to pull the thread that would unravel the whole. "Do you suppose any of the other students would know?"

Peggy looked toward the stairs and figured aloud. "Let's see. Paul has a nine o'clock. Mary, too. Johnny goes to work at seven. Chris has a ten o'clock. Edwina works in the mornings and has all afternoon classes." She turned back toward Annie and Max. "I don't think so. I don't think anyone would have been here to see Emily leave. But, if you'd like, I'll ask them."

They made their thanks and were at the front door when Max asked abruptly, "Do you suppose we could see her room?"

Peggy looked uncertain.

"We won't bother anything," he said quickly.

She hesitated for an instant longer, then shrugged. "It can't hurt anything. She didn't have any family. She grew up in an orphanage not too far from here." Turning, she led them upstairs, talking as they climbed. "That's why she was older than most of the students. She'd worked her way through school, all on her own. She was almost twenty-five and would have been a senior next year. So there isn't anyone to come and get her things. I thought I would ask the police what to do. If it's all right, I'll give whatever's usable to the Salvation Army."

Emily's was a small room at the very back of the second floor. Mrs. Simpson unlocked the door, turned on the light, and stood aside for them to enter. She remained in the hall. "I don't think I want to come in. Not right now. You won't touch anything, will you?"

"We won't," Max said reassuringly.

The room smelled like chocolate, doughnuts, and licorice. There were food containers everywhere, everything from pizza to wonton soup cartons.

"She didn't need to go down for dinner," Annie commented to Max.

"Do you suppose it was always this messy?"

"Probably," Annie said. "It looks like it's been this way for a long time."

Magazines and paperbacks littered the floor and the two chairs. Copies of *Cosmopolitan* and *Redbook*. Stacks of romance novels. Huge caftan-style cotton dresses were draped over chair backs, flung carelessly on the floor.

Careful not to step on anything, Max prowled the circumference of the room, looked under the bed, peeked into the wardrobe, checked beneath it, stood on tiptoe to scan its top.

Annie watched him curiously, then surveyed the room and its contents carefully. What was Max looking for? What was there to see but evidences of uncontrolled gluttony, sloth, and loneliness?

She waited until they had made their good-byes and were almost to the car before she asked. "What were you looking for?"

He looked at her soberly. "Any traces of gunpowder."

Annie stopped short, stared at him.

He opened the car door for her. "I didn't find any."

As Annie climbed in, Max said quietly, "But maybe she was very clever indeed."

The auburn-haired secretary stared at them superciliously over half-glasses. "You don't have an appointment?"

"No," Max said agreeably. "But I think President Markham might like to talk with us. Will you give him my card, please, and tell him that Miss Dora Brevard, the trustee, has asked us to investigate the problems in the journalism department."

The secretary returned quite quickly. "If you'll come this way, please."

Charles August Markham's office was magnificent. The college buildings may not have been built until after World War II, but they were a reflection of the glory days of South Carolina. The doorways echoed the formal design of the three-quarter windows. Slender recessed columns with decorative acanthus capitals were set off by an architrave with iris and honeysuckle in relief. The iris-and-honeysuckle motif was repeated in the ceiling plasterwork. A shower of light from a glittering crystal teardrop chandelier illuminated the delicate cream-and-gold design of the Aubusson rug and the rich green of the floor-length silk damask curtains.

Markham rose from his desk as they entered and came around to greet them, hand outstretched. "Mr. and Mrs. Darling."

His grip was firm and warm. He was tall enough to stoop a little in his greeting. White-haired and blue-eyed, Markham had the genial countenance of a gifted fund-raiser, the domed forehead of an intellectual, and the tweedy air of a scholar.

This time they accepted coffee, and it came in a silver server on a silver tray and with china cups.

It was almost as good as the coffee at Death on Demand. Annie began to feel cosseted and in perfect equilibrium with her surroundings. She studied Markham with fresh interest. Here he was, a college president with an unholy mess unexpectedly dumped in his lap, and he appeared completely relaxed and unruffled.

After a ceremonial sip, he set down his cup and studied them. "I've always found Miss Dora, in her own original fashion, to be quite perceptive. She has supreme confidence in both of you." He toyed with a bronze letter opener. "We have some very serious problems. A murder. Perhaps a second murder. If not, then an accidental death as a result of what I feel can rightfully be termed terrorism. And I have to wonder if the fault is mine."

They looked at him in surprise.

He picked up the letter opener, tapped it against his palm. "An administrator is responsible for everything that occurs within his domain. Both successes and disasters. Why has a department chair been murdered? Why has the office of the student newspaper been attacked? Did my hiring of R.T. Burke result in these horrors?" He balanced the letter opener on upturned fingertips. His blue eyes gazed without seeing at a bewhiskered old gentleman in an oil painting over the Adam mantel with its classic figures in stucco relief. "I had no sense"—now he looked at them directly, his eyes ablaze—"of such a possibility when I made the appointment. I know my faculty members. Oh, not perhaps as well personally as I might like. But I know of them, their work, their temperaments, their strengths. And their weaknesses. And I had no sense at all that I was introducing an insupportable strain upon the infrastructure of that department." A dry smile. "I knew, of course, what I was doing. And I intended it. That department was losing its support from the state newspapermen. There was a sense of too much cerebration, too little professionalism. We need a balance. An educational institution must have the scholar's work as its lifeblood, but, in this very real world we inhabit, there must be due appreciation of practicalities, especially in professional programs. For example, it's all well and good to examine the criminal justice system as a dynamic societal institution. It's also quite necessary for budding police administrators to understand precisely what procedural rights prisoners have. There must be a balance between the theoretical and the practical. I felt R.T. was the perfect man to tip the balance in the journalism department once again toward the professional. He was, as you may know, a superior newsman. Intelligent. Perceptive. Honorable. Reasoned. Relentless. And a man with a passion for language. He had a love of

writing when I knew him as a young man in the war and he never lost it."
The letter opener slipped from his fingers and thumped on the desktop. "I
expected controversy. I expected a furious faculty, which, hopefully, would
be galvanized into an expression of creativity. I never expected murder."

A sonorous, soft boom from the grandfather clock in the corner tolled
the half hour.

"R.T. Burke probably generated controversy all his life," Annie suggested gently. "He came to my store—" she looked at Markham inquiringly and he nodded "—and asked me to teach this class on the mystery. I
felt as if I'd been brushed by hurricane winds by the time he left."

"And when Annie and I saw him Thursday morning, he was hell-bent
to find out who had leaked the information on the faculty to the student
editor," Max added.

Markham nodded. "Yes, I talked to him on the phone early Thursday.
He was determined and he had every intention, if he could, of filing
charges against that person."

"Charges?" Annie asked.

"Yes. Theft isn't confined to objects," Markham explained. "Information which is adjudged confidential can also be termed stolen, if taken by
someone not authorized to have access to it."

"Oh yes, of course," Max said, with rising interest. "Sure. People can go
to jail for stealing information. But it gets pretty ticklish saying it was
stolen if the person who released it learned of it in an official capacity."

Annie translated that. Burke would have a hell of a time convincing a
prosecutor that the information was stolen if Kelly's informant was a
member of the personnel committee. Garrison, Moss, Norden, Tarrant,
and Burke himself had every right to know the information. Could it be
argued that releasing it without authorization constituted a form of theft?
(She wasn't sure this exposure to academia was doing much for Max's
ability to communicate.)

"So if Burke discovered the informant's identity and made it clear he
was going to file charges, that could be reason enough for someone to kill
him," Annie figured.

"That would also explain why the murder was apparently unpremedi-
tated," Max said.

Markham raised his white eyebrows. "Why do you believe it was unpre-
meditated?"

Annie beat Max to it. "Because of the weapon," she explained briskly. "It looks like someone decided in an instant that Burke had to be killed and grabbed up that iron bar."

"Or, of course, perhaps the murder *was* premeditated and the decision made to use the bar *because* it was there and would indicate a lack of planning," Max said.

Annie almost spoke, hesitated, then charged ahead. "Dr. Markham, we've made a lot of assumptions. But it occurs to me that there is another possibility."

The college president looked at her attentively.

"What if Burke fed that confidential material to Kelly? What if someone killed him because *he* leaked that information?" Even as Markham was shaking his head, she persisted. "Burke was a scrapper. He went all out in everything he did. Look at the awards he'd received as a journalist. And before that, in the war. He was a fighter. Maybe he was frustrated by the intractable opposition of the faculty. Maybe he decided to blow it wide open, let some public pressure build to support him in his efforts to revamp the program."

Markham stopped shaking his head and stared at her soberly. "R.T. was a hell of a fighter. You're right about that. And I know that the faculty was infuriating him, dragging their heels at any suggestions of course revision, trying to block changes in internal unit review procedures that would accord equal weight to professional attainments. But I would be astounded if he took such a backdoor approach."

"Someone leaked that stuff," Max said reasonably. "If it wasn't Burke, then the list of possibilities is pretty short: the members of the personnel committee or a faculty member with a master key."

"What about the young woman who died in the blast?" Markham asked. "She was the department secretary. Couldn't she have obtained the material?"

"She could have." Annie shook away Max's muttered objection. Obviously, Emily could have prowled in that file closet when Burke wasn't there. It could have been done. "But why would she? She had nothing to gain by it. Besides . . ." She described Emily's distress about the revelations and Mrs. Porter's subsequent suicide. "According to her landlady, she was truly distraught. So, I can't see Emily as Deep Throat. Why would she try to hurt a professor she admired?"

"So that brings it back to the faculty," the administrator said heavily. Markham sighed. He tapped a stack of folders. "I've been looking over their files this morning." He picked up the first one. "Malcolm Moss. Wanted to be chair, of course. An able man with an enviable record of scholarly publications, considered an authority on consumer behavior in response to advertising campaigns. But he has no rapport with state editors. And if he chairs the department, it will be a triumph for the academic over the professional." He closed the folder. "However, he is the senior member of the department and I asked him this morning to serve as interim chair."

"Did he accept?" Max asked.

"Of course."

Annie leaned forward in her chair. "Would he kill to head the department?"

"A week ago, six months ago, Mrs. Darling, I would have found that question absurd. But the fact remains, someone did kill R.T." Markham's silvery brows drew down in a frown. "Malcolm certainly does have an inordinate will to power. He must dominate every situation." He picked up the next folder. "Victor Garrison. Clever. Quick. Complex." A thoughtful pause. "A man who thinks well on his feet." Another folder. "Sue Tarrant. Sue doesn't have tenure. She serves at the pleasure of the chair." He stroked his high-bridged nose pensively. "I heard her speak recently at a meeting of Women in Communications. She made what I considered a rather bitter presentation about the difficulty older women face in the marketplace. I have always felt that Sue has a rather angry nature beneath a charming exterior. She has often expressed the view that her undoubted professional competence hasn't received the respect it should. Perhaps she lost patience with the pace of R.T.'s struggle with the faculty." He went on to the next folder. "Kurt Diggs." He tapped the cardboard reflectively. "I do not care for Professor Diggs. He is, in my considered opinion, self-indulgent, amoral, a sensualist. I believe he would always do whatever he felt was necessary to further his own interests." A pause. "I regret intensely that he was awarded tenure." A wry headshake at the next folder. "Professor Crandall. It's fascinating, really, how unworldly some people can be." His observant eyes challenged them. "Not a state restricted to academia. It's rather easy really to judge Frank to be a weak person. But in this case, it might again be that familiar phenomenon, the cornered animal fighting with true ferocity." He arranged the folders in a neat pile, picked up the last one. "Josh Norden. A fine man, a fine intellect. And a living example of the evils of alcohol. I do feel very strongly that Josh would never have done anything to cause distress to Charlotte Porter. They were old friends. Dear friends." A troubled sigh. "But I cannot be at all certain what he might do if he discovered the person whom he considered responsible for Charlotte's death. . . ."

"Like an opening night," Annie yelled in Max's ear. "Everybody's here —if you care about that sort of thing."

Max twisted in his seat to look back over the auditorium. Every seat was taken.

"Hell of a deal," he shouted back. "I never dreamed there would be this kind of turnout."

Nor had Annie.

Almost fifty news correspondents perched restlessly in the first five or so rows. Television crews and print photographers jockeyed for better positions. Students craned to see past them. Annie spotted all the journalism faculty members except for Moss.

The best seat in the house was front row, center section, center seat. Miss Dora occupied it as to the manner born. She appeared oblivious to the restless audience, sitting ramrod straight, of course, black gloved hands atop her ebony cane. She was all in black this morning, even to the three feathers atop her hat. She had the wild and predatory air of a scavenging hawk.

The sight of Miss Dora always produced sensations of discomfort in Annie, an uneasiness akin to setting out to cross a fun house, knowing full well that any resemblance to normality was deceptive.

Max tugged on her arm. "Over there. By the fire exit. Is that Henny?"

Untidy dark hair. A middle-aged woman in a shabby sweater, tweed skirt. A knitting bag with khaki, blue, and navy wool protruding. An air of insouciance.

"Tuppence, of course. When she was older. During the war. Finding spies and things. I'll bet Henny's about to burn up in that outfit."

Their glances met.

Henny gave a sporting, thumbs-up wave.

So it came as no surprise when Annie spotted Laurel, except that Laurel could always be counted upon to provide distraction. She was entering the auditorium on the arm of Dr. Markham, who bent attentively to listen as she spoke.

Annie would have loved to overhear that conversation! She leaned close to her spouse. "Bet she'll have a date with him before the session is over."

Max looked at her reproachfully. But he didn't say a word.

The auditorium doors closed. The hum of expectant conversation intensified.

A lectern stood at the center of the stage apron in front of the closed royal blue curtains. There was a ripple in the curtains and Malcolm Moss stepped out, followed by Brad Kelly. Camera shutters clicked.

Moss's half-smile never wavered as he strode to the speaker's stand. His curly blond hair glistened in the harsh light. The jacket of his blue suit pulled across his massive chest, emphasizing his bulk. Kelly wore a navy blue blazer, soft blue cotton shirt, red-and-blue rep tie, and khaki slacks. He might have been the year's outstanding graduate stepping forth to receive kudos except for the paleness of his face, a spatter of freckles distinct across his snub nose, and the tight set to his mouth. His eyes blinked rapidly. He clutched several pages of typewritten copy in shaking hands.

Moss surveyed the auditorium. Gradually, the crowd quieted.

"Good morning." His voice was deep, assured, confident. "Chastain College and the Department of Journalism have suffered grievous losses: our chair, R.T. Burke, our colleague, Charlotte Porter, and our student and staff member, Emily Everett. The college will be closed in their honor on Monday, November fourteenth. Services will be held that day at ten A.M. in Emmanuel Baptist Church for Chairman Burke. A private memorial service for Professor Porter is scheduled at two P.M. Services will be at three P.M. at the Baptist Student Center for Miss Everett."

The scratch of pens, the whirr of cameras.

"Chastain College has been shaken to its core by these tragedies. However, as interim chair of the journalism department, I wish to make clear the department's goal and the goal of Chastain College. Both institutionally and on a personal level, we are committed to doing everything within our power to aid the authorities in their efforts to ascertain who murdered our chairman and who destroyed our newspaper offices, thereby causing the death of a student and staff member.

"It is with these goals in mind that we are cooperating this morning in the appearance of the student editor, who will provide further information about problems which had occurred within the department in recent days. However, I wish to make it clear that the department is not responsible for views of or acts committed by the editor of *The Crier*. The student newspaper is, in accordance with bylaws promulgated by the Board of Trustees, independent of the journalism department, although, of course, it serves as a training ground for many of our students. On that basis, I present to you the editor of *The Crier*, Mr. Brad Kelly."

Moss stepped away from the lectern, nodding at Kelly.

The young editor walked stiffly to the lectern, carefully placed his notes on it, and gripped the sides of the lectern. Annie knew he was holding on tightly to hide the tremor of his hands, and she felt a pang of sympathy.

Kelly took a deep breath, lifted his head, and looked out into the flashing lights of the cameras and the sea of waving hands.

"Mr. Kelly, who's behind this exposé?"

"Is somebody trying to kill you?"

"What was Emily Everett doing in your office?"

"Who made the bomb? Do you have any idea?"

Kelly swallowed jerkily and spoke in a rush in a high, strained voice. "I wish to make a statement, then I will respond to questions." He cleared his throat, and looked down at his sheets:

"I am Brad Kelly, editor of *The Crier*. I was elected to the editorship by the student body for the winter and spring terms in an election held in late October." He paused, took another deep breath. "So at that time it became common knowledge that I would be the new editor, beginning with the issue of November fourth." He licked his lips. "On Tuesday, November first, I received a letter. It had no signature. It contained a message made up of letters which had been clipped from magazines and newspapers. The letters were of varying type styles and sizes. There were approximately five lines. As well as I can recall, this was the message: *Come alone to Scarrett Pond gazebo two A.M. November three. Burke's plans, faculty scandals revealed. Confidentiality essential. Go for the gold.*"

Pandemonium broke loose.

"Is Scarrett Pond the one here on the campus?"

"Who was there? What did you find out?"

"Where's this letter now?"

"Is this for real? Sounds like a lousy spy novel."

"What faculty scandals?"

Kelly swiped sweat away from his upper lip. He held up both hands. Slowly, the questions subsided.

"Scarrett Pond is here on the campus. And, unfortunately, I didn't keep the letter. I should at this time explain that I was aware, as most students were, of tensions in the journalism department. It was common knowledge that Chairman Burke was unhappy with the direction of the school and hoped to make substantial changes. As I understand it, he had a great deal of authority and could add or drop courses with the approval of the academic dean and without approval of the faculty. But I wasn't aware of any scandals concerning faculty members. My first instinct was to ask Mr. Burke—and I'd like to state that I now regret very much that I didn't do so. But I was afraid he would refuse to comment at all on personnel matters and that I would not be able to learn anything from him about any serious personal problems faculty members might have. And I thought I owed it to the readers to find out what was what. Personal matters affect the way people teach—and what they teach. So I decided to go to this meeting suggested in the unsigned letter."

He straightened his papers. "That meeting was early on the morning of Thursday, November third. I left my apartment about one-thirty and walked onto the campus. I was hoping to be in place before the letter writer arrived and perhaps be able to catch a glimpse of him. Or her. But it was a cloudy night and dark." He gripped the sides of the lectern. "God, it was dark." For the first time, his voice lost its rote tone, sounding instead young and awed. A titter of laughter swept the auditorium. "Anyway, I got there. I couldn't see a thing. I had a flashlight in my jacket but I didn't want to use it. I thought maybe I could surprise this guy and find out who was pulling the strings. So I sort of felt my way out there. See, you can follow the gravel path and reach the bridge. I did that and hung onto the railing and kind of crept over there. Then it's just a couple of feet more and I was at the gazebo. I sat on the steps and listened. I didn't hear anything but the sound of the wind in the trees, kind of an eerie, creepy sound and the plop of things in the water. I don't know what. Too late in the year for snakes and turtles. I sat there and sat there. I didn't know what time it was but I began to think that somebody'd jerked me around, played a joke on me, then all of a sudden there was a bright light and it stabbed right into my eyes and this high whispery voice told me not to move, if I made a single move, tried to get close or anything, it was all off. See, I was outmaneuvered. He had the flash and had me pinned in the light like a bug. Then he started talking, fast and high, and—" another swipe at the sweat beading his forehead now "—told me all this stuff about Professor Porter and how she'd taken money and they'd covered it up and then a lot more stuff about Burke and how he was going to outsmart the faculty that wouldn't play ball—Garrison and Moss—and make them teach courses on practical stuff, whether they liked it or not. They had tenure, but he could set the course work. And then some stuff about Professor Crandall and"—he lifted his head and the skin stretched tautly over his cheekbones—"his girlfriend, a student. I couldn't take notes but I was listening like crazy. Then, the voice said, 'Get started on a series about the faculty. I'll get back in touch with you with some more interesting information next week.' When he said that, all of a sudden the light switched off and I could hear running footsteps. I yanked out my flashlight, but all I saw was some shrubbery kind of waving like it'd been brushed. I knew it wouldn't do any good to try and catch him so—"

"You keep saying 'him,'" the AP reporter broke in. "Was it a man? How could you tell?"

Kelly rubbed the back of his neck. "I don't know. It could have been a woman. Whoever it was kept whispering. I guess I thought it was a man because—because—"

"Because?" Miss Dora prompted in her dry, crackly voice.

Kelly looked defiantly around the auditorium. "All right. I'll just come out and say it. The odds are it's a man. There was only one other woman on the faculty besides Mrs. Porter and I didn't think it was her. Ms. Tarrant wants the department to emphasize professionalism."

The questions erupted like rifle fire, but Kelly stood his ground. No, he didn't know it was a faculty member. But who else knew the kind of thing he'd been told? Who else would try and expose the problems in the department?

It was the CNN reporter who fastened on that. "You think this was part of the chairman's campaign to restructure the department? Are you saying R.T. Burke spilled the beans?"

"I don't know who did it," Kelly insisted. "I'm just telling you what I know."

UPI: "Did somebody stiff Burke because he set up this exposé?"

Kelly ignored that and continued doggedly, "Mr. Burke told me Thursday morning he was determined to discover the identity of Deep Throat. That's what he called him, after—"

"Yeah, yeah, yeah," came an impatient chorus. There was no need for Kelly to inform this audience about Deep Throat, that famous and still-unidentified player during Watergate.

"So Burke was acting like he was furious over the whole deal. And he was mad at me, too. Said I hadn't handled this right, that I should have contacted Porter, Garrison, and Moss. And him, too, I guess. I did call Mrs. Porter, but she wouldn't talk to me. But there wasn't a thing he could do about it. I'm elected to be editor, not appointed by the department. That keeps me independent. And I intend to stay that way."

"Do you think you'll stay alive?" a local television correspondent shouted. "Pretty deadly around that place. The chair dead. A student killed in an explosion in your office. Do you figure somebody's after you?"

Kelly hunched his thin shoulders and balled his fists. "I'm not going to be easy to take. Believe me. And I'm going to check any funny packages that show up."

"Too late for Emily Everett. How come she was in your office? Where were you?"

Kelly yanked a handkerchief from his pocket, swabbed his face. "I think she was just in the wrong place at the wrong time. Look, here's what happened. Emily came lumbering into the newsroom and she was breathing hard and kind of crying, said she didn't know what to do, but she thought maybe she knew who had leaked the stuff and she wanted to see if she was right. See, she thought I knew who I'd got the stuff from. But I told her real quick I didn't know." He gnawed at his lip. "I made a mistake. I should've tried my damnedest to get her to tell me. I mean, that was a hell of a story, too. But I thought I was in a bind. That letter said it had to be confidential and it seemed to me that by showing up and listening, then using that stuff in a story, I'd pretty well made a bargain. And just a couple of months ago an appeals court held a newspaper liable for a couple of hundred thousand dollars because they'd spilled the name of a source after they'd promised to keep it confidential. So I didn't want Emily to tell me. And she was goosey. She wasn't sure, see. So, she kept sniffling and she was so damn upset. I told her I'd go get her a Coke and a candy bar. Make her feel better. Then I was going to decide what to do. I started down the hall and I stopped at the john. I didn't hurry. I thought she could use the time to settle down. I was washing my hands when all hell broke loose. I mean, the goddamnedest explosion. I didn't know it was my office, but I sure as hell knew it was close. I ran down the hall, then I met up with some people—a woman who's teaching a mystery class—and there it was, the office blown to hell. We tried to get to Emily. But we couldn't. Anyway, I think maybe it was just damn bad luck she was in there." He took a deep breath. "And I don't think anybody was out to get me. I don't *think* so. I shouldn't have been there either. I'd dropped in to do a little work after my eleven o'clock, but usually I don't get to the office till around three."

Emily Everett. Short on luck. Very short.

The oh-so-familiar husky voice surprised Annie, it carried so well. But Laurel always managed to be heard.

"Mr. Kelly," came the throaty call. It would make almost any man immediately envision a South Sea island, swaying palms, languorous music, and other idyllic images not easily described in the media.

Annie studied her mother-in-law. For God's sake, how did she do it?

The magic touched Brad Kelly. He lost his haunted, tense look and managed a wan smile. "Yes?"

"A young man such as yourself, so eager to play a role in determining public policy, so devoted to the pursuit of truth, I feel confident you are acutely observant."

Kelly tried hard to appear acutely observant.

"Tell us more about Emily Everett. How was she dressed when she came to your office?"

"Dressed?" Astonishment lifted his voice. Then, awkwardly, he tried to explain. "Emily didn't—she wasn't—she always wore the same kind of thing, great big dresses. Emily was—she was fat."

"Was she carrying a large bag?"

Kelly's brows drew together. "Yeah." He spoke slowly. "Yeah. She was. This great big damn thing, kind of a striped canvas."

"Was it large enough, Mr. Kelly, to contain an explosive?"

Annie had a skittery feeling down her spine. Like mother, like son.

Kelly didn't say anything for a long, long moment. Then he shook his head impatiently. "That doesn't make sense. I mean, even if she was bananas enough to blow away *The Crier*, she sure as hell wouldn't have planned on being there!"

"A curious thing about bombs, Mr. Kelly. I've been doing some research." Annie heard Laurel's soft, husky voice with a definite sense of unreality. It was like hearing Little Red Riding Hood discuss guerrilla warfare. "So often it's the maker who gets blown away. A car bomb goes off and it turns out the driver and passenger hadn't intended to still be in the vehicle. Bombs have an ugly habit of exploding unexpectedly. And you're certain she had the bag?"

A frenzied thumping and Miss Dora's voice rose in a determined screech. "Irrelevant. Immaterial. Young man, the crux of the matter: why did Emily Everett come to you? Why not to Mr. Burke?"

Kelly gripped the lectern again. "Look, I don't know why she did anything. All I know is what she told me, that she thought she knew who dumped on the faculty and she wanted to see if she was right. But since I didn't know, I couldn't help her."

"Perhaps it's the age-old answer," Laurel offered dreamily. "A handsome young man. A young woman attracted to him even though she lacks physical charm and grace. It isn't only the beautiful who fall in love." Her lovely Grecian profile reflected the essence of tragic love.

"Oh, now wait a minute," Kelly erupted. "I hardly knew her."

"Oh now, Mr. Kelly, you're so modest about your kindnesses," Laurel trilled. "I've heard from some of the girls who knew Emily that she thought you were quite wonderful, a knight in shining armor, a perfect example of journalism's finest."

Kelly's face flushed a bright crimson. "God, I just tried to be nice to her. Poor old thing. She wanted to be a reporter, but, my God, you can't look like that and get a job. I told her to think about free-lancing. She could've done that. I mean, she might have had some problems with interviews but a lot of stuff can be done by phone or mail. Oh, hell, she was pathetic."

Laurel beamed, "Ah, but you were kind to her, Mr. Kelly. No doubt that is why she came to you—in addition, of course, to her hope that you could confirm or refute her identification of the individual responsible for leaking the information from those files."

Kelly shook his head vigorously and his ears continued to flame.

Miss Dora's white hair fairly flapped in indignation. "Irrelevant. Immaterial. What did the young woman know? That's what we must determine. Mr. Kelly, did nothing she said give you any idea at all as to the person she suspected?"

"No idea," he said quickly, positively.

Annie looked at him closely. That tone was so positive. He'd expected that question, been prepared for it, planned to sound forthright, conclusive, convincing.

Was it a lie? Did he have some idea? But, if he did, he most certainly didn't intend to share it. Why did she suddenly have a bone-deep sense that Brad Kelly had stage-managed beautifully today, that he had presented himself in the best possible light, and that he knew a good deal more than he planned to admit?

He stood so stalwartly behind that lectern, his pale face composed and serious.

A rustle at the far left of the auditorium and Henny stood up, gesturing for attention with a balaclava helmet. "Mr. Kelly, do you have any idea who may have killed Burke? Or who put the bomb in your office?"

"None." He slammed a balled fist against the lectern and his papers flew to the stage floor. "But I intend to find out. I'm going to ask questions and poke around and tell everybody what I discover. That's what good reporters do. And I'm a good reporter." He took a quick breath, then half turned to confront Moss with a jutting jaw. "And as a beginning, I think it's time the Department of Journalism told some hard truths. What else is in those personnel files that rightfully should be made public? What kind of quarrels are tearing this department to pieces? Do we have faculty members who aren't doing their jobs as they should? What's in these files? I demand that they be made public! Now!"

Moss stepped forward. "There is always in journalism a fine line, a very fine line, between the public's right to know and the individual's right to privacy. Men of good character differ strongly on this matter. Some would support the efforts of our young editor, others oppose him." Those thick lips still curved in that half-smile. Did Moss see the world always with sardonic amusement, or was it a trick of musculature? Blandly, without the least appearance of discomfiture, he added, "In this present instance, the question turns out to be academic. Those files have disappeared."

15

MOSS LED THE WAY up the back stairs of the journalism building. Even these steps had a fine film of dust. "It's safe enough. The building will be reopened Tuesday, but it has to be cleaned first and they want to do some bracing before students are permitted inside." He unlocked his office door and waved them to seats in front of his desk. He took off his suit coat, tossed it carelessly over a coatrack, then settled at his desk. His short-sleeved shirt revealed heavily muscled forearms. It would take a tough customer, like Rob Kantner's PI, Ben Perkins, to take him on. Moss leaned back at his ease in his oversize brown leather armchair. His office was all oversize leather: the couch, the chairs, even a dark brown footstool. The massive furniture emphasized his powerful physique. He was an intimidating man in a background intended to reinforce that image.

Max, of course, Annie was pleased to note, wasn't the least bit intimidated.

Nor, she assured herself, was she, although she did find overlarge people discomfiting.

But Moss was on his good behavior today. He even managed a genial smile as Max finished speaking.

"I certainly will do everything in my power to be helpful to Miss Dora."

His tone was agreeable, but Annie realized she found him even less likable when he was attempting to charm than when he was openly contemptuous as he'd been at that faculty meeting held in response to the revelations in *The Crier*. Sensing her hostility, he fastened heavy-lidded blue eyes on her. His half-smile widened. "You look a little skeptical, Mrs. Darling. How can I convince you of my good intentions?" A rumble of deep laughter. "You are, I suppose, an ardent feminist, and I must assume you took umbrage at the meeting when I twitted dear Sue a bit."

Annie opened her mouth to attack, but twisted her lips into a polite smile at Max's warning glance. After all, she wasn't here to engage Moss in combat.

"Actually, we're hoping for a frank appraisal of your colleagues," Max said encouragingly. "This isn't the time for tactful responses."

"I'm not known for those." Another rumble of laughter.

"So you won't mind if we take a hard look at your faculty—starting with you. Are you Deep Throat, Professor Moss?"

He was still genial. "Funny you should ask. That's the first thing Burke said to me when we talked Thursday. I'll give you the same answer. No. But I wish I'd thought of it. I've never seen so much excitement generated about this department. As we say in advertising, any public notice— even critical—is better than none. And I would enjoy a public discussion of where this department should go. Burke meant well, but he was living in another age. He was a throwback to the era of Floyd Gibbons and Webb Miller. Those were the days of typewriters and Western Union and extras. Those days are gone. We need sophisticated approaches to marketing and to news gathering. But you young people aren't interested in hearing about the philosophy of journalism education."

"Not unless it supplied the motive for murder," Annie said sweetly.

For an instant he stared at her with cold blue eyes, then he laughed robustly. "I can't rule it out, but I'll tell you now, I didn't bash his head in. I might have enjoyed it, but I didn't do it. As a matter of fact, Sue Tarrant can vouch that I left R.T. alive and on the warpath. She was coming in as I left." A feline smile lifted the corners of his full lips. "And I'd say she was looking for a fight."

"Burke was on the warpath? Trying to find out who leaked the information from the files?"

"That's what he said." There was the faintest inflection on the last word.

Annie pounced. "Do you have any reason to doubt his sincerity?"

"Not altogether. But I will say that he is—was—the newcomer to this faculty. He was determined to change the direction of this department. He had no great affection for any of us. And although he did decide quickly to permit Charlotte to make restitution, I was never convinced that he cared about her personally. I felt, rather, that he saw the shortage as just one more problem but not a major one, not central to his task, and that he made his decision solely on the basis of what would be most helpful to him. A scandal would not have helped."

"Then why would he feed the information to Kelly?" Max asked.

"Perhaps he'd changed his mind at this point. Perhaps he decided it would be more helpful to his campaign if he got rid of Charlotte, named her replacement, thereby picking up support within the faculty. Or perhaps he intended to reveal all the circumstances of her theft at the news conference which didn't occur and thereby cast himself in a rather heroic stance, protector of a loyal faculty member who had committed a crime because of an intolerable personal tragedy. And, of course, he could continue feeding information to Kelly that would embarrass the rest of us."

"You can come up with a lot of maybes, when he isn't here to defend himself," Annie said tartly.

"Oh yes, I'm good at that," Moss said amiably. "On the other hand, I can equally easily believe that he was not responsible, but that he discovered the informant's identity and it caused his death."

"In that event, who do you think leaked the information?" Max asked.

Moss frowned. "I would assume, Mr. Darling, that what I say will be held in confidence. I should be very unhappy to pick up the local newspaper and read any report of this discussion."

"The local newspaper will not hear about any of this from us," Max assured him. "But I don't know what the local police intend to reveal."

A relaxed headshake. "I don't believe they intend to reveal much of anything. They have made their arrest. And, in passing, I might say I've had that young lady in class. I find the proposition that she is a violent murderer to be absurd. But, back to your question. My candidate for your villain is the same now as when Burke and I talked. I've always felt that Kurt Diggs likes to live on the edge. Garrison's cautious. Norden's out of control. Crandall's a fool. Now Sue," he said ruminatively, "Sue's a dark horse. Hot-tempered, perhaps a little unstable. Perhaps Sue. But of them all, Kurt's the one with a wild streak." He stroked his chin, but his massive fingers didn't quite hide his salacious smile. "I understand he was tried for rape and acquitted when he was in the military."

"Would that have been in his personnel file?" Annie asked.

A shrug of those bulky shoulders. "I have no idea." He held up a meaty hand when Annie started to speak. "Although I was on the personnel committee, I certainly wasn't cognizant of every piece of information in every file."

Max poised a pen over his notebook. "What can you tell us about those missing personnel files?"

"Not much more than the fact that they're missing. I went through the offices with a police lieutenant this morning. Now, I don't know what was in Burke's files. I couldn't help them there. But the minute we got to the middle office, I knew there was trouble. Those files are kept in a locked closet which can be opened by a master key or by a key on a bunch kept in the secretary's desk. In Emily's desk. By the way, her keys were there. I suppose any faculty member would have known about her keys—but no faculty member would have needed them, because we all have master keys. In any event, the closet was open—and it shouldn't have been. I checked immediately and the current personnel files are gone."

"What do the police think?" Annie asked.

A supercilious glance. "I'm not in their confidence."

Annie decided Moss would have had his head bashed in years ago if he'd been foolish enough to keep an iron bar handy.

Max hurried to forestall an outburst. "What do *you* think?"

Moss didn't answer directly. "That door was closed when I left Burke's office shortly after ten. That is no guarantee, of course, that the files were in there. But I think it's likely that the door was left open when the files were taken. I would assume that happened at some point after I left and before the explosion."

"Do you think the murderer took the files?" Annie asked.

Those sardonic blue eyes looked amused. "Isn't that what we are supposed to think?" He shrugged. "But what else is there to think? And what good does it do anyone to remove those files?"

"For one thing, it prevented their being made public to the press today," Max suggested.

"True. But it has also focused the attention of the world on those files —and their presumed contents. As any journalist knows, once questions are raised it's so easy to find answers." Was there a satisfied lilt to his heavy voice?

"Are you willing to give a public description of the contents of those folders?" Annie asked sharply.

He was bland but definite. "Of course not."

"To protect yourself or the school?" Max inquired.

"The files themselves, if they still exist, have substance," Moss pointed out. "The uncorroborated memory of a committee member as to their contents is worthless. If, as acting chair, I am asked to release the files, should they become available, that is a decision I would have to make. Under no conceivable circumstances could I be expected to rely upon memory to recreate them."

"So it gets you off the hook?" Annie said.

"What hook?" he asked lightly, but his blue eyes were cold.

"I do not like thee, Dr. Fell," Annie chanted as they completed a fruitless round of the other faculty offices—nobody home—and started down the stairs.

Max chuckled. "That doesn't surprise me a lot."

"Sexist asshole," she amplified.

"Elements of that," Max agreed.

As they stepped out into a sharp wind, Annie shivered. "Did you notice his arms? He could bash anything to pieces."

She grabbed Max's elbow as they ducked against the wind on their way to the Student Union. She didn't need support, of course. But it made the cool misty morning so much cheerier.

Over coffee and doughnuts (even Max, which surprised her, but maybe he needed a boost, too), they studied their sheet of faculty addresses and wrangled over their next step.

Annie won. "Crandall was there!" she insisted heatedly. "At or just before the critical moment."

•   •   •

The pampas grass behind the bed of pink flowering impatiens rippled in the freshening wind.

"Storm coming," Annie, the old salt, announced, leading the way up the shallow front steps. Not every house in Chastain was old, of course. This boxy red brick ranch house was in a subdivision a good five miles from the campus. Drawn drapes in the front windows gave the house a forbidding appearance, but light from a lamp glowed behind the living room picture window.

Max poked at the doorbell. "Good day to be home in front of a fire."

The warm image he had evoked dissipated immediately when the door opened. A sharp-featured woman with thin, heavily carmined lips, jutting cheekbones, and dark, brooding eyes stared out at them.

"Is Professor Crandall home?" Max asked.

"No." Her eyes darted from Max to Annie and back again. "Who're you? Why do you want to see him?" Her voice was sharp.

Max lifted his eyebrows ever so little, to indicate polite surprise at her query. Lord Peter couldn't have done it any better, Annie thought.

"Mrs. Crandall?" Max inquired.

"Yes. Who're you?"

"We're working for one of the college trustees," Annie said smoothly, "trying to discover what's gone wrong in the department."

Those thin lips twisted. "A little late, aren't you? And I suppose you're going to whitewash that Burke man, turn him into a hero?"

"Not at all," Max said swiftly. "All we want to do is discover the truth."

"He was a jealous, hateful man. *That's* the truth." She glared at them. "He laughed at me. I know he did."

"Were you here on Thursday, just before lunch?" Annie asked.

The brooding eyes flashed with anger. "I wasn't over there, I can tell you that. I don't know anything about it. I play bridge on Thursdays. All day."

"Your husband was there," Max said quietly.

"Of course Frank was. He teaches there. He had every right to be there."

"Certainly," Max said soothingly. "But he did talk to Burke Thursday morning. In fact, he may have been the last person to see him alive. That's why we want to see him. Can you tell us when he'll be home?"

The tight mouth trembled. She tried to speak, but couldn't. Tears splashed down her cheeks. She shook her head and turned away, slamming the door against them.

The grass needed mowing. A shutter hung loose and rattled disconcertingly as the wind swept the verandah. The sea pines quivered, whispering of the coming rain.

They had almost turned away, having knocked three times, when the door slowly squeaked open. Josh Norden filled the doorway. He was a bigger man than Annie remembered. He looked at them blankly.

"Professor Norden, sorry to bother you at home. You remember we talked early Thursday morning? Yesterday."

"Certainly I remember, young man. Is there any reason why I shouldn't remember?" His diction was flawless. If he'd been drinking, and he probably had, he was well within his capacity.

"We won't take much of your time," Annie said quickly. "Could we talk to you for just a few minutes?"

It hung in the balance. But, finally, with a curt nod, he held open the screen door. The antebellum house followed the usual pattern, deep rooms opening to either side of the hall. They followed Norden into the room on the right.

The long drapes hung open. The gloomy day pressed against the windows, providing the only illumination in the dim room. The room was cluttered with books, books on the floor, books in chairs, books scattered on tables. Open books, closed books. Norden cleared two chairs, gestured for Max and Annie to sit. He took a wing-back chair opposite them. Shoving his sliding horn-rims higher on his beaked nose, he said brusquely, "Well?"

"Professor, what did you and Mr. Burke discuss yesterday?" Max asked quietly.

His nostrils flared. A flush rose in his chalky cheeks. "It was a matter of decency. That's what I told him. The only honorable thing to do. And he had the gall to say that he didn't need for me to instruct him on how to act."

"What did you want him to do?" Annie asked.

"To announce to the world the circumstances of Charlotte's use of those funds. It's hideous for her friends to think she was no better than a common thief. And that's little enough to do for her now."

"When we talked to him, before you saw him, he was considering whether to do just that. Had he decided against it?"

"He had made no final decision. But he said that on reflection it seemed to him that any revelation from those files was an invasion of privacy. I told him not to be a goddamned fool. Charlotte didn't need privacy any longer." His hands clenched. Then his voice smoothed. "Moss will see it my way. He'll take care of it."

"You quarreled with Burke." Annie's tone was declarative, not accusatory.

Norden responded angrily. "I quarreled with him, but I didn't kill him."

"Do you think he could have been the one who gave that information to Kelly?" Max asked.

Norden's blue eyes weren't glazed this morning. They burned with unsated fury. "If I'd thought that, I'd—" He broke off. He looked at them sharply. "Is that what you think? That he was the informant? God, it would serve him right then, wouldn't it?"

The rain slapped against the windshield. "What's the number over there?" Max asked.

Annie rolled down the window and peered through the slanting rain. "That's it. The second complex."

Despite Max's majestic black umbrella, they were damp and, consequently, shivering by the time they struggled against the wind up outside stairs and reached the unprotected second-story balcony and the door to apartment nine.

Max pushed the doorbell.

At the second ring, a peephole opened. "Yes."

Annie stepped closer. "Professor Tarrant, may we speak to you for a moment?"

"Sue," a man's voice called nervously, "who is it?"

The peephole closed.

Sue Tarrant was divorced. That was in her vitae, but it gave no hint, of course, of her life, her friends, her lovers. Or lack of them.

The door jerked open. Tarrant faced them, unsmiling. She wore a blue jersey dress that emphasized voluptuous curves, but her face was ashen beneath her makeup and her brown eyes were angry.

"Who gives you the right to hound people? Miss Dora may be a trustee, but she doesn't have any control over my private life. Frank can come here if he wants to, for God's sake."

Frank Crandall paced toward the door. "Did my wife send you?" he demanded. He jerked his head toward the living room. "Come on in, for God's sake. Let's have it out."

Since Max had an unfortunate propensity for the truth (Annie had told him and told him that creative obfuscation was *not* lying), Annie shot ahead of him. She stood dripping in the middle of the small living room and announced baldly, "Your wife is really upset."

Crandall shoved a trembling hand through his mop of shaggy hair and looked helplessly at Tarrant.

She hurried to him, put a reassuring hand on his arm. "Frank, none of this is *your* fault. Please don't be upset." She faced Annie and Max like a tigress protecting a favorite cub. "Look, you've got to understand the background. That Finney girl has hot pants."

Crandall winced. "No, no. No. She's a nice girl. Really, she is. I didn't —she is so gentle, so kind. So pretty."

Tarrant's eyes glistened like ribbons of steel on an August day.

"But Burke wasn't having any, was he?" Max said crisply, obviously less than enchanted with Professor Crandall. "Burke didn't want his faculty messing with students, right?"

Crandall clawed at his knitted tie, loosened it. "I had a nice talk with him. We agreed that everything was going to be all right." His face brightened. "In fact, he said he was going to recommend me for tenure."

It was like watching a cartoon character as the light bulb turns on. Annie knew, as surely as if she'd perched in his head, that the idea had just occurred to Crandall that no one could contradict his version of that final conversation. And he was going to position himself as well as he could.

"Certainly Frank will get tenure. I'm sure Malcolm will be all for him," Tarrant said quickly.

"Moss doesn't care much for women, or about women, does he?" Annie asked sharply. "He won't care if Professor Crandall's having an affair with a student."

Tarrant snapped, "That's in the past. It's all over with."

Max stepped closer to her and spattered rainwater on the rug. "How much does it mean to you for Frank Crandall to receive tenure, to stay on this faculty?" Then he whirled on Crandall and another fine spray whipped from his coat. "Why don't you tell us the truth? You and Burke had it out. There wasn't going to be any tenure for you, was there?"

"I don't know what you're talking about," Crandall said weakly.

"The witness who saw you hurry out of Burke's office said you were upset." Annie ignored Max's reproachful glance and was glad Tarrant and Crandall were too shaken to notice. "You might as well tell us the truth." Inspiration struck. She had to wonder if perhaps Georgia Finney had a guardian angel strumming her wings in Annie's vicinity. "That's why Georgia went in his office, isn't it? She saw you and you were obviously distraught. She hurried in there, hoping to be able to set things right with Burke, perhaps take all the blame for the affair. You seem to have plenty of women willing to do all they can for you. Anyway, Georgia went in and found him dead and she was terrified you'd done it. That's why she grabbed up the bar and ran away with it, hoping to be able to get rid of it and protect you."

"He was such a bloody shit!" Crandall exploded. "He wouldn't even talk to me! Told me he'd deal with me later, that he thought I was—" His lean face flushed.

"Yes?" Annie encouraged.

"Frank, we know what he was like," Tarrant murmured.

"He said I was a sorry bastard and he didn't want anybody like me on his faculty. So, yeah, I was upset and I slammed the goddamn door as I went out. Why should I have to listen to stuff like that? I swear he was all right. He was brushing me off, didn't have time for me, too busy talking on the phone. And he's the one who set up the appointment, insisted I come! But he was all right when I left, I swear."

"How long were you in his office?" Max asked.

"Two minutes maybe. He couldn't wait to get rid of me."

Annie was trying to work out the timing in her mind. "Okay. You came out of his office around eleven-eighteen or so? What did you do then?"

"I went outside. I needed some air. I needed to get the hell away from there for a while."

"Did you see Georgia?"

Crandall cracked his knuckles. "The cops asked that."

"Did you?" Max pressed.

Crandall looked at Tarrant for support. Her eyes glittered, but her voice was smooth. "If you saw her near Burke's office, you should say so, Frank."

The better to incarcerate her, my dear, Annie thought. Was there any limit to what Sue Tarrant would do for Crandall's attention?

Crandall swallowed jerkily. "Yeah. Well. I told the cops I didn't see her. I mean, they might think—" He swallowed again. "But the thing about it is, I saw her, but I didn't want to talk to her. Hell, everything was all screwed up. I don't like for things to be shitty," he said plaintively.

Annie decided she wasn't enchanted with him either, despite his sensitive face, appealing mop of brown hair, and nicely fitting khakis.

"I thought you told the police you went to the Union for coffee," Max objected. "Couldn't she have caught up with you easily?"

Crandall turned and walked away. He banged against the sharp edge of a glass coffee table. Wincing, he grabbed at the calf of his leg.

Tarrant was at his side immediately. "Oh, Frank, that damn table. I ought to get rid of it. Here, sit down," and she urged him toward the overstuffed couch. She knelt down and began to massage his leg.

"Where *did* you go when you left the journalism building?" Annie prodded.

"To the Union," he said defiantly. Then his glance slid away from her. "But not straight." He nodded appreciatively at Tarrant and patted the couch. She gave his leg one last lingering stroke, then settled beside him.

"Not straight," Max repeated. "You burst out of the journalism building. Upset. Furious with Burke." Crandall started to interrupt, but Max charged ahead. "Okay, you see Georgia, but you don't want to talk to her. How did you avoid it?"

"She was behind me. She called out once, but I'd told her we couldn't be seen together on the campus. So I walked faster, then I cut across the avenue and hurried into the woods around Scarrett Pond."

Scarrett Pond. Dark, dismal, and dank in November, a place of shadows and impenetrable shrubbery, saw palmettos, dwarf huckleberry, willow oaks, red cedars, and ringing the pond, the brooding, majestic cypress. Strange plants flourished there, blasphemy vine and false boneset, toadflax and devil's walking stick.

"Did she follow you?" Annie asked.

Once again, Crandall looked to Tarrant for support. She took his hand and squeezed it.

But he wouldn't look at Annie and Max and his voice was a mumble. "I heard her behind me, but I hurried and turned off to the right, a path that isn't used much. She stayed on the main path and she called out for me."

"You didn't answer." There wasn't much inflection in Max's voice, but Crandall flushed.

"I was upset." He gave Annie a hostile glare. "I didn't want to talk to her. And in a few minutes I heard her coming back down the path. I waited until there wasn't any sound at all, then I went to the Union."

Annie reached over and flicked on the heater as Max started the car. "Brr. Is there anything soggier than a steady November rain?"

"Frank Crandall," Max replied crisply.

She grinned.

Max slowed, peering through the rain at a street sign. "Do I turn here?"

She checked the open city map on the seat beside her. "Right."

Max shot her a bemused glance. "What's that guy got? Why are women drawn to him like filings to a magnet?"

Annie knew better than to try and explain. Max would never understand a sensitive face and pleated khakis. So she merely shrugged.

"He's too much of a wimp to have done it himself," Max said derisively.

"Maybe." Annie wasn't convinced. "But sometimes weak people will fight like demons when they're threatened. Just like the killer in *A Murder Is Announced*. But Max, more importantly, if Crandall didn't do it, he drew Georgia away from the building long enough for the murder to have occurred."

Max nodded grudgingly. Clearly, he thought a noose would fit nicely around Crandall's neck, but Max was always willing to be impartial, at least for a moment. "We've got options," Max agreed. "One, Crandall killed him. Two, Crandall found him dead but is too scared to say so. Three, Georgia killed him. Four, unknown murderer entered after Crandall's departure, killed Burke, got the files, and departed before Georgia arrived."

Annie rolled the window halfway down and peered out. "This is it."

As they ran through the rain, she heard him murmur, "Forty-eight seconds."

That was how long somebody in a hurry, a real hurry, could make it from the second-floor faculty offices to Burke's office.

Although it might take Norden a little longer.

But not if he'd hidden in the file closet.

A cheery fire blazed in the hearth. Victor Garrison was at his ease, a professor in his study, floor-to-ceiling bookcases filling two walls. It was a comfortable room, with two brightly slipcovered sofas, a Navajo throw rug, a dartboard on one paneled wall, a family portrait over the mantel. Garrison's children looked bright and happy and his wife was slim and pretty with dark hair drawn back behind a green bow that matched laughing green eyes. Garrison glowed with good health and positive thinking.

"A little odd to be home on Friday morning, but I'm taking advantage of it." He gestured at the legal pad on his desk, and Max recognized that neat, precise writing. "Not, of course, a welcome break." He shook his head solemnly, ruing the uncertainty and dark twists that life could take.

"Totally unexpected, of course," Max said.

Garrison smoothed back his short blond hair. "Violence is *always* a shock, Mr. Darling. But unexpected? Frankly, I knew trouble was coming. I didn't foresee the form it would take. But people have been known to dig their own graves. I think that's what happened to R.T. Burke."

"He brought it on himself?" Annie asked. "Is that what you mean?"

Garrison leaned back in his swivel chair. "It's always a mistake to put someone who has no interpersonal skills in charge of a group. Now, we're all quite willing to recognize Burke's achievements as a newsman. He was quite skilled at investigative reporting, had the requisite qualities to excel there: persistence, quick intelligence, ability to marshal facts, aggressiveness, toughness, combativeness. But, as do we all," and he offered a charming smile, "he had the defects of his virtues. He was not empathetic. He was impatient with failure, whether it be moral, intellectual, or physical. I believe this entire matter can be very simply put to rest, and that lovely child Georgia Finney released, if the authorities will only look at the principals involved, Charlotte Porter, R.T. Burke, Brad Kelly, and Emily Everett."

Annie wanted to object to Emily's inclusion as a principal, but Garrison barreled ahead.

"Burke made a serious mistake, a profound misjudgment of cause and effect, when he leaked that material on Charlotte to Brad."

So Garrison tabbed Burke as the informant, no ifs, ands, or buts.

"He couldn't know, because he hadn't been here long enough, that Emily Everett adored Charlotte." He gave a little shrug. "Though perhaps he can't be faulted there. I'm one of the few who knew. Charlotte had gone to bat for Emily, insisted that the bylaws be changed and a part-time student be permitted to serve as president, ironically enough, of the Student Press Association, the same group from which she was later to embezzle those funds. But the point is that Emily was from that time forward Charlotte's partisan. I don't suppose anyone had ever gone out of their way for Emily before. So, there is the background. Emily, a morose, unhappy creature, plodding along, doing her class work, working in the office, but remembering that moment of glory when she served as president of the group. What happens when that story comes out in *The Crier*? Emily must have been furious, both at Brad and at whoever gave him the information that hurt Mrs. Porter." Garrison reached for his pipe, began to fill it. "I don't suppose we'll ever know how she discovered Burke to be responsible. Perhaps she'd seen him recently in the confidential files. Perhaps it was simpler than that. She looked at who would profit from such a disclosure and came to the same conclusion I reached—R.T. Burke."

"So she killed Burke and planned to blow up Kelly? Why did she get blown away instead?" Max asked.

"I would think Emily must have been very upset by the time she reached the *Crier* offices. And she couldn't, of course, force Kelly to remain there, if he excused himself. Perhaps the bomb was set for a later time and she thought he'd be back and she'd be gone. Perhaps it wasn't set at all but misfired, killing her. Perhaps she was in the act of setting it when it exploded. That is so often the way with bombs." He smiled modestly. "I covered a good deal of that sort of thing in the seventies. Bombs are damn dangerous—especially to their makers. You remember that town house in New York?"

He flicked a lighter and lit the tobacco, and the woodsy smoke curled through the den. He smiled complacently.

"When you saw Burke Thursday—just before he was killed—did you accuse him of being Deep Throat?" Max asked swiftly.

Garrison puffed at his pipe and eyed them cautiously. "As a matter of fact, Mr. Darling, no."

Annie looked at him in disbelief. "Didn't the two of you talk about the leakage of information from the files?"

"Oh, of course. In a sense. Burke was busy playing sleuth. He asked if I had done it. I said that was absurd. He seemed to accept that. Then he wanted to know who I thought might be behind it."

"Surely this was the time for you to accuse him, wasn't it?" Max demanded.

But Garrison was unruffled. In fact, he chuckled. "Disappointed in me, Mr. Darling? Do you know," he sucked contentedly on his pipe, "I don't seek confrontations. I've always thought it better policy to keep my own counsel. I don't," and his smile was satisfied, "tell everything I know, Mr. Darling."

"Oily." Max put the car in gear.

"Odious." Annie searched in her purse for a tissue to pat against her wet hair.

"But such a tidy solution." The car zoomed to forty-five and Max eased up on the accelerator.

"Certainly please our Professor Garrison, wouldn't it?" Annie observed. "The devil of it is, he may be right. Max, was Burke really Deep Throat?"

From the fake leopard skin sofa with its two extra large downy throw pillows to the glossy white throw rug in front of the fireplace to the scented candle stubs lining the mantel, it had the air of a genuine love nest.

Kurt Diggs reveled in it. His suggestive glance stroked Annie, bringing a tight set to Max's mouth. Diggs leaned casually against the mantel. His Levi's fit like fresh snake skin, his magenta-striped sports shirt was unbuttoned to midchest. A heavy gold chain glistened at his throat. He held a whiskey glass in one hand and his eyes lingered on Annie.

"Don't you ever drink before lunch, sweetheart? Drop around by yourself sometime and I'll introduce you to its pleasures—and maybe some others too."

Max looked like he'd enjoy twisting that gold chain right into Diggs's windpipe.

Annie hastened to divert him. "My morning hours are all spoken for, thanks. And I don't need whiskey to have fun. Too bad you do. But speaking of pleasures—wasn't Burke planning on shortening your list?"

Diggs grinned and his large, even, white teeth gleamed against his tanned skin. He took a swallow of his drink. "Yeah. Just shows what happens to do-gooders, doesn't it? Jesus, he was hot to banish sin and lust from his department. Biggest prick I ever met. But it just goes to show, nice guys sure as hell finish last, just like they should."

"Is that how you see him?" Max asked. "A do-gooder?"

"Jesus, did you ever *talk* to him? One goddamn platitude after another." Diggs recited in a high falsetto, " 'Success without honor is the ultimate failure, a man's word is his bond, a journalist must rise to a higher standard than the society he serves, the public's right to know ends where the right to privacy begins, character is destiny.' " He took another stiff drink. "He made me gag."

"What sayings do you prefer?" Max asked in disgust.

Those white teeth flashed again. "How about: 'Shit happens'?"

Annie ignored that skirmish. "So you think impressing his values on the department mattered most to him. Would that justify in his own mind leaking those files to Kelly?"

Diggs arched a dark eyebrow. "Hey, I thought you had some brains. But I guess you're just another pretty broad." Annie reached out and grabbed Max's arm. "Hell, didn't you hear me? He was a goddamn crusader, lady. I kept expecting him to break out in that stupid song from *Man of La Mancha.*" He hummed a bar of "The Impossible Dream." He downed the rest of his drink and laughed. "Hell, that's rich. Burke as Deep Throat. No way. Not that Holy Joe prick. No way."

16

IT RAINED for two solid days, a sodden, gray world with the damp chill of coming winter. Gorgeous November days would come again with temperatures in the seventies, and Annie and Max were quite likely to play badminton on Christmas afternoon, but lovely weather was only a memory that Saturday and Sunday. Actually, Annie and Max both enjoyed rainy weekends. The homeyness. The jolly good-fellowship. Afternoon delight. Not, unfortunately, that the latter pastime seemed possible. There didn't seem to be enough time between telephone calls. The weather, however, didn't discourage wintering swallows. Annie insisted they visit the forest preserve despite the dripping skies when Ingrid called Sunday afternoon to report excitedly that the bird club had spotted a huge flock, five hundred strong, feasting on the bayberry shrubs. Max was moderately enthusiastic. It was to be admitted that he would have welcomed almost any outing at that point for some respite from the telephone.

Annie kept a record of the calls. Should one of her three most enthusiastic students demand an accounting of how extra credit was earned (and she conceded that these three would expect extra credit for their efforts despite the cancellation of the class project as a whole), Annie intended to present the telephone log as clear evidence of who did what.

Then, rather as in the manner of baseball statistics, the log became a matter of fascination to her in itself.

The keeping of the log began at Death on Demand:

2:04 P.M. Saturday: "Where *are* those files? Surely the two of you in your journeyings yesterday did at the very least address this question?" Miss Dora's crackly voice oozed contempt. "I have before me the list of those believed to have been in the building just previous to the explosion, but *not* accounted for in a class. It includes, as I would hope you know, Professors Moss, Garrison, Tarrant, Norden, Crandall, and Diggs; the victims, Burke and Everett; and that querulous infant, Bradley Kelly. It is, I hope, not superfluous to note that none of the above could have made provision for the files *after* the explosion."

3:16 P.M. Saturday: "So disappointing when one's picture of plucky young lovers disintegrates from the pressure of reality. In truth, reality often robs Cupid of his arrows, I'm afraid. However," and Laurel's voice cheered, "I feel confident that love—or perhaps the lack of it—may be the root cause of our tragedy."

4:49 P.M. Saturday: "It's just the same thing as when that peck of shrimp disappeared from Mrs. Fothergill's shop. If I *think* on it, I'll know what happened. After all," Henny's accent was quite crisp, "it all comes down to character, doesn't it?"

The calls continued that evening at Annie and Max's tree house:

6:42 P.M. Saturday: "Brad Kelly was seen on the main avenue of the campus late Wednesday night. When queried today, he said he was on his way to a second meeting with Deep Throat at Scarrett Pond, but no one showed up. He didn't mention this, he said, at the press conference when he revealed his knowledge, however paltry, about the informant, since nothing came of the second meeting. He did admit to seeing Mrs. Roethke running from the journalism building and thought it strange but was hurrying to reach the pond on time so didn't stop to investigate. What does this signify?" A pause, and Miss Dora sniffed in disgust. "A woman of her age" (Annie knew Laurel would have found this reference quite offensive) "has *no* place in a drinking establishment frequented by students. Quite unseemly."

Annie admitted to Max that this piece of information was intriguing, in part because it indicated an awesome ability for information retrieval on Miss Dora's part. It provoked them into constructing a timetable of events. (Max would gladly have opted for other, more intimate activities, but a timetable could withstand the assault of the telephone. As for the possibility of unplugging the phone or stuffing it under a pillow, Annie apparently found this a psychic impossibility which all women would understand immediately.)

Annie insisted on beginning at the beginning:

Tuesday, November 1: R.T. Burke comes to Death on Demand, persuades Annie to teach a class on the mystery.

Thursday, November 3: early morning clandestine meeting between Kelly and informant at Scarrett Pond.

Thursday, November 3: Annie attends her first faculty meeting.

Saturday, November 5: Charlotte Porter visits Death on Demand, bringing the first issue of *The Crier* with its nice picture of Annie.

Tuesday, November 8: Annie teaches her first class; *The Crier* is published with the article revealing Charlotte Porter's misuse of funds.

Wednesday, November 9: Max is hired to discover who leaked the confidential files to Kelly; Annie attends emergency faculty meeting on the exposé; Charlotte Porter's suicide discovered. Late that night, Kelly goes to Scarrett Pond but his informant doesn't show up; the *Crier* offices vandalized, Laurel arrested.

Thursday, November 10: Annie and Max spring Laurel from the city jail; Annie and Max talk to Burke about the leaked information; Kelly schedules news conference; Annie's class picks outside research project (later canceled); explosion wrecks *Crier* offices, kills Emily Everett; Annie discovers Burke's body; Georgia Finney arrested; Annie and Max in conference with three eager students at the Palmetto Inn.

Friday, November 11: Annie and Max (awakened by the telephone, of course) make an early morning survey of Burke's offices, discover open door to file closet; Emily Everett's landlady describes Emily's last hours; President Charles August Markham ponders the effects of his choosing R.T. Burke to head the journalism department; Kelly reveals what little he knows about his informant at a jammed press conference; Annie and Max try to flesh out their picture of R.T. Burke.

Was or was not Burke Deep Throat? Annie tapped her pencil on the card table they'd put up in the middle of the living room to hold all of their materials about the crimes. "Max, why didn't Deep Throat show up Wednesday night? Had he already decided to kill Burke the next day?"

"That's assuming someone other than Burke is the informant," he cautioned.

Annie wildly ran her hands through her hair. "Dammit, there it is again. Who is Deep Throat?"

"Or was," Max augmented.

Their construction of the timetable and discussion of questions it raised occurred, of course, with intermittent interruptions.

7:15 P.M. Saturday: "Oh, the human heart, and the dark and tortuous impulses generated when love is so desperately sought." Laurel's husky voice trailed off for a moment. "The tragedy. The heartbreak."

"Yes, Laurel?" If Annie wanted aphorisms, she could read Kahlil Gibran.

"And the young are so ruthless, are they not? It scarcely seems possible that it should have happened. Although, of course, you would think a woman the age of Sue Tarrant would know better." From the intonation, an unknowing listener would have assumed Sue Tarrant to be *much* older than Laurel.

A lengthy pause.

Annie couldn't resist. "What happened?"

"A student of Professor Tarrant's discovered, somehow, that she belonged to one of those long-distance conversation clubs. You know, for lonely people. And the student put it on a bulletin board."

Funny. Annie wasn't struck so much by the student's cruelty as by Tarrant's desperation.

9:03 P.M. Saturday: "The quest continues." Henny gave no evidence of fatigue. In fact, she sounded absolutely chipper and, of course, very British. Dame Beatrice Bradley? "When Victor Garrison was an undergraduate, he lost an election to the presidency of the Student Council. A few weeks later, an anonymous informant accused the newly elected president of plagiarism on a term paper. The charge was substantiated and the student expelled. A new election was held and Garrison won. Interesting psychological parallel, don't you think?"

10:15 P.M. Saturday: "I've met the loveliest young man. His name is Peter Strawn," Laurel caroled. Annie tensed. Surely— "He works part-time for the student police and he claims there were three figures fleeing the journalism building the evening that I was there. I do believe Peter— he plays football and is *so* attractive—will be very suitable for Georgia when we succeed in clearing her."

11:06 P.M. Saturday: "Want a thing done and done well, do it your-self!" And wasn't the old devil pleased with herself, Annie thought. Miss Dora's crackly voice was plump with satisfaction. "President Markham escorted me. Kept looking nervously at the ceilings. By God, if the build-ing hadn't fallen by then, why should it? And he turned absolutely beet red at the urinals. But I grew up with chamber pots. The urinals held no interest for me. It was the trash cans. The trash cans!"

"The trash cans," Annie parroted obediently.

"Of course. Do you think maintenance engineers—and what a silly damn fool name for a trashman, used to be just custodians, now it's building maintenance engineers—do you think they *look* in trash barrels? Not likely. So I did and there they were."

Annie didn't have to ask. So, the missing personnel files had been found. By Miss Dora. In the first floor men's room, stuffed in the bottom of the trash sack in the waste barrel.

6:03 A.M. Sunday: "Newspaper people are so difficult to track down. But, of course, it's seven hours later in London. Nice young woman. Used to think the world of R.T. Burke, but upset when a good friend of hers, who had been a financial writer, found it impossible to get a job because of Burke. Seems the young man, Somebody Smith, profited financially from a story, delayed turning it in so he could buy some stock. Well, he made restitution and all that and even served a couple of years in the Peace Corps, but Burke said, 'You can't make a crooked stick straight,' and kept him from getting another job in journalism." Henny chirped, "I guess the moral is, watch out if you bat a sticky wicket." The British accent fled. "Annie, what the hell *is* a sticky wicket?"

That call awakened them, of course. They made the early church ser-vice for the first time. Max thought being up early on a Sunday kind of fun. Annie was grumpy.

11:20 A.M. **Sunday:** "This is in total confidence, of course. My sources are impeccable but must remain unnamed." A trill of laughter. "Oh, don't you think I might do well as a journalist? I've always thought it would be so exciting to know an unimpeachable source or a highly placed executive or an administration spokesman. Do you think I should consider a new career?"

"Heavens no, Laurel." Fearing she'd lacked in tact, Annie added swiftly, "You're so busy as you are. So involved." She forbore to say that the nation's news-gathering infrastructure would never survive an onslaught by Laurel.

"That's true, my dear. Oh, Annie, you are such an inspiration to me. I believe I have found my niche in life. Understanding the Mystery." Her tone elevated it to a high calling. "We can encompass all experience within the purview of the Mystery, which serves as the morality play of our time."

Annie gripped the receiver. Oh God, what was she going to do about Laurel?

"But I am *drawn* to the excitement, the drama, the behind-the-scenes delving of journalism." That husky voice dropped even lower. "And I do have previously unreleased information. From a source I cannot reveal, I have learned that Georgia Finney has broken her silence. She denies emphatically that she had anything at all to do with the splashing of blood on the door of the *Crier* office on Wednesday night. Rather, she insists that she went to the building late in the evening because she hoped to enter when it was untenanted and search the electronic files of the paper to determine if Mr. Kelly had written a story on Professor Crandall. However, she was unable to make that search. She said that after she entered the building, she realized there was another figure near the door. Abruptly, there was a crashing sound, as of glass breaking. Frightened, she broke into a run. She skidded on some sticky substance. Fleeing from the building, she hid in a line of pines to avoid detection by the campus police. She returned to her sorority house and discovered at that time that the soles of her shoes were stained with blood. She was frightened and hid the shoes on the roof behind a chimney. Poor, dear child. Such a traumatic week, but I've sent her flowers. With a picture of that handsome Mr. Strawn tucked into the bouquet."

Over a leisurely lunch at the Island Hills Country Club, Annie and Max began work on a definitive motive summary. They made every effort to complete this task during the afternoon. When not engaged on the telephone.

2:17 P.M. Sunday: "The Sunnymeade Home for Children is eighteen miles from Chastain. My pleasure to serve on the board of trustees there. The superintendent was only too happy to give me particulars about Emily Everett. Child came to the home when seven. Never knew her father. Abandoned by mother. Obese upon arrival. Hated sports. Always reading. In trouble often for hiding novels in her schoolwork in class." A portentous pause. "Favorite holiday: Fourth of July."

Annie was tempted to ask if Miss Dora had also uncovered Emily's favorite color, favorite food, and favorite pastime. But, as a native-born Texan, she had learned early on never to rile a rattlesnake, so she kept quiet.

"Next door to the orphanage," and Miss Dora's voice bristled with import, "is one of the largest fireworks factories and outlets in the South."

That, Annie knew, meant fireworks on a magnitude of which nonsoutherners would never believe. Thousands of pounds of fireworks. Big ones. Little ones. Fireworks for every taste and every pocketbook. Fireworks that were sold every day of the year. In the South, fireworks are not relegated to the Fourth. Having a party? Why, dazzle the night sky.

"A fireworks factory," Annie said thoughtfully.

Then, in the evenhanded tradition of Lord Peter, Miss Dora added grudgingly, "Of course any real southerner knows all about fireworks."

Real or, perhaps, adopted. Even outlanders could learn.

Fireworks. Made of gunpowder. And easily, so easily, obtained in the sovereign state of South Carolina.

Annie and Max enjoyed their outing to the forest preserve. Of course, they were soaked by the time they got back and quite cold. A hot shower did wonders for their morale. (The ringing of the phone couldn't be heard in the shower. Max would gladly have remained in there, cramped as it was, until their skin turned to crepe paper, but Annie did think enough was enough.)

6:11 P.M. Sunday: "Never would read those *Fletch* books after I started the first one and he'd thrown a cat out of a seventh-floor window."

"Humor, Henny," Annie replied.

"Black. Anyway, Josh Norden would've fixed his wagon. Three years ago he was arrested for going after his next-door neighbor with a bullwhip."

"Professor Norden?" Annie's voice rose in shock.

"He heard dogs screaming. That's what he told the police, screaming. Norden went over there. His neighbor was whipping the dogs with coat hangers."

Annie shuddered.

9:02 P.M. Sunday: "Sometimes I think Emmett hasn't the intelligence God gave a sea cucumber and less spine. Acts like one, too. Tries to roll up into a ball and refuse to talk. Well, I can tell you, I won't put up with that." Emmett. Emmett. Oh, of course. Miss Dora's unwilling accomplice in Chief Wells's office. "I gave him what for when he told me about the fingerprints. For pity's sake, it should have been among the first information he provided!"

"Fingerprints?" Annie wondered if a Greek chorus ever got bored.

"There weren't any! Now put that in your pipe and smoke it."

"Weren't any. Where?" Annie asked wildly.

"On the cabinet holding those confidential files. Been wiped shinier than a presidential limousine."

They did get to bed fairly early, but, in one sense, to no avail. It's difficult to sleep well or enjoy any of the other joys of bedtime when the inner ear is ever-cocked for the telephone—whether it rings or not.

Monday morning dawned clear and bright, and the day held promise of warmth. They wouldn't need sweaters today. They fled the tree house early, enjoying breakfast at the grill at the Island Hills Country Club. Max even indulged in an egg. Boiled, of course. They lingered over coffee, but had time to spare to catch the nine o'clock ferry. They arrived in Chastain a good twenty minutes before R.T. Burke's funeral was scheduled to begin. Parking in the shade of a live oak, they watched people arrive: Moss in a somber black suit, accompanied by a slender woman with melancholy eyes; Garrison politely shepherding his wife, his face suitably grave; Tarrant clutching Crandall's elbow; Norden alone, his shaggy white eyebrows drawn in a tight frown; Kelly, clutching a notepad, and the girl with the long braids, almost unrecognizable in a denim skirt; Diggs in a blue blazer, his concession to formality. Annie spotted President Markham, escorting Miss Dora. She was willing to bet that frosted Laurel. But Laurel was walking with a very handsome young man in a letter jacket. Annie only hoped this was the romantic interest Laurel had selected for Georgia Finney, and not . . . But it was better not to borrow trouble. She decided to make no comment to Max. His mother and such a young man might very well be a coupling Max would find unpalatable.

They found a place in the last row. The church was full. Burke had evidently had many friends from all walks of life, who had come to pay their last respects. The faculty sat together in the row behind President Markham and Miss Dora.

During the sermon, the minister offered this tribute: "R.T. Burke was a man of honor, a man devoted to his profession, seeing in it the opportunity of serving his fellow men, his state, his country, and his God. He saw the profession of journalism as a noble endeavor, the earnest effort to protect freedom and democracy by providing to the citizens in a fair, honest, and decent manner the information necessary to conduct their lives. He valued fairness and he treasured the truth. He began this life . . ."

There were six eulogies by newspapermen who had worked for Burke. At the service's end, there was scarcely a dry eye as the attendees filed out. Except for members of Burke's faculty. Annie watched them pass, their faces impassive, and knew there were no mourners among them.

Outside, Max tugged at Annie's arm, then nodded toward Moss, his wife, and Kelly, who were surrounded by a group of well-dressed men.

They drifted close enough to hear Moss invite a number of the state publishers to join him and Mrs. Moss and Kelly at the Faculty Club for lunch, after the drive to the cemetery.

As they walked back to Max's car, Annie murmured, "The king is dead. Long live the king."

The Student Union wasn't Max's pick for lunch, but Annie finally persuaded him. No one would bother them. They could eat, then organize their thoughts until it was time for Emily Everett's funeral. Charlotte Porter's memorial service was, of course, to be private.

The lunch was not memorable. Max poked unhappily at a square slab of fish with a ratty slice of orange as a decoration. Annie forbore to point out that anyone who ordered fish in a school cafeteria deserved what they got. She, of course, opted for a burrito, chili, and a root beer. Max averted his eyes.

It was a fine place to spread out their papers, however. They settled down with coffee, not Kona, and, with only occasional bickering, got to work.

About two, Annie lifted her head and looked at Max uneasily. "What do you suppose they're—"

But Max reached out, placed a cautionary finger on her lips, and murmured, "It isn't that I believe in genies but let's just not talk about them. They're silent, quiescent, perhaps spirited away to another plane."

It was almost two-thirty when they finished. Annie looked at their efforts with pride, then they reread the report together.

THE MURDER OF R.T. BURKE: MOTIVES

1. MALCOLM MOSS. To gain the chairmanship of the department. Or Moss could have leaked the confidential information to Kelly and killed Burke to escape disclosure. Why would Moss reveal the contents of the files? To cause difficulty in the department, embarrass Burke.

2. VICTOR GARRISON. To regain control of the department, stymie Burke's effort to switch the emphasis from the academic to the professional. Or, if he leaked the confidential information to Kelly and Burke discovered it, to prevent disclosure.

3. SUE TARRANT. To protect Frank Crandall's job, because she is in love with him and would do anything to keep him on the faculty. Unlikely to be Deep Throat as continued revelations could only harm Crandall. Might attack Burke in a fury if convinced he had engineered the leak.

4. JOSH NORDEN. To revenge Charlotte Porter's death, if he decided Burke provided Kelly with the information about her embezzlement. Or in an angry frenzy because Burke refused to announce the reasons behind Porter's theft.

5. FRANK CRANDALL. To prevent disclosures about his personal life if he thought Burke was Kelly's informant. Or in anger because Burke made it

clear there was no likelihood of tenure on account of Crandall's involvement with a student.

6. KURT DIGGS. Because Burke threatened his pressure on coeds for sex. Or because Burke discovered Diggs was Kelly's informant. But pushing Burke's problems with the faculty, including Diggs, into public discussion should be the last thing Diggs would want. However, interesting to note that the informant had nothing to say about Diggs in the meeting with Kelly and never showed up for a second meeting, at which, presumably, more dirty linen would have been aired.

7. EMILY EVERETT. To avenge the death of Charlotte Porter, if Emily thought Burke was responsible for the revelations. Emily, despite access to the closet key, could not be suspected of leaking the information, because she, like Josh Norden, would never intentionally have harmed Charlotte Porter.

There was no crowd at the Baptist Student Center for Emily's funeral. No more than a half-dozen students gathered. Josh Norden was the only faculty member there. Sudden tears pricked Annie's eyes when she saw Laurel approach the closed casket with a delicate spray of white roses and baby's breath.

The youth minister, Joe Bill Hankins, spoke quietly, recalling Emily's hard work, her determined efforts to gain an education, her hopes of becoming a reporter. There were no stories here of friendship or love. But, at the end of his eulogy, he said hopefully, "Emily seemed happier these last few weeks than I can ever remember, and we can hold that memory to us, and find solace in it, that Emily in her last few weeks had a kind of bloom about her. And we thank God for that."

It was almost closing time when they reached Death on Demand. Agatha was aloof. Only a single visit on Sunday and neither sight nor sound of Annie until after dark on Monday was absolutely beyond excuse. She didn't even come back to the coffee bar (of course, Ingrid always overfed the beast) until Annie opened a can of salmon. Finally, after Annie had called cajolingly, Agatha strolled slowly into view, surveyed her dish, and emitted a grudging purr.

With mugs (Annie chose *Whose Body?* and Max selected *Murder at*

School) of freshly made Kona coffee, they spread their papers on the table nearest the coffee bar. Agatha leapt smoothly to the tabletop and settled to watch. Annie reached out to pet her and was rewarded with a flick of claws. The lack of attention had yet to be forgiven. They worked in silence broken only by the irritated swish of Agatha's tail, then exchanged their efforts, Annie handing Max her conclusions on Burke's murder and Max giving her his judgments on the explosion.

ANNIE SUMS UP RESULTS OF BURKE'S MURDER:

1. Moss, at least for the moment, has the chairmanship.

2. Garrison will probably keep intact the present program of the department, because he will have Moss's support.

3. Tarrant will still have the opportunity to see Crandall because Moss will probably support his efforts to win tenure.

4. Norden. No definite result, unless it means he can win approval from Moss for the full story on Porter to be released.

5. Crandall may win tenure.

6. Diggs won't face, from Moss, pressures to change his lifestyle.

7. Everett. No gain.

MAX SUMS UP MOTIVES FOR BLOWING UP THE *CRIER* OFFICES:

1. Moss—Although he claimed he would enjoy a public discussion of department differences, he might have feared Burke's position would be strengthened if the faculty were pictured as obstructionist in the exposé.

2. Garrison—Infuriated by student editor's admittance to faculty meeting.

3. Tarrant—To prevent further disclosures about the faculty, especially Crandall.

4. Norden—To avenge Charlotte Porter.

5. Crandall—To protect his job.

6. Diggs—Ditto.

7. Everett—To revenge Charlotte Porter.

MAX SUMS UP RESULTS OF THE *CRIER* EXPLOSION

1. Emily Everett killed. Was Brad Kelly the intended victim? Was he lucky and Emily unlucky? Could Emily have been the intended victim? Could Emily have intended to destroy *The Crier* herself and been a casualty of her own design? Or could Emily have intended to be blown up with *The Crier*?

2. No publication for a period of several weeks. Therefore, no further exposés, but the press, once alerted, is probably seeking information at the present moment. The story certainly won't die.

3. Kelly is under police protection and surfacing only long enough to reveal the story behind the exposé. He is receiving quite a bit of attention from the press.

The phone was ringing when Annie and Max left Death on Demand to go to dinner at the country club. Annie fretted over who the call might have been from. Max merely said, "You can't imagine?" That did seem to answer the question, so she relaxed and enjoyed her fried scallops, insisting that they had no more fat than Max's with a cream sauce.

The phone was ringing as they unlocked the front door to the tree house. Annie, of course, sprinted for it.

8:46 P.M. Monday: "Moss took that young whippersnapper, Kelly, to lunch at the Faculty Club, along with a half-dozen of the state's most prominent publishers. I was invited, of course. From a newspaper family." Miss Dora paused, then admitted reluctantly, "Young Kelly handles himself well. On the other side of the fence from me when it comes to ethics. Shame to see grown men fawn over him." She gave an irritated sniff. "Well, time for a report. I do assume you have not frittered away your weekend. Who is the depraved creature who revealed that highly confidential information to that young idiot?"

Annie handed the phone to Max. "Your client, my love. Wants to know what the hell we've figured out."

Max approached the telephone with all the enthusiasm of a Jim

Thompson addict being presented with a crate full of Dorothy Gilman novels.

Annie propped her feet on the coffee table and sank back against a stack of soft cushions. But she had to hand it to Max. He was as suave as Sir Percy Blakeney, a/k/a the Scarlet Pimpernel.

"We have almost completed our investigation." A pause. "Certainly, but we must tally up all the facts first. When? When?" He looked desperately at Annie, then made the plunge. "In the morning. We will make our final report in the morning."

It was exceedingly quiet after he hung up. He avoided Annie's eyes. "Well, dammit," he said, gesturing at the stack of paperwork they'd dropped on the coffee table as they came in, "what else is there to know? Annie, the answer has to be there. Now, come on. I'm not going to admit to that old harridan that we can't figure it out." He looked at Annie accusingly. "You've read more mysteries than H. R. F. Keating. Who did it?"

They reread their notes, studied the timetable, and analyzed the suspects: what they were like, what they would do and would not do. But at midnight they finally turned in, exhausted and thwarted, no solution in view. As Max turned off the light, he said wearily, "Maybe inspiration will strike in the morning."

It was impossible to sleep. Annie twisted and turned and then lay resentfully listening to Max's even, regular, *relaxed* breathing. How could he sleep? Why couldn't they figure it out? Sleep did come finally, that on-the-edge, skittery kind of sleep when every nerve is tensed and the mind races, image piling on image: Burke's choleric face when he railed against gutter-sniping journalism the day they'd met; tears streaming down Josh Norden's cheeks but suddenly the face was Emily's, red and gross and swollen; Brad Kelly looming into view through the writhing clouds of masonry dust; bloody footprints leading out of Burke's office; Malcolm Moss's smug half-smile and Victor Garrison's sleek facade; Sue Tarrant's passionate defense of Frank Crandall; Kurt Diggs's sardonic appraisal of Burke.

Fragments of the phone calls rippled in her mind, too, a sentence here and there, Laurel's husky voice, Miss Dora's irascible tone, Henny's crisp accent. The three had retrieved bits and pieces, odds and ends, like silky black feathered crows, keen eyes noting the smallest vestige of movement.

Smallest vestige of movement . . .

Annie sat bolt upright in bed.

Movement.

What had *happened* since Friday?

Very damn little.

Her three most dedicated students retrieved information, little pieces here and there, but all the drama had occurred on Friday.

Why?

The luminous dial of the clock glowed in the darkness.

Time.

Why did everything happen in such a short span of time?

The explosion was the result—had to be the result—of careful preparation.

Every fact, from the snatched-up weapon to the use of Burke's raincoat as a shield from blood, argued for haste and immediacy in Burke's murder.

Two acts antithetical in their origin, one done with careful craft, the other a desperate response to immediate threat.

It was obvious, wasn't it, that the bomber intended at the least to destroy the *Crier* offices and at the most to injure or kill Brad Kelly. That could have happened at any time that day.

But why did Burke die when he did? What prompted his attacker to don the coat, grab up the iron bar, and bring it crashing down upon his head?

A wavering, tremulous moan, plaintive and forlorn, wafted on the night air. Annie's heart pumped until the *hoo-hoo* sounded again. A screech owl. Winter belongs to the owls in the low country, but knowing this did nothing to lessen the prickling at the back of Annie's neck as the moan sounded again. Taking care not to disturb Max, she slipped out of bed.

Laurel would nod and murmur about lost souls, questing for justice. Annie, of course, was not superstitious, but she moved with brisk determination to the coffee table. Thumbing through their notes, she recreated in her mind Burke's office as it was in the moments preceding his death. And the owl continued his mournful calls.

Burke's office. Emily Everett's name scrawled on his legal pad. Emily Everett arriving at the journalism building, her face swollen from hours of crying. Emily lumbering heavily down the hall to the *Crier* offices.

A bombing already planned. A murder committed in haste.

"Oh my God. Of course," she said aloud. She knew the identity of the killer now, the necessity for murder. She knew why vicious blows rained down on Burke's head. She knew why Emily Everett died.

And Henny was right. It all came down to character.

Whirling, she raced back to the bedroom. "Max, Max, I know who did it. I know how it happened."

He struggled to wakefulness and listened. When she finished her reconstruction, he nodded.

"It makes sense, Annie. It makes all kinds of sense." He looked at her admiringly, if still a little sleepily, and she attempted to appear humble. Then came the damper. "How are you going to prove it?"

But she had an idea there, too. Max wasn't convinced it would work, but, what the hell, it was worth a try.

He cleared his throat. "Only problem . . . you'll have to have some cooperation."

"Miss Dora can swing it."

"Sure. But will she?"

"For extra credit, I'm sure she will," Annie said demurely. Then she trotted back into the living room.

Max joined her as she picked up the receiver.

"Annie, it's three o'clock in the morning! Who're you calling?"

"Miss Dora," she replied happily. It had scarcely ever given her such exquisite pleasure to dial a telephone number.

17

ANNIE STEPPED BACK to look at her handiwork. The chalk-drawn floor plans of the journalism building weren't scale, that was for sure, but they were easy to understand. She labeled Burke's office, the middle office with the file closet, the *Crier* offices, and the men's restroom on the first floor and the faculty offices on the second floor. Then, with a brisk nod, she wrote "48 seconds" by the stairwell.

When she turned to face the class, almost every seat was taken. A little surprisingly to Annie, all twelve members of her class were in attendance, from Pink Hair to Mr. Jessup. Although perhaps the last was to be expected. He sat directly behind Laurel and the rest of the room might not have existed. Brad Kelly scanned the assemblage eagerly, making notes in an open spiral. He wore a blue blazer, cream shirt, and tan worsted slacks. Annie wondered if the crusading young editor had more media interviews scheduled for today. The regularly enrolled members looked puzzled at the sudden expansion of the class size, except, of course, for the three. Annie wondered vaguely if ever after she would think of them as "the three."

Laurel was a vision of nautical grace in a blue-and-white cable sweater and white linen slacks. She was every man's vision of the perfect companion on a slow boat to summer. She leaned forward, her cameo-perfect profile turned to the best advantage, and fixed Annie with an attentive, *supportive* look.

Miss Dora's eyes glittered like lumps of burnished coal. Her silver hair was bunched beneath her wide-brimmed gray velvet hat, throwing her yellowish, crumpled face into greater prominence, emphasizing the sharp hook of her nose and the jut of her determined small chin. Her dress and gloves were gray today too. Mother-of-pearl buttons gleamed at her tiny wrists. She sat in her accustomed place, first row, center seat, with her customary unbending posture, gloved hands locked on the silver knob of her ebony cane.

Henny's rust-colored cardigan seemed even more stretched out than usual this morning. She must have crammed the pockets with apples. She flashed Annie a hearty smile, lifted out a MacIntosh, and took an enormous bite.

It was one of the few smiles around.

Chief Wells stood across the room, his back to them all, staring out of a window. The hunched set of his massive shoulders proclaimed his extreme reluctance to be there.

But he had come. (Miss Dora was awesome, indeed.)

And Chief Wells had brought with him Georgia Finney, who sat between Laurel, who occasionally gave her a reassuring pat, and tiny, balding Jed McClanahan, the world's greatest trial lawyer, who surveyed the scene with bleary eyes, and kept repeating, "A little class on murder, what the hell's that? And why's it so goddamned early in the morning?" He sucked unhappily on a can of Mountain Dew and glared at the clock on the wall. The little lawyer dismissed the Death on Demand contest paintings with a bored look.

Georgia stared down at the desk, her cheeks flushed. She wouldn't look behind her where the members of the faculty sat, all in a row. Her red hair hung straight and limp, and fatigue marked dark circles beneath her eyes.

There was no way Annie could have compelled the faculty members to come. She found it interesting that all had responded to her invitation. As she had phrased it, "I know you are concerned about the dreadful occurrences on Thursday. I know what happened and why. If you want to find out, you are invited to attend my class this morning." And like the suspects in a Nero Wolfe novel, each had shown up at the appointed hour.

Sue Tarrant sat beside Frank Crandall, her hand possessively on his arm. He slouched unhappily, staring at the back of Georgia's bent head. Malcolm Moss made the student desk look pint-sized. His china blue eyes were alert and watchful. Victor Garrison surveyed the room, his unlit pipe cupped in his hand. His cheeks were ruddy, probably from an early morning run. Josh Norden's bleak face, his mouth pinched with anger, his eyes somber, was the clearest reminder that death had stalked the campus. Kurt Diggs leaned back insolently in his chair, a Marlboro man unwillingly corraled.

The bell rang. Max closed the door and dropped into the end seat next to it.

Silence fell.

Annie knew she would never again capture the attention of a class quite so completely. She found it exhilarating, and understood why Nero Wolfe arranged for every suspect to be present as he revealed all.

"I appreciate the cooperation of the college,"—Miss Dora nodded complacently—"the Chastain police,"—Chief Wells continued to look out the window—"the faculty of the journalism department,"—a row of wary faces—"and the members of my class. Especially," she managed not to sound grudging, "three of them."

Laurel moved just a little and a shaft of morning sun highlighted her flawless profile. Miss Dora's tiny, pursed mouth *might* have moved in a smile. Henny hoisted out another apple, looked at it with loathing, and stuffed it back in a bulging pocket.

"Each of these three students—Mrs. Roethke, Miss Brevard, and Mrs. Brawley—contributed to the solution of the crimes that occurred in this building by focusing my attention on three important elements—emotion," (Laurel sighed delicately), "circumstances," (Miss Dora thumped her cane), "and character" (Henny lifted her chin and was the image of indomitable British spinsterhood).

Max pantomimed lifting a telephone receiver. Annie ignored him.

"Let's begin with character. As Charlie Chan might have said, When leopard changes spots, see sun rise in west."

Max winced. The student with the black braids looked bewildered. Chief Wells's craggy face curdled in utter disgust. Annie wasn't sure whether it was directed at her or a result of his unsuccessful search for a spittoon.

"Why did R.T. Burke have to die? What kind of man was he? If we look at his life, his acts tell us a great deal. He was a superb investigative reporter. He had no tolerance for what he saw as unethical acts. He never forgave or forgot. He was determined to instill in the journalism department his principles of professionalism. Why, then, would this leopard suddenly change his spots and leak confidential information, even if it might help him in his campaign to change the program? The answer is simple. He wouldn't. That would have contravened every tenet he'd held sacred throughout his life. Leopards don't change their spots. R.T. Burke was not Deep Throat. So why was he killed? Because he posed a threat to the futures of several faculty members? Or was it because he discovered the identity of Deep Throat? And why Friday morning, within minutes of a massive explosion?

"These two considerations, Burke's character and the timing of his death, set me on the right track. Burke died because he was stubborn, vindictive, if you will, and intransigent when he made up his mind."

Henny nodded approvingly.

"But what provoked that brutal attack? This is when I looked at the circumstances." She nodded toward Miss Dora. "Professor Crandall"— his head jerked up and he looked at Annie with wild eyes—"saw Burke Friday morning but they had a very short conversation. Burke was on the telephone and not at all interested in talking to Crandall.

"This is where we must look closely, because we are in the last few minutes of Burke's life. A phone conversation. With whom? It could, of course, be anyone, a tennis friend, a stockbroker, a wrong number. But when Max and I saw Burke that morning, the phone was driving him mad." (And didn't she appreciate that feeling.) "His secretary, Emily, had called in, saying she was sick, and he had to answer the phone himself. In fact, while we were there, he turned it off. He was concentrating solely on his search for Kelly's informant to the exclusion of any other concern. So I suggest that he was pursuing this goal on the telephone, that he had made a phone call and it had reaped an unexpected bonanza—*because he now knew how that confidential information was obtained.*"

Her listeners scarcely breathed. The silence was oppressive.

"Whom did he call?"

She looked at the row of faculty.

"He had just talked to most of the faculty members, Professors Moss,

Tarrant, Garrison, Diggs, and Norden. He didn't want to talk to Crandall. Those are the names in his appointment book. Another name is scrawled across his legal pad and circled. He called Emily Everett, who was distraught over Mrs. Porter's suicide and vulnerable to questions. Here is where emotion came into play, the emotions of loss, guilt, and grief. Burke knew how to ask questions. He asked them, because he was a thorough man and he covered all the possibilities. And he discovered the source of the ugly story on Charlotte Porter.

"I'm not certain of the exact sequence of events. Did Emily then alert Deep Throat? Did Burke call Deep Throat? I think perhaps the latter, because Burke was committed to one of the basic tenets of journalism, get both sides of the story. Burke wouldn't have made a final move, to call in the police, to press charges, until he heard the other side of the story. Because Emily could have been lying.

"But she wasn't lying. Imagine the shock, then, when the phone rings in Deep Throat's office. There is the demand for a meeting. Deep Throat hurries to Burke's office. Burke announces that Emily is on her way to the school at Burke's request, that a thorough investigation will be held, that Burke intends to call the college legal counsel and press charges.

"Deep Throat whirls around, grabs the coat, grips the bar with a sleeve, and bludgeons Burke to death.

"But Deep Throat isn't safe yet. There is Emily. Of course, she will know immediately who murdered Burke. There must have been a sense of panic, but there was a way out, oh God, such a clever way out!"

She looked at Deep Throat.

He saw the certainty, the total confidence in her eyes. He jumped up and plunged toward the front of the room.

Miss Dora's cane shot out.

Brad Kelly stumbled and swore as he careened to the floor.

Chief Wells and Max together had to pull away a shouting, cursing Josh Norden from the struggling editor.

18

IT TOOK TIME for the arrival of a deputy to escort Brad Kelly to jail and for Chief Wells to take Annie's statement, but not a single member of her class or any of that morning's guests departed.

As Wells gave a final nod, saying, "That should cover it," he glowered at Georgia Finney. "If people would call the police when they discover a crime and not mess with the evidence, we'd all be better off. I damn well ought to file charges."

Georgia's eyes filled with tears.

Laurel sprang lightly to her feet. "Chief," she murmured. She lightly touched his arm, smiling tremulously up at him. "We all remember when we were so young and our hearts ruled our heads. I know a wonderful man such as yourself has many dear memories of those years. You *will* be kind, won't you?"

Wells's corrugated face turned a bright pink. It was like seeing Inspector Battle blush.

He made a strangled noise deep in his throat, and Laurel, of course, took it for assent. She stood on tiptoe and brushed his cheek with her lips.

Chief Wells fled.

As the class began to file out, Jessup paused by the lectern. "Mrs. Darling, I don't understand how you knew Kelly was Deep Throat."

Laurel surged to join them. "Dear Mr. Jessup." Annie thought the little man might faint from happiness on the spot. "Don't you see, there never was a Deep Throat!" She whirled toward her daughter-in-law. "That's what confused everything, didn't it, dear?"

That was one way of putting it, and, Annie thought, as good a way as any.

"That's right," Annie agreed. "Kelly had made friends with poor Emily, who was, obviously, always starved for attention from anyone. He must have flattered her, told her she had the makings of a wonderful reporter. When she trusted him, he persuaded her to make him a copy of the keys to the office and to the confidential files. He may have stressed what a service this would be, uncovering the evils in the department—for example, Crandall's relationship with Georgia. You can bet that would have pleased Emily, to see Georgia and Crandall in trouble. So, she gave him the keys. He probably crept in late one night and had all the time he needed with the files. Emily, of course, had no idea there was anything discreditable in Mrs. Porter's file. She would have laughed had anyone suggested it. As for Kelly, he showed what a bastard he was, because he used that for his first story, and, as a matter of fact, the files included the reason why Porter took the money. He didn't use that because the story was stronger without it, indicating a real cover-up on the part of Burke. When the story came out, Emily was devastated. When Mrs. Porter died, she was hysterical. And that wasn't a normal response, even if Mrs. Porter had been her only friend. The violence of her reaction indicated more than grief. It indicated guilt. What could Emily be guilty of? She couldn't be Deep Throat herself. She thought too much of Mrs. Porter.

"But Emily had access to the keys. Not a single faculty member needed keys to obtain that information. Whom did that leave? Brad Kelly.

"And Brad Kelly was the only one with everything to lose if it came out that he had been in the files. He could be charged with theft. If he went to jail—and you can bet Burke would have bent every effort to send him there—he would lose his post as editor. Further, it would probably cost him his Fulbright. So when Burke wormed the truth out of Emily, he signed his own death warrant. After killing Burke, Kelly once again did his best to focus the crime on the faculty, by stealing the confidential files. And where were they found? In the men's room right across the hall. And that's where Kelly claimed he'd gone when he left Emily in his office."

Annie turned and traced the path on her blackboard. Then she pointed at the faculty offices on the second floor. "There they all were, but there they stayed. Here was the murderer," and she crossed an X in Kelly's office.

"As for the bomb, that was part of Kelly's long-term plan. First he obtained the information and broke the story. That attracted attention. Then he splashed blood on the office door. It was fortunate for him that Georgia Finney once again was where she shouldn't have been. He threw the blood. It was seen as another attempt to frighten the stalwart young editor of *The Crier*. His fame was spreading. Then he prepared the bomb. He planned, of course, for it to go off when no one was there, but it would look as though an effort had been made to kill Brad Kelly. Instead, driven by desperation, when Emily came into the building, he diverted her to his office, perhaps with some story that Burke was going to join them there and Kelly was going to write a story admitting the hoax and apologizing. Emily followed right along. The bomb was there. He triggered it, then excused himself, saying something like he'd go and tell Burke she was there. He went down the hall into the men's room, waited, and bang, Emily was dead. And as a delicious plus, Brad Kelly was hailed for his bravery in persisting in his efforts to reveal the truth about the journalism department."

"Not a very nice young man. Wanted his own way at all costs. Reminds me somewhat of Jacqueline de Bellefort in *Death on the Nile*," Henny observed sagely. "And without even love as an excuse."

"But it's love or the lack of it that caused so much of the unhappiness here," Laurel murmured throatily. "As Mary Roberts Rinehart would have understood so well."

"An interesting exercise," Miss Dora said sourly, "but nothing to match any of Miss Sayers's books. No *intellectual* conversations." She sniffed, rummaged in her carryall, and plucked out a sheet from an old-fashioned children's writing tablet. She thrust it at Annie.

Unfolding the paper, Annie saw the spidery, spiky handwriting. She was enchanted. Wait until Henny saw this: Miss Marple to the life. Then she began to read. As she did, she realized a crisp voice was echoing the very same information in her ear and there was a scratchy sound of chalk against the blackboard.

"First painting: *File for Record* by Phoebe Atwood Taylor writing as Alice Tilton.

"Second painting: *Home Sweet Homicide* by Craig Rice.

"Third painting: *God Save the Mark* by Donald Westlake.

"Fourth painting: *Fletch* by Gregory Mcdonald.

"Fifth painting: *Malice in Maggody* by Joan Hess."

Annie looked at Henny, standing by her side, gesturing victoriously at the paintings.

"Certainly gave me a run for my money. But I came up with it. I certainly did. *Fletch.* I knew I'd track it down." Henny sighed, almost giddy with relief. "Sure glad I figured it out first, saved my autographed copy of *The Mysterious Affair at Styles.* I would be sick if I lost it. Plus, I get a bonus. That great copy of *The Beast Must Die.*"

Annie hated to puncture her euphoria. "Henny, gosh, I'm sorry, but just the instant before you told me, Miss Dora handed me the answers. See," and she proffered the tablet paper with the spiky handwriting.

Henny grabbed the sheet and her bony shoulders slumped. "Oh." She swallowed. "Oh, well. That happens, doesn't it. I'll get the book for you."

"Oh no, no, this was a tie, Henny. I wouldn't dream of taking your *Styles* away from you."

"Annie, you are a sport!"

"And you were so much help with the class and solving the murder, why, you can have your bonus book!"

"Annie!" Henny embraced her.

The staccato thumping of the cane broke them apart. Miss Dora, her eyes glittering with bloodcurdling determination, demanded, "And my bonus book?"

"And mine, I should think," a husky voice warbled from the blackboard as Laurel pointed winsomely at her own list of titles. They were, of course, right on.